PREGAME KISS

"Do you have any pregame rituals?" she asks.

Jared stares out the window. "I don't know."

"I heard about this one guy never washing his shirt before a game or another guy who ate almond butter with breadsticks before a game. Stuff like that. What's yours?"

It takes him a few seconds to respond. "I have a key chain that I have to touch before leaving the dressing room." He slows down to turn the corner, checking in his side mirror and watching the road in front of him. He pulls to the side of the road. "I have a few superstitions."

Meghan raises an eyebrow. "You pulled over to tell me that?"

"I have to kiss a girl the night before the game."

She lowers her chin, staring at him. "You're kidding."

"Nope." He's leaning in closer.

Meghan glances out her side window and when she brings her head back to meet Jared's, he has brought himself closer. She swallows hard, staring into his eyes. She can feel his breath on her face.

"I don't want to be just a girl to kiss. That means you've had plenty and that's not for me," she whispers, looking at his clean-shaven face and cheekbones. His eyes are what's drawing her in. She bites her bottom lip. Jared leans into her and grazes his mouth on hers. What she thought would be a quick peck turns out to be an enjoyable reaction. She kisses him back, feeling her body sink into the seat a little more. . . .

Books by Charlene Groome

HIS GAME, HER RULES

COLD AS ICE

PRACTICE MAKES PERFECT

Published by Kensington Publishing Corporation

PRACTICE MAKES PERFECT

CHARLENE GROOME

LYRICAL PRESS
KENSINGTON PUBLISHING CORP.
http://www.kensingtonbooks.com

LYRICAL PRESS is published by

Kensington Publishing Corp.
119 West 40th Street
New York, NY 10018

All Kensington titles, imprints and distributed lines are available at special quantity discounts for bulk purchases for sales promotion, premiums, fund-raising, educational or institutional use.

Special book excerpts or customized printings can also be created to fit specific needs. For details, write or phone the office of the Kensington Sales Manager. Attn.: Sales Department. Kensington Publishing Corp., 119 West 40th Street, New York, NY 10018. Phone: 1-800-221-2647.

Lyrical and the L logo Reg. U.S. Pat. & TM Off.

First Electronic Edition: August 2015
eISBN-13: 978-1-60183-348-8
eISBN-10: 1-60183-348-2

First Print Edition: August 2015
ISBN-13: 978-1-60183-349-5
ISBN-10: 1-60183-349-0

Published in the United States of America

For Jared,
my husband and best friend.
You always have my heart.
xo

ACKNOWLEDGMENTS

I am so blessed to be able to share my stories and work with talented individuals who share the same passion for books.

I would like to thank my agent, Dawn Dowdle of Blue Ridge Literary Agency, for her immense dedication and always being there when I need her.

To my editors, John Scognamiglio and Gary Sunshine, thank you for your hard work and making this book all that I envisioned. I appreciate everything you do.

And thank you to the marketing team at Kensington Publishing, I am forever grateful for the generous support you give me.

To Karen Christiansen, the director of charitable and corporate events for the Vancouver Canucks. Thank you for answering my questions and giving me a peek of what you and your team do.

Many thanks to you, my reader, for taking time to read my book. I hope you enjoy.

Chapter 1

"You're late!"

"I'm sorry! Sorry!" Meghan fingers a long strand of hair away from her face. "I couldn't find parking." She hopes to get away with it considering she's never parked at the old stadium before. It's home to the Vancouver junior hockey team, but today, the ice was taken out, leaving just a concrete floor where a Warriors fund-raiser is taking place. "And there's a line around the building."

"I noticed the crowd when I drove by on my way to work," Keri, the events director, tells her. "You have a parking pass."

First day as the public relations coordinator and already Meghan's got a strike against her. She blows out a breath. "It was full."

"Full? Really? The players must be arriving. Hurry, we still have stuff to do." Keri waves her hands around. She's wearing a gray skirt and blazer, reminding Meghan of a stewardess. Her hair shapes her round face, resting at her collarbone, and her makeup is minimal, except for her bright red lips desperately in need of another coat. "Tables need to be set with name cards. They each need a Sharpie pen and water cups, and the stanchions have to be placed properly. Do you have your checklist?"

Meghan reaches into her briefcase and pulls out a paper protected by a plastic cover.

"What happened to your shirt?"

Meghan flicks her hand at her chest as though it will magically come off. "Coffee. I'm having one of those mornings." Well, that's strike two. Maybe she should be carrying extra clothes in her car.

"How many cookbooks did you order? I don't think we have enough."

"Five thousand." Meghan's heart starts to race. "Just like we talked about."

"It looks like we may only have half the order. I can't tell."

"What? Only half?"

"You need to find the rest of the order."

"I double-checked the delivery."

"Unless you know where else they could be." Keri seems to get sidetracked by an employee carrying a water cooler. "Over here!" She scurries over to lead them where she wants the station set up.

Meghan skims her checklist. Her feet are killing her. She wiggles her toes in her new shoes. She should have worn ones that were broken in.

"Meghan!"

Meghan sees a girl race toward her. "Where do you want these potted mums?"

"One between every table. There needs to be room for fans getting autographs. We don't want clutter. We also need these name cards at every seat." She hands over a stack of printed cards from the clear bin in front of her and walks with a soft step, trying not to put pressure on her foot. She shouldn't have bought the plain black heels because they were half price. Cheap shoes. Her baby toe is throbbing.

"Meghan," another voice calls out. "What should I do with these doughnuts?"

"Doughnuts? Who are they for?"

"The players, I guess."

"I don't think the players will eat them. You can put them at the beverage table."

Meghan shuffles her foot as she walks to the perimeter of the arena, where there is a stack of boxes. She takes count of how many there are and clearly a few thousand cookbooks are missing. She stands, staring at the boxes. What went wrong? Did she mess up the order? It was a lot of work getting each player to submit his favorite family recipe in time to have the books designed and printed.

Meghan kicks off her heels and runs to where she left her briefcase. She takes out her phone and scrolls for the confirmation e-mail. As she looks through her messages, there are men trailing through the arena. Casually dressed men wearing jeans and T-shirts and some in button-down shirts. Meghan's stomach flutters. The team is here, and she doesn't have enough books. She can't call off the event. There's a line of people outside of the arena who have been waiting for hours to come in, and if she doesn't have an adequate number of cookbooks to give away, she will most likely be demoted. How could this happen?

"When do we open the doors?" a blond-haired girl with hot pink tips, asks.

"Fifteen, twenty minutes. I have to figure something out, Deanna."

"Dana."

"Dana, sorry. Can you please make sure the players are in the right seats and tell me if there are any players missing?" Meghan catches two girls standing around talking and turns to them.

"Can I get both of you to offer each player a beverage? There are doughnuts, too, if they want any."

The girls snicker.

One of them asks, "Where are your shoes?"

"I . . . um . . . have to put them on. My feet were sore." Meghan excuses herself and rereads her e-mail. Yep, five thousand cookbooks were delivered. Then where is the order?

Meghan takes a quick look at the players taking seats. Her stomach tightens. It will be a nightmare if the missing books don't show up in the next few minutes. She has to track down the rest of the order. Meghan makes a quick call to the office. Nobody is answering, so she goes back to recount the boxes to make sure there wasn't a mistake. She slips on her heels and hurries through the building to find the rest of the order.

"Meghan," a voice calls out across the room, pinning her attention. She is stunned at hearing her name paged again, when her boss, Keri, is standing within arm's reach.

Meghan's heart beats faster and she sweeps her bangs away from her eyes. "Yes?"

"You asked me to check off which players are present and it looks like Alex Price and Jared Landry are still missing." Dana holds up the guest list to her face. "Everyone else is here, sitting down and ready to go."

"I'm sure they're on their way."

"Alex will be here. Jared may or may not show." Keri digs through her clear bin. "Where did my pack of Sharpies go?"

"He has to show!" Meghan says.

"It's the chance we take. Have you seen the pack of Sharpies?"

"They're already on each place setting like you asked," Meghan says.

"Awesome! Thanks." Keri closes the lid. "We have to get these players something to drink. They can't just sit down with nothing!"

"Done!" Meghan turns to Dana. "Do you want to put these cookbooks at the entrance with the rest of them? How does the line look to get in?"

"It's wrapped around the building. Some people have been here since early morning."

"I heard. Just to buy a cookbook." Meghan shakes her head. "Insane." At least some people will appreciate the effort she's put into this.

"Yeah, but they get to meet the players. Well worth it. I hope Alex Price shows up. Is he on your list?"

"I think so."

Dana exhausts a sigh and throws her head back. "Ah, what I would give to have him for a boyfriend."

Meghan chuckles. "One that doesn't last."

Dana arches an eyebrow.

"It's true! I've heard the rumors." Meghan gives a sideways grin. "I'm sure you have too."

"A girl can dream, right?" Dana sprints across the room to the line of tables with seated Warriors.

Meghan's phone vibrates on her hip. She looks at the number. A text from Stu: I have to cancel tonight. Sorry.

She blows out a breath. Right. Probably playing Xbox with his cousin again. She needs to break up with him. Tonight. The relationship is going nowhere and it's boring. Stu's boring. All he wants to do is go for motorbike rides or to the movies. There's nothing new. It's the same as their first date five months ago. Does he even care about her? She's wondered about this for weeks now. It only came to light when her friend Brie asked if she and Stu wanted to join her and her boyfriend, Mike, on a day trip to Mayne Island. Stu was the only one who said he didn't feel like walking over on a ferry. Meghan loves the outdoors and exploring nature. She was bummed she couldn't get Stu to budge. At first she thought maybe he wasn't feeling well, then Meghan found out he was driving his dad to the airport. Like he couldn't have gotten his sister to do it. She still lives at home.

"They're opening the doors," someone yells.

"The books." Meghan turns to Keri. "I don't know where the rest of the order is. I checked the order and five thousand are supposed to be here."

"How many are here?"

"Thirty-five hundred."

"They have to be here. Did you check the loading zone? Maybe they were left there."

"Good idea. I'll check."

"No, get someone else to look. We have to make sure the players have what they need."

"Dana made sure they have everything."

"The crowd will be coming through any moment. Alex is here, but I guess Jared isn't showing up." She walks toward the tables one last time.

"I gotta get those books to the front of the line." Meghan gets two employees' attention and has them open the rest of the boxes.

Meghan escapes down the hallway to see if she can find the rest of the order. She makes another call, this time to Eddie, one of the coordinators who's at the office, working on another assignment.

"Eddie, it's Meghan. Listen, we seem to be missing a couple thousand cookbooks. Have you noticed a stack of boxes in the boardroom? Storage room? Someone's office?"

"I haven't noticed, but I can look around for you."

"Would you do that? Thanks." Meghan talks with her head down, walking fast to the nearest room, except she doesn't know exactly what she's expecting. There aren't offices, more like a hallway and the referee's changing room. She stops and lowers her cell phone to her side. Where else can she look? Are there any other rooms? It's such an old arena and she doesn't know her way around. *The change rooms!* Of course! They have to be empty, so why not store the boxes there? It is like an aha moment. She attaches her phone to her side and leans into the bright blue door with an unlocked latch. She opens it a crack and peers in to get a better view. She doesn't see anybody, so she opens it wider until she's sure the room is empty. It smells of sweat and wet rubber, except the floor is dry. She looks around at the empty room and nothing catches her eye, so she leaves to make it down the hall to the next door. It's a locked room.

"You won't find anything in there," a security man tells her. "It's the janitor's closet." He chuckles to himself. "Can I help you find something?" He glances at her lanyard hanging from her neck.

"I'm missing some boxes that were delivered here. They haven't arrived for the signing yet, and I'm wondering if they're stored in the wrong place."

"Haven't seen any." He walks away.

Some help he is.

Meghan walks across the hall to the next door. The word HOME is painted across the wall in yellow paint. The door is unlocked, which leads her to believe she won't find anything that belongs to her in there, but there are only so many places to store boxes. Meghan leans her shoulder into the door, takes a peek, and begins to step inside.

"I wouldn't go in there if I were you," a male chuckles.

As she turns around, a guy's walking past her. He is wearing jeans and a polo shirt. Meghan doesn't recognize him. His deep-set blue eyes and the curl of his upper lip stun her like she's seeing something breathtaking for the first time.

"I'm looking f-for something." She rests her weight on the door.

He stops, makes eye contact with her, which makes her breathe just a little bit harder and stare just a little bit longer. She gulps.

"I haven't heard of a dressing room being used for anything else. I wouldn't go in unless you have to." He pauses, butts his lips together as though he's thinking about something, and takes a step closer. "I've heard about people like you."

"Like me?" Her voice rises with concern.

"Yeah. Sneaking into the dressing room to get a selfie and post it on social media."

"What?"

"Oh yeah. I saw one posted once. There was a girl in Brampton, where I'm from, and she snuck into a dressing room. I don't know how she did it, but she managed to get a shot of herself in a player's cubby."

"Never heard of it."

"So if you want a picture," he says, turning around. His feathery blond hair falls softly to his neck, the typical hockey cut as it's called. "Go ahead. I won't tell. Do it quick."

She raises an eyebrow. *Who does he think he is?*

"Does it look like I'm about to take a selfie?" She holds up her lanyard with a swipe in the air and puts it down. Is he trying to be funny?

"I guess not . . . I didn't notice . . . Sorry."

"I'm just checking whether something was left here." She opens the door all the way to take a look. Nothing. She closes her eyes, bites her bottom lip, and turns on her sore foot to leave. These shoes are going into the garbage can when this event is over, even if she has to drive home barefoot.

He chuckles. "You might want to check upstairs for the lost and found."

She shakes her head as he saunters down the hall toward the arena. *Who is this guy?*

"Excuse me."

Automatically Meghan steps to the side to let a man pulling a flatbed dolly with stacks of boxes on it through.

"Wait!" she shouts. "Are those cookbooks?"

The man slows. "I heard they were books." He shrugs.

"Okay, great! Do you know where you're going?" Meghan tries to walk with him but is falling behind. The dolly takes up most of the hallway.

They get to the arena where thousands of people are waiting in line for their chance to have a cookbook signed or have something auto-graphed by their favorite player. People have come dressed in Warriors attire. She scans the tables. Every player is there. She notes that Jared Landry's place is occupied. From where she's standing, she can't tell who is who.

"Where do you want them?" the deliveryman asks.

"Follow me." She walks away from the crowd to a place near the front of the line. Security is letting people through. People only get a few seconds with each player, but it looks like the event is running smoothly and Meghan can breathe easily now that there are more cookbooks to give away.

The man unstacks the boxes and puts them with the rest. Meghan calls some employees over to help open the boxes and get them ready for the public. She's happy she made the decision to keep the limit to one item signed per player, whether it's the cookbook, a hockey card, or a jersey. She couldn't expect the players to sign everything. That would be asking for too much, and she wants to be on everyone's good side, especially when there will be many more team events. Meghan helps out at the front of the line and then strolls the arena to make sure the event is running the way it was planned. So far, so good. People are smiling, laughing, and having a great time meeting their icons, and the players seem to be enjoying themselves. Meghan walks around the facility, making sure everyone is doing their job and the players have what they need.

By the afternoon, the crowd thins and Meghan instructs security to lock the entrance and to warn people the event is coming to a close.

There are still around a hundred people trying to get through to have something signed.

"Good job today," Keri says. "I'm heading back to the office to finish up on a few things. See you tomorrow."

"Yes, see you tomorrow." After Keri leaves, she kicks off her heels and hides them under a table with her briefcase. Instant relief. She sighs and throws her head back as she wiggles her toes.

"Exhausted?" Dana makes a pile of the crushed boxes.

"I'm okay. It's my feet. They're killing me."

"You look like you could use a nap."

"It will be an early night for me, that's for sure." Meghan takes out her cell phone to check the time. "It's three already!" Meghan touches her stomach. She missed lunch. Early dinner, early bedtime. "We can start cleaning up. The event is over. You can tell the players to wrap it up. I'm going to start clearing off the tables."

"Did you need me to sign any extra books?" a guy asks.

Him again!

"They're for charity, right?"

This guy really is stuck on himself.

"I think we're okay. Thanks." She continues to collect the Sharpies.

"Do you need a hand?"

"No, I'm fine, thanks." She ignores him as he clears off his place setting and hands her his name card. Jared Landry. It had to be him. She takes the card.

"I thought this went until four."

"I sent out the updated notice. It ended at three." Meghan throws his card in the tote and places it with the others on a nearby table, where Dana adds the other name cards to it.

"That was you? You sent the e-mail?" Jared picks up a potted mum. She stares at him. Is he for real?

"You're Meghan." He extends his hand while holding the plant at his side. "Jared Landry."

"Meghan O'Riley." She places her hand in his with a firm shake and releases it, going back to clearing the table of garbage and used Solo cups.

"Are you taking that?" Dana points to the plant.

Jared flinches and hands it over. "No."

"I can take it." Dana leaves with it.

"Sorry if I offended you back there. I didn't know who you were."

"And that makes a difference?"

"It does. We kinda work together. Don't want to damage our relationship."

Meghan snickers. "Damage our relationship?" *What relationship? This guy is too much.*

"Let me help you." He reaches for another plant.

"No, I'm okay. Really. Thanks. I'm fine." She tries hard to grin, even though she wants him to leave and not bother her again. She starts clearing the tables.

"The least I can do is give you a hand." He puts the plant down as Dana comes for it and takes it away.

She raises an eyebrow. "Don't worry about it. Thanks. I've got it. I'm sure you have things to do."

Jared scratches his temple, looks around, and starts to stack the empty Solo cups that line the tables before tossing them into the garbage.

"Are you always this helpful?"

"I don't mind helping out."

"You don't have to feel guilty for accusing me of being some random woman checking out locker rooms."

"I didn't know who you were."

This guy's not letting up. Why is he still here?

"That makes a difference? Is that what you like to do, spy on people?" She stares into his eyes. She swallows, waiting for an answer, but he, too, is gazing at her as though unsure what to say.

"I was walking by. I wanted to make sure you weren't lost."

She bursts out laughing. "Okay."

"Seriously."

"It was nice meeting you." She turns on her toes. *There is no way this Jared guy is going to think he's God's gift to women, the way he cocks his head and smiles at me. No way will I fall into that trap of forgiveness. What does he want?*

"Are you having a bad day?"

She looks at him inquisitively. "No, I'm not."

His eyes skim her outfit and he stares at her bare feet.

"I was wearing new shoes."

"You spilled something." He points to his chest, mirroring her reflection.

Her shoulders sink. "Thanks for pointing it out. I spilled my coffee on the way to work. Will you be at the next event?"

He nods.

"Good. Well, I'm sure you have things to do. I've got this." She pulls off a white tablecloth.

"I tried calling you on my way here and I got pulled over—"

"You tried calling me? Why?"

"To tell you I was coming. I was running late . . . and then I got pulled over for holding my cell phone."

"Don't tell me, you got off."

"Yeah." His top lip tightens into a grin.

Typical.

"It was close. I got a warning."

Meghan ties the Sharpies together with a rubber band. "It happens, right?" She throws them into the bin. *Probably happens all the time.*

"It's never happened before."

Yeah right. Is he reading my mind? I hope not because I'm thinking his biceps are incredible and his chest is probably just as tightly chiseled.

"I better go. Looks like you're done here." He backs away. "Get your boyfriend to look after you tonight and give you a foot massage."

Her cheeks feel suddenly warm. As if Stu would even think of doing such a thing.

Boyfriend. Breakup. I gotta leave so I can get in touch with Stu and tell him we're through.

Jared saunters across the concrete floor without a care in the world. He probably has a nice girlfriend and a nice life.

Chapter 2

Meghan wakes up to the sound of her phone ringing. Her eyes pop open, staring into the darkness, and she realizes she's not dreaming. Her heartbeat quickens as she sits upright and looks at her alarm clock. It's 12:02. She grabs for her phone that's sitting on her night table. Who would be calling her at this hour?

She brings her phone to her ear and says hello with a sleepy voice.

"Megs!" the voice says, bringing her attention to his dramatic tone.

She puts her hand to her forehead. It's Stu. He started shortening her name after he heard Brie call her that a few times, but for some reason when he says it, it doesn't sound genuine. It's forceful, like he's trying to blow up an already-full balloon.

Meghan reaches over to turn on her sidelight. "What's going on?" she asks. "Is everything all right? I tried calling you at dinnertime, but you didn't answer and then I tried calling again before I went to bed. Did you get my message?"

"I just got home from the hospital."

"Oh, no! What happened?" She brings her hand to her cheek; suddenly she's not so angry with him. "Are you okay?"

"I broke my leg in an accident."

"Your motorbike?"

"Yeah," he says. "My motorbike."

"Is it totaled?"

"Looks that way."

"How are you feeling?"

"I'll be okay. Some bruising and cuts from the road. I'll be fine."

"How did it happen?"

He exhales, taking his time. Why does he have to play cool when she just wants to hear the answer?

"I tried to pass a car and there was an oncoming pickup. I don't know . . . I swerved to miss it and went into the ditch."

"Were you not paying attention?"

"The truck was coming so fast."

"You're driving a bike! You think you're invincible!" Meghan says. "You drive like you own the road."

"I don't."

"Cars shouldn't have to give you the right of way. Jeez. Good thing there was room or you'd be a pancake," she says, letting off steam. "Why do you think you can drive like that?"

"I'm lucky."

"Yes, you are! And you just have a broken leg?"

"Amazing, isn't it?"

"When did this happen?"

"After work."

"Where were you going?" Suddenly Meghan calculates the time. What has he been doing for the past six hours?

"Oh, uh, just for a ride."

"So after work, instead of going home, you decided to go for a ride?"

"Yeah."

Meghan lets out a breath. "Must have been a long ride."

"The weather was decent."

"Where were you going?"

"Um, to a friend's."

"Who?"

"Why the questions? I'm hurt! Don't you care that I have a broken leg? I could use some TLC."

"Who were you going to see?"

"Someone from work," he snaps.

"When did the accident happen?"

"What's with the questions, Megs?"

"Doesn't make sense that you would spend all that time with a guy friend, that's all."

"What? You don't believe me?"

"It's kind of odd, isn't it?"

"No. I ride all the time. You know that. I keep asking you to come along, but you never do."

"Motorbikes scare me." *And the way you drive.* "Fortunately, I wasn't with you."

"I'm home now."

"Are you doing okay?"

"I could use some company."

"I can come by tomorrow after work." Why does she feel so annoyed?

"Why not now?"

"Now? I need to be sleeping. I have to get up in six hours."

"That's right, you need your beauty sleep," he mocks.

Meghan flinches. This is one of the reasons they aren't compatible. He's needy and she's bored of him. Stu asking her to come over should excite her, but instead she'd rather be sleeping.

She has to break up with him. They can't go on like this. They're not even a couple. They barely see each other, and when they do, it's about riding. She doesn't even care to see him, not now, not after work. . . .

"Who were you going to see?" Meghan asks.

"Can't a guy go for a ride?"

"You worked until seven last night, usually when you work later all you want to do is go home."

"Megs, Megs, it's not what you're thinking."

"What am I thinking?" She's grinning at the fact that he's acting like he's hiding from telling her who his new friend is. "You're friends with Thomas, the computer genius. You used to call him The Geek, now you guys are friends. I should have seen it coming when Thomas was asking you about your bike."

He lets out a chuckle. Why does he find humor in this?

"You don't have to be shy about it. I know you don't want to be labeled as friends with Thomas, but it's fine—"

"It was Tori."

"Pardon?"

"I was on my way to see Tori."

"The intern? What for? Never mind. I don't want to know. I can't do this anyway."

"Do what?"

"See you anymore."

"What do you want?"

Someone who cares to call me when an accident happens. Someone who needs me and I need them.

"We're not serious, is that it?"

"Maybe that's the problem," she says, thinking out loud. "You don't treat this relationship like it means something to you."

"You're not thinking marriage?"

Not with you.

She lets out a sigh. "No."

"Then what is it?"

"I'm not feeling this, us, being together. Clearly, I don't mean anything to you."

"What do you need?"

To call because you need me, love me . . .

"I'm not feeling the connection, the bond, the feeling I should be feeling. I don't know what it is. I just know we need to move on. We're done."

"You're breaking up with me over the phone?"

"I hardly see you!"

"I just asked you to come over!"

"Yeah, to have sex with you!"

"No, we can talk."

"Since when do you do all the talking?"

"I can't change your mind?"

"What for?" Meghan asks, her temper flaring.

"We can't break up," he says.

"Yes, we can."

"We're just getting to know each other!"

"It's been five months! Besides, I don't like being cheated on."

"I didn't sleep with her!"

"Seriously, Stu? That's going to make me stay? You were probably on your way to her house to sleep with her. We don't see each other anyway, only when it's convenient for you."

"You don't want to give it another shot?"

Meghan hangs up the phone and lies awake, wondering if she'll ever feel connected with someone enough to see him in the middle of the night and trust that she's the only one.

Chapter 3

Jared grabs his wallet and puts it in the back pocket of his baggy black shorts. His other hand is holding his cell phone as he walks out of his house.

"I told you, Jare, you don't have to send such extravagant gifts for Beckham," his sister Jane tells him over the phone.

"Does he like it?"

"What four-year-old wouldn't like a powered Porsche Spyder—a replica of his uncle's—make that two Porsches because you had to buy one for his friend. Who does that?"

"At least when he's playing with his friend, they don't have to share. What kid wants to share?"

"That was really generous of you, thank you."

"I like the pictures you sent."

"He's proud of his new race car."

Jared smiles imagining his nephew putting the powered toy in full speed and ripping up the driveway.

"We're coming out next week, remember?"

"Your rooms are ready."

"Becks tells everyone he has his own room at your house."

"Well, he does."

"He makes it sound like he lives with you."

"This house is too big for me. I don't know what I was thinking when I bought it."

"Didn't you say it was perfect for a family?"

"It is."

"One day you'll fill the rooms," she tells him.

"I don't know about that. A couple of kids and I'd still have extra rooms."

"Anybody would love to live in your house."

Jared knows he's fortunate to own such a beautiful estate, but he knows it's his career that's afforded him such luxuries. He hasn't forgotten his roots, and if he can spoil his nephew and give his family things they don't have, then he's happy.

"Becks is really looking forward to seeing you."

"Can't wait either. Don't worry about packing skates to use for one afternoon. I'll have some here for you."

"You didn't buy him a pair, did you?"

"I'd like Beck to come to the rink."

"He'll like that too. Jare?"

"Yup."

"Your girlfriend won't corner me again and ask to take me shopping?"

He laughs. "No. Definitely not."

"Good. I don't have the energy for that anymore. Last time, she told me I needed to wear skinny jeans and smaller hoop earrings were in. She's like the fashion police. I know she's your girlfriend, so I think I've been pretty fair with her, but if she tells me I need to cut my hair into a bob one more time, I think I'm going to tell her to mind her own business."

"Ex-girlfriend," Jared says, chuckling.

Jane exhales. "You two broke up? When?"

"Yeah. A month ago."

"Thank God. She was a nutcase."

"You're telling me."

"What happened?"

"She tried to move in."

"Like stay over and not leave?"

"That and bring her stuff over and just leave it here. I found some candles on the living room mantel along with a picture of us in a frame. Never seen it before. And in my bathroom she left her makeup bag and toothbrush in a drawer. Don't women hold on to those things?"

"Usually."

"Then she started talking marriage."

"No!" Jane shouts.

"She had big plans for us." He laughs.

"I assume you broke it off? How did that go?"

"Not good. Does it ever?"

"By the sounds of it she's obsessive."

"A little possessive, too," he adds. "And, I've lost a garage remote."

"You think she took it?"

"I hope not. It's probably around the house somewhere."

"Does she have a house key?"

"No."

"Do you think she's impulsive? Do you think she would hurt you?" Jane's voice is electric. "You have to be careful."

"No, I think it'll be okay," Jared says, but the tightness in his stomach tells him otherwise.

"Make sure your gate is locked and Loretta knows not to let her in."

"Yeah, I'll tell her," Jared says about his housekeeper.

"You're going to need a new girlfriend."

"I'm not in a hurry."

"You need to find someone new before Ms. Obsessive comes back into your life."

"If you're worried that I'd take her back, I won't."

"She's smart. She'll find a way to be with you."

"Nah, it's over," he says.

"Because you told her it was over?"

"I gave her her things and told her we don't belong together."

"Did she cry?"

"Yeah, she cried. She sobbed. Told me I was making a big mistake."

"It's her way to rope you in. I didn't like her the moment I met her. There was something about her. She has those crazy eyes. I don't trust her. Maybe when I'm there I can help you find someone."

"I do fine on my own."

"Sure you do. That's why you're single and attract women like Ms. Obsessive."

"This is why I don't tell you half my life story because you're so critical of my decisions."

"Someone has to look out for you. You're living in Vancouver all alone."

"I'm on the road most of the time."

"I suppose. Do you miss home?"

"I haven't been home since I was fifteen. I look forward to company." Jared stares out at the water fountain that's situated in the middle of the driveway. When will he meet someone genuine who will love him for him? He loves this house, but would love it even more if it was filled with his own family. "I don't know why I bought this house." He scratches his head. Buying it might have been a mistake. He could have bought a penthouse downtown; it would have had little upkeep. When he was presented with the house among many others, he was drawn to the four-car garage, games rooms, and home theater. "I have an empty swimming pool, five bedrooms—three that are left empty—and dishes I've never used."

"You have a beautiful home," Jane says softly. "People dream about living like you do."

"I don't take it for granted."

"It's how we were raised. You've earned it. Don't forget your dedication and hard work that went into paying for what you have."

"I don't remember my late teen years. I was on the ice for most of them."

"Look where it's gotten you," she says.

"Sometimes I feel lucky." Jared rubs his forehead. "I still think about Luke."

"So do I."

"Lately I've wondered why I lived and not Luke."

"It wasn't you who was in that boat, Jare. When are you going to stop blaming yourself for what happened?"

"I tried helping . . ."

"I know you did. You did everything you could."

Jared sighs, getting into his car. It was a time in his life he couldn't forget. Every detail, every scream that came out of his mouth trying everything to get Luke to respond to him was burned into his mind.

"It's been ten years," he says, trying to justify his loss.

"I know. It's still hard. Doesn't seem that long ago."

"I remember the day like yesterday."

"Where does the time go?"

Jared is quiet. As the years go by it's harder to accept that Luke will never experience all his hopes and dreams the way Jared's life was going for him. He thought he'd be stuck on some farm team and Luke would be the one playing in the NHL. Now Jared can see he has the life his cousin wanted, just not a family he thought he'd have by now. Most of the guys on the team were married with kids. From the stories he heard from teammates, most guys had children in their twenties.

There was nothing stopping them when they had the money to make their dreams come true. Why wasn't Jared so lucky with women? They came and went like the rain on the West Coast: some stayed longer than planned. There was never anyone he felt he could be with for the long-term.

"Ten years isn't that long," she says. "Not when you miss someone."

Jared scratches his forehead, elbow resting on the steering wheel. "I don't know where the time has gone." Calgary, Carolina, and now his second season with Vancouver.

"If you have a girlfriend by the time I come out, I want to meet her."

"So you can grill her?"

"Someone has to. The last one got away with too much."

Jared throws his head back and stares out at the cloudy sky.

Meghan comes to mind. Her red toenails pressed against the carpeted concrete floor. He remembers, without her heels on, she stood up to his chest. Petite, but made of fire. He wants her. He is sure he can make her putty in his hands, starting with a foot rub. She turns him on. She is pretty with green eyes and a soft glowing complexion. He wants to know who Meghan is. Although he won't be with just anyone; he learned that recently and won't go down that road again. He is done with the immature dating. He wants someone he can count on. A woman who is willing to stand by him. Love him for who he is and is secure with herself. There have been plenty of women who have thrown themselves at him. It's sometimes flattering like the time he had a few too many beers and the woman he met at the pub was a gorgeous blond who knew what she wanted and what she could give him. That was the old Jared. This time, he wanted someone real. Someone he could count on and connect with. He didn't know Meghan, but she kept playing on his mind. She was sexy and if she didn't know it, he wanted to show her how he felt about her. That was the challenge. He needed to show her that he was attracted to her. Would she be interested in him?

"Do you remember Lindsay? The one I used to work with? She was asking about you."

"Lindsay? I don't recall."

"She wanted to know how you were doing. Next time you're home I'll set you up."

"That won't be for a while."

"When you play Ottawa, maybe there might be a night."

"You know I don't have much time when I'm in a city. We play a game and depending on how far it is, we fly out the next day. You know that."

"She's nice, you'd like her."

"Why are you bringing this up now? You didn't mention her when I was visiting in the summer or any other time I'm there. Is she newly single or something?"

"Yeah, she just broke up with her boyfriend."

"Okay, Jane, I have to run. I gotta get to an event."

"I expect you to introduce me to one of your lady friends."

"My lady friends?"

"I want to make sure you're on the right track."

"Thanks for that." Jared hangs up, satisfied that Jane called. It always means a lot to him when his family calls, making them feel not so far away.

Jared drives to the event held at a car dealership located on the outskirts of town, where the Warriors Heroes Campaign is taking place. Meghan had sent an e-mail to all the players asking if they could attend. He replied with a yes, knowing that he needs to continue to make some appearances in this city if he wants to be liked.

Jared gets out of his car and checks his phone because Meghan had specific instructions where to park, what entrance to use, and where the Warriors' tent is set up. Jared sees the blue tent a mile away, including balloons and music from the dedicated parking lot.

For the beginning of October, the weather is blue sky and cool. He walks through the lot, taking in the amount of people there and what exactly is going on. A clown is playing with balloons creating a buzz around the children's tent and the salesmen have their hands behind their backs, pacing the lot, smiling, trying to make eye contact with the guests at the event.

Jared stays focused, getting closer to the Warriors' tent, where he sees his buddies chatting to one another. Security is making lineups for people to talk to his teammates and by the looks of things, it's going well. There is one woman, hanging about, mostly to the side of the tent. The toe of her boot is circling the pavement, her hands tucked into her coat pockets, looking every bit model-ready with her straight blond hair and light-knit hat she wears for a fashion statement. Given that it's

October, it's still not cold enough for gloves and hats, unless they were back home, but even still, Easterners were used to the autumn chill.

Jared takes one more step and realizes that the woman is someone he knows. His stomach tightens and he puffs out his chest, unwilling to walk farther. He doesn't want to see her. She'll make a scene, act like they're together when they're not and she will insist on going home with him. The idea gnaws at him for a second or two, until he reminds himself that she wouldn't leave willingly. He had a hard enough time breaking up with her. Even if he wanted affection from a woman, he certainly didn't want it from his ex-girlfriend. He'd have a hard time getting rid of her once she saw that he was there.

With a quick turn on his feet, he hustles back to his car, trying to hide behind trucks as he dashes away. As much as he wants to make an appearance for the fans, he can't stand there knowing she's watching his every move. He can only imagine her response when he joins his teammates under the tent. He doesn't want to face his ex-girlfriend and listen to her whine about him. He needs to be away from her now and hopes that, given time, she will forget about him, too.

"Hi, Keri," Meghan says, as she walks past her boss's office, heading next door to her own.

"Meghan, hi! How did the event go?" Keri asks.

Meghan is stepping away when she hears the question being asked. She steps backward so that she's in Keri's office doorway. "Good. I think we raised a lot of money."

"Did they give away a car?"

"They did!"

"Good. They said they would."

"Even if they didn't reach the minimum?" Meghan asks.

"Regardless. It was great publicity." Keri crosses her arms at her chest. "Sorry I missed it. I had too much work to do. I knew you could handle it though."

"I'm happy with how it went."

"On our end, how did it go? Players got enough attention? No crazy fans?"

"All players who were scheduled showed up, except Jared Landry, even though he e-mailed me and told me he would be there."

"You can't make a player do anything they don't want to do," Keri says.

"Yeah, but they should show up to events when they're scheduled. That's what's expected from them."

"Ha! Don't expect anything from any player." She gives her a stare. "What they do and what they show up for is because they genuinely care. Someone like Jared, there's no use spending time trying to convince him to go to events. He does or doesn't. The only one I'd push him on is the black-tie event at the end of the year. Every player is expected to show up at least for an hour to show their support for Children's Hospital. We're making a huge donation. The whole franchise will be there. It's the least they can do."

Meghan crosses her arms at her chest and leans against the door rame. "They are placed on pedestals in this city and this country for that matter, and make millions of dollars to play a game. A game. Hard to believe," she says, shaking her head. "The least they can do is make appearances."

"All the power to you. But just remember, they are celebrities and are what make up this organization and our jobs."

"We're doing what's best for the team and have to show support for our community."

"I like your thinking, I really do, but if you make a player do something he doesn't want to do, he'll be unsupportive and hard to get along with. You don't want that." Keri gives her a sharp eye. "Jared's the only one that chooses which events he shows up at. At least all the players cooperate."

"Why doesn't he show up? Who does he think he is?"

Keri double taps her pen on her desk. "I don't know. He used to. He's never said."

"I'd understand him if I knew what was going on in his world."

"Like he's going to tell you." Keri giggles.

"Well, maybe he doesn't like big crowds," Meghan concludes.

"He's not shy," Keri says.

"What do you think it is?"

"I don't know. Maybe it's personal?"

"I'm going to ask him."

Keri raises an eyebrow. "You're going to ask him why he doesn't come to events? But he does make it to some."

"What makes him pick and choose which ones? You would think he likes the attention."

"You would think," Keri says.

"Okay, well, I'm going to find out what the reason is."

"And do what?"

"He'll have to show up for everything or I'll make it uncomfortable for him at the events he does go to," Meghan challenges.

"You're not going to win."

"I'm just going to tell him that I won't advertise him at events if he doesn't bother making an effort to show up. I have fans ask me where he is. I'm making excuses for him and I don't even know the guy!"

Keri bursts into laughter. "That won't happen. Before I forget, I'm having a girls' night next week, after the reading campaign at the library. We're all meeting for dinner and drinks. You're welcome to come."

"Sounds like fun."

Keri hands her a binder. "I need you to look at this. It's the black-tie event. We need to confirm some details before announcing the schedule."

Meghan takes the red binder and brings it to her chest. "When is it?"

"December thirtieth. You're gonna love it. It's a good excuse to go shopping and buy an outfit."

"What kind of outfit?" Meghan asks.

"Formal."

Meghan purses her lips.

"If you don't have anything, it's a good excuse to buy something." Keri flips open her notebook-style agenda. "I've got to make a phone call before it gets too late."

"And I have reading to do," Meghan says, lifting the binder in the air. She also has to find an outfit to wear since she can't think of anything hanging in her closet. The only dress that comes to mind is her beloved wedding dress she never got to wear.

Chapter 4

"Can you make it to the stop sign?" Meghan asks her best friend, Brie, who is running a stride behind her.

"It's a block away!" she says breathlessly. She wipes the sweat from her forehead. "My legs feel like they're gonna fall off."

"You can do it!" Meghan tells her. "Almost there!"

Brie blows out a breath. "Easy for you . . . to say . . . you're conditioned."

"So are you!"

"Twenty-minute jogs don't count." Brie slows down her pace.

Meghan takes a leap to the stop sign, jumps up, and stretches her arms to the sky. "You did it!"

Brie catches her breath, hunches over, puts her hands on her hips, and marches on the spot. "Plus, you have longer legs."

"Thanks for the company," Meghan says, smiling.

"You're going to have to find someone who can keep up with you," Brie says, breathing hard. Sweat is dripping off her neck, visible from her ponytail. Her blue headband rounds her face, making her brown eyes vibrant with her red cheeks.

"I usually go by myself."

"I'm going to a yoga class tomorrow night, wanna come?" Brie asks.

"I don't think so." They are wearing identical capri workout gear and sports tank tops. The pair walk together, across the road to Meghan's place.

"Come on! You never go."

"That's because the last time I went I did some pretzel move and hurt my knee. I couldn't run for a week!"

"You know what to expect now," Brie says. "I think it would be good for you . . . a chance to stretch out your body, relieve stress."

"Why don't you ask Sara? She'll go. She does that hot yoga thing."

"I always wanted to try that! I think you would really like it, Megs."

"I like running." Meghan opens the front door of her apartment building. "Yoga is boring. If I'm going to work out, I want to do cardio, really sweat, you know?"

"You'd like it," Brie tells her. "I'll see if Sara wants to do it. It would be nice to go with someone."

Meghan shrugs. "She'll probably go. Do you want to come in and grab a drink?"

"Sure. Maybe for a few minutes. How's the job working out?"

"Great! Everyone seems to be okay to work with. I'm not used to working with celebrities though. Some of the guys think they don't have to show up for things because of who they are."

"Oh, yeah? Like who?" Meghan opens the door to the staircase. "You're really making me work my cardio," Brie says, as they both climb the stairs.

"It'll give us a good stretch," Meghan says, opening the door to the second floor. "Don't say anything, I'm sure Mike tells you stuff anyway, but there's this one guy, who I just met, and he's really getting on my nerves. I mean, he shows up after the event, saunters in like it's no big deal."

"Did he forget the time or something?" Brie asks.

"No, he said he got pulled over for trying to call me on the way there. I don't believe him."

"I'm sure they're full of excuses." Brie flips her hand. "Although they can't be forced to be somewhere if they don't want to be."

"I don't know. He did promise me he'd make an effort next time."

"Who is he?"

"Jared Landry."

"Yeah, I heard he does what he wants to."

Meghan gets out her house key and inserts it into the lock. "What do you mean?"

"I'm not really sure and I shouldn't repeat this, but I heard that if he doesn't feel like doing something he doesn't. There was some charity thing at the hospital and he refused to go on television because his stitches were still visible on his face."

"What else does Mike say about the players?" Meghan wants to know.

"Not much, he doesn't really talk about it. He tells me stuff he hears from his coworkers. Mike deals with international and national media relations, so he doesn't have a direct relationship with them like you do."

"Some relationship." Meghan laughs. "I communicate by e-mail and even then I'm not sure if they receive it. Most of the time I don't get a reply."

"They probably assume that you know they'll show up."

"I appreciate Mike getting me the job." She takes off her shoes.

"You earned it."

"I know, but he put in a good word for me and I owe him that."

"Mike's glad to help. He said they needed someone with promotional experience. They need you."

"Tell him thanks, again."

"Megs, you've told him. He knows you appreciate it."

Meghan pours two glasses of filtered water from the jug in the fridge. "I'm glad to be out of B & B Communications."

"Because of Stu?"

"There's that." She hands Brie a glass. "It's hard working with a boyfriend who checks up on you constantly. I couldn't make a phone call without him hovering at my desk. Besides, I wanted the senior position and I didn't get it." Meghan gulps down her water. "They're all in cahoots with each other. I didn't have a chance." She fills her glass again. "Better to get out while I could. I'm lucky you're dating a guy who has a killer job."

"You have a killer job."

"I do now. Thanks." Meghan smiles, filling Brie's glass. "So, things are going well for you two?"

Brie nods and then says, "Really well. It's weird. Before Mike, I was dating some guys who I liked but there was something missing, you know? Then I meet Mike and my whole life has changed."

"I'm really happy for you guys. You think you two will get married?"

"I think so. Do you miss Stu yet?"

"No," Meghan says, and laughs. "I'm glad it's over. I should have broken up with him months ago. I feel bad for doing it over the phone though."

"Why? He didn't feel bad for cheating on you."

"True. When you and Mike first got together did you think, 'I like this guy, I can see myself with him for a long time'? Or, did you think he was just another guy to date?"

"I knew we'd be together. I felt it. We love being together. He makes me laugh and is easy to talk to. We just fit."

Meghan sulks.

"Don't worry, it'll happen to you," Brie says, patting her friend's arm. "You definitely need to find someone new. Someone cuter, stable, ready to get off the couch and run with you."

"And where do you suppose I'll find him?"

"Work?"

"That's where Stu and I met. Look what happened."

"You're not there anymore. You're at a new place with new men, new potentials."

"I don't work at a dating service," Meghan says, giggling.

"You work with a lot of hot men. Men with careers. Men who are all business, looking for a smart woman to complement them. Let's not forget about the gorgeous hockey players you work with. Your guy is there, right under your nose, you just have to open your eyes to see him."

"That's false advertising," Meghan says. "Just because I work with guys doesn't mean there are any available."

"You're smart and too pretty not to have a guy with similar interests. Now that Stu's out of the picture, you can start finding a decent guy, someone who's not going to take advantage of you."

Meghan sighs. "I'm not in a rush. I should give it some time. Clear my head. Think about what I want in a guy."

"No!" Brie jumps. "You don't need time. You need to get back into the groove. You're already in dating mode, you might as well find someone else."

"And if I don't want to?"

"Please. You can't tell me you don't want to be in a relationship."

"I do. Of course I do, but if I don't find anyone that's okay, too."

"You're just saying that. You need to practice your flirting skills. Get confident in your abilities. I think Stu stole that from you."

Meghan laughs. "I don't flirt." She settles onto the couch.

"You have to if you want a man to be interested in you. You need to practice talking to guys. I think Stu was a guy you went for because he was there and you hung out after work."

"It was convenient."

"Exactly!" Brie snaps. "You need to practice getting to know guys who aren't so non-boyfriend material."

"Stu was okay."

"He wasn't for you. You need to get back into the scene and show that you're available."

"I'd like to be single for a little while. I could probably use a break anyways."

"Why? What for?"

"I don't know."

"Look, you need options. I bet there are guys at work you could practice on."

Meghan stares at her friend. "No."

Jared.

"Is there someone in the office?"

Meghan shakes her head.

"How about a player? I'm sure there's someone."

Jared.

"There's no one."

"Not one?"

"Nope."

"Come on. Seriously? I don't believe it. There has to be guys who are single and looking."

"Looking for what? Not a relationship." Meghan laughs.

"They're human too. They want to settle down I'm sure."

"No one I've seen or talked to," Meghan says, although Jared keeps popping into her head. She doesn't know why. She doesn't even like him, but his blue-eyed stare seems to sink into her body the same way her body soaks up the sun: with a pleasurable warmth and acceptance.

"You're not giving yourself a chance."

"Since when do you care about my relationships?"

"I've always cared."

"You didn't like Stu, did you?"

"Not really."

"How come you never told me?" Meghan asks.

"Would it have made a difference?"

"I don't know. What don't you like about him?"

"You don't suit each other. You don't show interest in the same things. Even when he held your hand it was like a chore. It didn't seem genuine."

Meghan thinks about this. "It was rare Stu would grab my hand or throw his arm around me, yet he didn't have a problem with kissing in public."

"I'm surprised it lasted as long as it did," Brie says. "You should have dumped him months ago."

"It was going okay."

"You should be out dating other guys."

"I'm just not sure where to start, let alone ask a guy out."

"That's why you need some practice. There's got to be some guys at work who you can have a conversation with and flirt a little to get your confidence up for the real thing."

"I don't really know any of the guys." *Jared.* "There's no one I'd care to talk to." *Jared.*

"You work with eighty percent men and nobody comes to mind?"

"Well . . ."

"There's someone? Tell me!"

"No one," Meghan says. "Can't think of one guy." She tightens her lips, shaking her head.

"Maybe you need some more time to get to know who's who."

"That's probably it."

Brie grabs for her cell phone. "You might be interested in this." She scrolls through her pages. "I follow a relationship expert and her latest feed is the flirt challenge. I tried this on Mike and it totally works."

"What's that?"

"I found I got his attention when I complimented him, told him he looks good, fixed his hair for him . . . he couldn't keep his hands off me. I swear!" Brie smiles wide.

Meghan giggles. "Really? You're kidding."

"You should find someone to flirt with and try these tips." Brie scans through her phone to find the article.

Meghan giggles again. Why does Jared come to mind? She doesn't even know him, or like him.

"Here it is!" Brie waves her hand around with excitement. "The first thing it says to do is lock eyes and then look away. If he doesn't look away," she says, "it means he's interested. The next thing, be approachable."

"I am!"

"Don't cross your arms. It makes you seem closed off. The other thing is, smile and laugh. If you come across as a happy person, chances are you'll attract him. People like to be around others who are joyful. It says."

Meghan lies back on the couch, resting her head on the puffy cushion. "Who do you think I'm going to flirt with?"

"I don't know. A guy in a coffee shop, at work, anywhere. When you see an attractive guy, try this out."

"You're into this, aren't you?"

"It works! It could help you." Brie puts down her phone. "I'll e-mail this to you."

"You think I need help with getting a guy? I just broke up with Stu."

"He's a loser and you're not wasting tears over him, thankfully!" She sighs. "He's not what you needed and you know that. Stu totally took advantage of you and stripped you of your confidence."

"Are you an expert now?"

"Oh!" She waves a hand. "It says to find ways to bump into him. If he sees you often enough, he's going to want to see you again. Maybe your man goes to that café you go to every Friday and you haven't noticed."

"I just started going there on Fridays. I treat myself to a mocha before work."

"You need to do this!" Brie clicks off her phone and puts it down. "You can thank me when you marry the guy who you win over with these moves. So the next time you see a guy who you find attractive, lock eyes with him. That's the first thing you do. If he stares at you, smile. Flip your hair or play with your necklace, something like that. You have to be direct. So when you're stirring your mocha and putting a lid on your cup, strike up a conversation, ask him a question to get him talking."

"And if he leaves?"

Brie shrugs. "On to the next guy."

"It's that simple?" Meghan smiles.

"Uh-huh."

Meghan thinks about this. "I'm not a flirt. I can't do this."

"Sure you can!"

"I can't just bump into a guy and start talking to him. I've never asked a guy out."

"You don't have to. Once you flirt, it will lead to him asking you out. You'll know if Jared is interested. Do you have someone in mind?"

"No."

Jared.

"I'm going to take off. I promised Mike we could have dinner together."

Meghan walks her to the door.

"Forget about your ex-boyfriends . . . refocus your strategy on finding a new man."

"I've never needed help before."

"Maybe you do this time," Brie says, walking into the hallway. "What are friends for?"

Meghan thinks about Jared. He's too stuck on himself. She could never go for someone like him—a gorgeous, famous hockey player, living in the same city, working for the same company. He may be too out of reach for her, she thinks, but flirting is harmless.

Chapter 5

"If you can score a goal like you did in practice, we'll kick some serious ass tonight," Alex Price says as he takes off his shoulder pads. "It would be a good feeling to win against Winnipeg early in the season."

Jared throws him a nod as he unlaces his skates. He listens to the guys talk around him. He'd rather keep to himself, that way he doesn't have to get into his personal life, and the less the guys know, the easier it is to try to move on.

"I was watching Sports National," Alex tells the player beside him. "They say Corey Wells might be coming here."

Jared perks up. He hasn't heard Corey's name in years. Suddenly a sick feeling is at the pit of his stomach. Wouldn't that be a nightmare if Corey played here? *I'd ask for a trade.*

"Mark?" Alex shouts. "I heard you might be traded."

"Don't believe them," Mark says, sitting beside Jared.

"I don't know," Alex taunts. "The media is all over it."

"Do you believe them?" Mark asks.

"Yeah," Alex says. "I do. You've been here for a long time."

"Six years," Mark says. "We'll see what happens."

Jared thinks about Corey. It's been ten years since they spoke to each other. Thankfully, they never played on the same team, always against. Every time they played, Jared steered clear of Corey and vice versa. It was like a secret code they shared. Although, there was a time when after Jared body-checked Corey into the boards he wanted to elbow him in the face, which would have started a fight and cost him a major penalty. He hadn't wanted his team to lose because of his decision, so he had left Corey alone.

"Hey, Landry!" a voice says from across the room. "You didn't make an appearance yesterday. Did you forget?"

"Nah, something came up," he lies.

"Too bad. Your girlfriend showed up looking for you."

Jared clenches his jaw. "She's not my girlfriend."

The guy whistles. "Oh, wow, she wants you bad."

Jared keeps a straight face, proceeding to take off his hockey shorts. This is what he didn't want from his ex, but then, she thrived on attention.

"Our promotions girl, what's her name? Meghan? Yeah, she was wondering where you were. Saw her checking her phone to make sure she didn't miss your call."

"How do you know she was checking for me?"

"She said."

Jared gives a sideways grin as he takes off his shin guards. "Is that right? I don't believe you."

"Now there's an easy target for you. She likes you."

"What did she say?"

"Called you a liar for not showing up."

"I never said I'd be there," Jared says.

"She was all bent out of shape about you not showing up."

"It's not a big deal, is it?" Jared asks as he heads to the showers. Once he's cleaned up and dressed, he exits the locker room and walks down the hall. Instead of taking the elevator down to the parking lot where his car is, he rides it to the third floor where the marketing offices are. He stands tall, trying to relax his shoulders, but the thought of talking to Meghan puts a little fear into him. Will she accept his apology? He doesn't know why he's nervous about talking to her, he talks to women all the time. He'll break the ice by telling her that his nephew will be taking part in the family skate. The elevator dings and the doors open. Then again, he can wait to talk to her. He can e-mail her. She's probably busy. He won't be able to find her anyway. That's what he will do. She must have a boyfriend or husband. A pretty woman like her wouldn't be single. She's damn hot. What he would do to get his fingers dangled in her wavy, auburn hair. Her green eyes glisten like the Mediterranean Sea and her body moves with grace. The doors are starting to close. Jared makes a quick exit, signaling the doors to reopen.

The third floor is surprisingly quiet. He's never been here before. Never had to. He looks from side to side trying to figure out which direction he should walk in. There are no signs posted to tell him which department is where, so he decides to go left. It's a stretch of hallway with office doors and framed action photos of past and present Warriors players. He stops to look at each one. He's not in a hurry anyway. No one is going to tell him he can't be here, so he takes the time to read the bronze engraved plate at the bottom of each picture. It's like being at an art gallery. There are so many frames lining the hall that he's interested in looking at each one.

"Can I help you, Jared?"

You know my name.

Jared looks to his side to see a short, dark-haired woman holding a handful of papers to her chest, dressed in a business suit.

"Uh, no, well, I was looking at these . . ." He points to the wall and stops talking. "Actually, I'm looking for the marketing department."

"You are? Everything okay?"

"Yup."

"It's the other way," she says, pointing her finger. "This side is sales."

Jared nods. "Thanks." He takes a moment to look at a few more pictures and then walks down the hall, passes the elevators to find Meghan's office. Does she have her name on her door?

He saunters down the hallway, passing people as he goes. People taking second glances at him as they walk by.

"Hey, Jared!" a guy in a business suit calls with a wide grin. "Can I help you look for someone?"

"Meghan?" If only Jared could remember her last name. He's read it on her e-mails, but hadn't paid attention, that was until he met her at the cookbook giveaway. What a gong show. Cookbooks. Who would have thought they'd be in demand. What happened to a signed hockey card? Or an autographed T-shirt?

"Marketing department?" Jared asks.

"The door at the end."

"Thanks!" Jared walks to the open door. The closer he gets, the more noise he hears. People chatting, phones ringing. No wonder this department is at the end of the hall away from everyone.

He stops at the doorway contemplating to go in. He could just e-mail Meghan like he planned. He doesn't have to interrupt her. She's probably really busy. . . . *Maybe I'll just walk in and see if I can see her. Nobody will know I'm there . . . I can always say I found the wrong door.*

Jared cautiously steps inside, looking around at all the staff gathered in small groups. *It's so loud and busy, people walking around, they won't even notice. . . .*

His eyes dance around the room to see if he can spot Meghan. It doesn't occur to him that he could be standing in the wrong place and interrupt this department's work agenda.

He walks in farther, and the room gets quieter until the only sounds are phones ringing. All eyes are on him. Even the girl on the phone has her mouth open and looks stunned as though he's dressed in a Halloween costume. *It can't be because of me,* Jared thinks, someone important must be behind him. Ted Walker? He looks over his shoulder. Nope. It's just him, standing in the middle of a large office with desks around the perimeter and a boardroom table in the middle. There is no privacy. The room is a wide-open space.

"Hi, Jared." A young guy in a suit walks over, holding out his hand. "I'm Eddie. Can I help you?" He extends his other hand to indicate the direction.

Jared shakes his hand and looks past the guy only to see Meghan standing at an employee's desk beside an employee with her hand on her hip.

"Meghan?" Jared asks. His throat is dry. He swallows and looks around. All eyes are still on him.

Meghan scoots over to him. The room returns to lower voices and whispers.

"I want to talk to you," she says.

He glances to her side to see a bunch of eyes fixed on him. "You do?" He rubs his prickly chin and smirks. *Maybe this is a bad idea.*

"Can we go to my office? It's next door," she says.

He nods slowly. "Okay."

"Follow me," she says, stepping past him.

His eyes travel from her tanned high-heel shoe to her muscular calf to the smoothness of her skirt on her backside. He can only imagine what her body looks like without the skirt and sheer blouse. Although she could keep the heels on. That's always a turn-on. He stares at her until she walks into the next room where there is one desk, a few photos, and a stack of binders. He could lay her down right here on the desk and have his way with her. He'd love to play with her hair as he kisses her neck. . . .

"I'm glad you came by," she says, waving to a chair. "Have a seat."

He shakes the fantasy out of his mind. "I . . . I don't want to sit."

"Okay." She leans against her desk. "What can I do for you?"

If she only knew.

"I'm bringing my nephew to the skate on Saturday." He looks around at her bare walls. Jared notes the empty, cold feeling of the white walls and empty desk. "Is this really your office?"

"Yes. Why?"

"Just wondered."

"I'm still getting settled," she says.

"How long have you worked here?"

She releases her arms to her sides and holds on to her desk, sliding her bottom back to sit. She crosses her legs at her ankles.

He notices she isn't wearing a ring on her left hand.

If he can get her talking, maybe he wouldn't have to leave so quickly. This conversation can end in a second and yet he wants to know who she is. Her eyes are bright, a little makeup, he guesses, but whatever it is, she is stunning. Her light skin tone is highlighted in pink at the apples of her cheeks and her auburn hair is pulled back into a ponytail, leaving wisps of hair shaping her oval face.

"Almost three months."

"You need pictures or something," he tells her.

"I haven't had time."

"You're busy with events . . . what do you do?" he asks, realizing he doesn't know what people in this department are responsible for.

"I organize public events and schedule players to attend—"

"That's why you're always e-mailing. You're in charge of every-thing."

"Well, not everything," she says, smiling now. "But I execute a lot." She pauses, staring at him.

He whistles. "Sounds serious. Execute. Killing events."

She sucks in her lips, but a burst of giggles comes out instead.

"That's what it means?" he asks, leaning against the wall so that he is looking straight at her.

"I'm guessing you didn't come here to see where I work," she says, picking up her pen and tapping it on her desk. "Funny enough, I have to talk to you about something."

"You do?" He's all smiles.

"I want to make sure that we are on the same page. If you can't make it to an event, I would appreciate an e-mail or phone call from you so I can get someone else."

His smile fades.

"I'm committed to the team to make these events happen and if players don't show up, it wouldn't be much of an event."

"Fair enough."

She gives a shrug of her shoulder and says, "If you can't make it, let me know. I spend a lot of time advertising who will be at an event and it seems like a waste if you don't show up." Her voice is sweet and light.

"Got it."

"So, what can I do for you?" She's all serious again, but her eyes look bright and happy. A good change from the women he's used to being around.

"The family skate. I wanted to tell you I'm bringing my nephew. That's all," he says, shuffling his foot.

"Okay. You can e-mail me, you know. You don't need to come all the way up here. I'm sure you have better things to do."

"I figured since I was at the rink that I'd come by your office, check out the place."

"Okay. Thanks for letting me know. I'm not keeping track of what players are bringing who. It's open for the players' families. I'm just scheduling it. There will be some refreshments and snacks, that sort of thing."

"Thanks for doing this." He pauses, putting his hand on his hip. "Did your boyfriend give you that foot massage?"

Her face flushes. Her green eyes widen. "No."

"Too bad. You were run off your feet that day."

"How did you know? You were busy signing autographs."

"I was watching, well, kind of." He swallows. "The crew. There's a lot of behind-the-scenes people," he says for a quick cover-up.

"Wasn't it like that in the last city you played in?"

"Not like here. The turnout is bigger. . . ."

"I'm surprised, but I guess Carolina doesn't have as many hockey fans as Vancouver."

"They have fans . . . good fans." He points at her and then brings his hand back to his side. "Wait . . . you knew I played in Carolina."

"I follow hockey." She shrugs.

Jared smiles. "Impressive."

"Not really." She shrugs. "I work with the Warriors, I need to know what's going on."

Even still, Jared is taken aback that she knew anything about him, let alone where he was traded. Didn't she say she had only been working here for almost three months?

"Trade deals go around in this city as breaking news," she says with a snicker. "Plus, I used to work with guys who that's all they talked about, trades and hockey pools."

Jared relaxes, enjoying the conversation. It doesn't bother her that he's in her space chatting about stuff that doesn't matter?

"And of course it's news when you're in the play-offs."

"You think we'll make it?" he asks, throwing the question her way to see how serious she is about his sport.

"I'm sure you'll make it." She gives him a seductive look that makes him imagine again just what he could do with her in his bed.

"You have faith in us. The season has just begun," he says, sizing her up.

"We have a strong team," she says, shuffling papers on her desk. "There's no reason why we shouldn't."

"I like your thinking," he says, and means it.

"When we're in the play-offs, that's when wagers start and people bet who don't normally gamble. I suspect the same will happen here in this office."

"I don't know. I've never been in this department before," he admits.

"Never?"

"I've never had a reason."

"You came by to see me?"

"I had to talk to you. Well, you probably have lots to do. I should get going."

"You have a game tonight," she says.

"I do."

"Do you go home and rest before?" she asks.

"Sometimes."

"Not today?"

"I will . . . I have things to do," he stammers, thinking how interested she is.

She is playing with her pendant, her hand at her cleavage, moving the jewel from side to side. She is such a distraction.

"You're busy," he says again.

He takes another step backward. "I'll see you at the skate."

"Yes and I'll see you at the Vancouver Library for the Warriors Reading Campaign."

"When's that?"

Her shoulders sink. "Next Tuesday." She looks down at her desk calendar and runs her finger over the dates. "Yeah, we're promoting literacy. It's an annual event."

Jared says nothing.

"I sent the e-mail."

"All right then."

"You need to be there. People are counting on you. You did get the e-mail?"

He nods.

"Good. I'm starting to think you're ignoring me."

"I'm not ignoring you. I apologize for not showing up yesterday—"

"What is it? You don't like publicity? Or are you too busy?"

"What time's it at?"

"Starts at ten."

"Until when?"

"Two. That's it. It's a short event."

"I'll be there in the afternoon."

"Why not when it starts?"

"I don't like being at these things the whole time."

"Come on! They're fun! You get to meet kids and talk to people. It's all about promoting you and the team."

"Who else is going?"

"Let's see," she says, looking down at her desk calendar. "Mostly everyone is supposed to go. You do like kids, don't you?" She looks up over the page she is holding and sees him nod. "It's an easy promotion. You just have to show up. The kids will be all over you."

"Am I supposed to bring something?" he asks.

"No," she says. "You just have to show up."

"Like the cookbook promotion?"

"Exactly."

"Does anyone really care about those recipes? People don't actually use the book, do they?" He chuckles. "That seemed like a ridiculous promotion."

"Not at all. It was successful," she says.

"Was it?"

"Of course. Any promotional item that has the Warriors brand on it sells. I'm sure it was like that in Carolina. Only here can you sell a cookbook."

He shakes his head.

"And run out of them," she says. "I had to turn people away because we ran out of five thousand copies."

He scratches the hair on his jawline. "Who comes up with these ideas?"

"Me."

He laughs. "Do you?" He lets out a blustery breath and walks backward until he's at the open doorway.

"When you show up to these events, it benefits you and the team. The public wants to see our stars as regular people doing good things."

"I'm here to play hockey. I don't care about appearances."

"No?" She raises her chin. "Then why did you come by to see me?"

"To tell you about the skate," he says matter-of-fact. "I wasn't sure if there was a requirement of how many people a player could bring."

"If you're only bringing your nephew, it's not a big deal. Some players have three kids, some are coming by themselves. It all evens out. Besides, it's for fun. There are no rules."

"Great." He walks backward out the door. "If you're free tonight after the game, bunch of us will be at Buckley's. If you're up to it."

"Bars aren't my thing."

"Oh. Okay. Me either. See you at the next event then."

"I'll try and make it," she says, playing with her necklace.

Jared is fixated on the way her necklace dangles between her cleavage. She smiles at him and just when he thinks to leave, she says, "Thanks for stopping by to talk. I appreciate it."

He steps out into the hallway, turns around. She is swinging the pendant over the gold chain. He holds her stare, feeling a moment of desire he doesn't want to let go of. Her green eyes have sucked him into wanting more of her. He can't pass her up. He has to find a way to get Meghan to want him and then maybe his ex will come to terms with the fact that they are really over. His ex-girlfriend still thinks she has a chance with him. She keeps showing up to events and expects him to give her all of his attention. At the beginning, they hung out like couples do, except, Jared didn't bring her to the rink or associate her with his teammates, afraid it would turn serious and he wasn't ready for commitment. She, on the other hand, wanted more. She began to call him often and even showed up in LA when he was on a road trip. That was when he told her they needed a break. Jared didn't hear from her for weeks. He thought he would never see her again, until he made an appearance at a Warriors event and she showed up telling him they belong together. What will it take for her to understand that there's not going to be a second chance?

He nods at Meghan in response. Jared gets one last look at her as he leaves. She has to be taken. Has to be, he tells himself as he saunters down the hall to the elevators.

Chapter 6

The Dome is closed to the public. Staff and the players are gathering around the rink. There are refreshments and snacks on oblong tables. Children are laughing, players are smiling, making the event an enjoyable place to be.

"Can you please add more bottled water to the ice bath?" Meghan tells an employee. "And we'll need another tray of layered dip and a bowl of chips over there." Her eyes skim the table for anything else that might be missing.

The food station is set up not far from the Zamboni doors. There's room to gather, plus the entrance to the rink is wide open for people to come and go.

"I'm here," a voice says, catching Meghan's attention. She makes eye contact with Jared.

Her stomach rises and falls. "Oh, hi, Jared," she says, smiling. She grabs hold of her bracelet and begins to twirl it around her wrist, remembering the flirting techniques. Her eyes drop to Jared's waist where she sees a little boy standing beside him, looking up at her with the same blue eyes. His blond hair is a lighter shade and falls to his neck. "Hi there," Meghan says, trying to guess the boy's age. She sees a strong resemblance. The boy could pass for Jared's son.

"I'm going skating," the boy tells her.

Jared taps the boy's shoulder. "This is my nephew, Beckham."

"I'm glad you could join us." Meghan crouches down. "Did you bring your skates?"

"Uncle Jare bought me some," Beckham says.

"He did? That was nice of him. You're all set, then." Meghan reaches over to grab a juice box. "Beckham, would you like a drink?"

The boy takes it and says thank you.

"You know, there are some games for kids starting in a few minutes," Meghan says."If you want to participate. There's a bench over there," she points. "If you want to put on your skates."

She smiles at Jared and then looks past him to see a woman with medium-length blond hair walking up to Jared. She is wearing a long coat with tiny pockets and big buttons. She has a pair of figure skates hanging over her shoulder.

"My brother's always looking out for him. I'm Jane," she says, extending her hand.

"Meghan."

"Meghan is the PR coordinator," Jared says.

The woman nods. "Where's Becks?"

Jared points to the bench.

"He'd get lost in this crowd. Gave me a scare at the airport. He wandered off when I was checking in."

"He needs a leash," Jared says jokingly.

"He'll learn," Jane says, hearing her son call for her help to tie his skates.

Meghan watches Jane walk away. "Your nephew is really cute. He looks a lot like you."

"So, you think I'm cute?" Jared teases.

Meghan blushes. "Well—"

"People do ask if he's mine," Jared says. "The Landrys have strong genes."

Jane returns. "He's ready to go. So you're the one who put this together?"

"I had help."

"I'm impressed."

"Don't be, it's a team effort."

"I'm ready," Beckham says, handing his mom his shoes.

"You can leave them at the bench with the others," Jared tells him.

"Are you skating?" Meghan asks Jared.

"Yeah," he says. "I'll go grab my skates."

"Where is Uncle Jare going?"

"He'll be right back," Jane says. "Probably going to the dressing room to get his skates."

"I wanna go!" the boy yells.

"Catch up to him, then," Jane says, watching her son walk as fast as he can in his ice skates. Beckham calls for his uncle. When Jane sees Jared stop to wait for the four-year-old, she smiles at Meghan.

"Does your son play hockey too?" Meghan asks.

Jane rolls her eyes. "Yes. He wants to be just like his uncle."

"Sweet."

"It's a little much sometimes, but we know he's proud of him. Do you have children?"

"No," Meghan answers. "Do you have other children?"

"We've been trying for another one, but it hasn't happened for us yet." Jane clutches her jaw. "Aren't you going for a skate?"

"I didn't bring mine," Meghan says. "Actually, I don't own a pair."

"Here, you can borrow mine," Jane says, and she takes the skates off her shoulders.

"No, it's fine, thanks. I'm working."

"Is it hard to organize this kind of event? It seems like a lot to do with a team and staff."

"This one was easy. Everyone wanted to be here, it makes a difference."

"I guess so. I'm surprised my brother wanted to come out. He's not really a social butterfly."

"I sense that," Meghan says. "It would be great if Jared could make more appearances though. He has a lot of fans here."

"He does at home, too."

"I bet."

"I'll work on him," Jane says with a wink of her eye. "Here he comes. We better change the subject, don't want him to think we're talking about him. Might go straight to his head." She smiles at her brother. "He could use a little grounding."

"Don't believe what she says," Jared says, approaching. "She likes to get me into trouble."

"I'm allowed to. I'm the oldest," Jane bickers.

"Uncle Jare took me into the dressing room!" Beckham exclaims. "I got to meet Mason Ward and Alex Price. It was so cool."

"It is pretty cool," Meghan says. "Did you see the center of the room? It looks exactly the same as the rink's center ice."

"You've been in the dressing room?" Jared asks, staring at her blankly.

"Does that surprise you?"

"Oh, well, I guess you have. I mean you work here . . . it's just that the room isn't open to anyone all the time and you're new . . . so—"

"I'm not that new." She holds a stare with the blue-eyed guy whose tasteful lips are parting as though he wants to speak, but can't seem to get the words out. Instead he smiles, just enough to show a glimpse of his top teeth that are not perfectly lined, indicating his teeth must be real. "Besides, you don't need to be a player to walk into the dressing room."

"I thought—"

"You do have to have credentials, which I do, and a reason for being there and I did." Her eyes are steady on his, making sure he gets the point that she's not just an employee but an important part of the franchise. Jane is snickering, and Jared is listening inattentively.

"I didn't mean it negatively," Jared corrects.

"Can we go now?" Beckham asks, tugging at his uncle's shirt, springing up and down.

Jared keeps his focus on Meghan. "I'm surprised, that's all."

"I have a lot to do with the Warriors that you might be forgetting," she says.

"I know what you do."

"Because you've been on the third floor, so you think you know what's going on?" she teases.

"I do now."

"And what's that?"

"You . . . you organize events."

"Uh-huh. And?"

"And you talk to different organizations."

"Yeah."

"Can we go!" Beckham cries. "Pleeeease."

"Okay, okay," Jared says to his nephew, trying to shush him with a wave of his hand. Jared holds his gaze with Meghan. "Aren't you skating?"

"I told Meghan she can borrow mine."

"It's okay, really, I'm not skating. Besides, I'm sure we're not the same size."

"I bet we are! What size are you?"

"Eight, eight and a half."

"I'm an eight! I told you! Now here, put them on." Jane shoves the skates at her.

"I shouldn't."

"There should be some perks to the job. Of course you should!"

"And just start skating by myself?" Meghan laughs nervously.

"Jared will take you. Right, Jare?"

"No, I'm fine," Meghan protests. "You better get Beckham. He's on his own."

"He's been skating since he could walk," Jane says.

"I'll be back," Jared says, walking to the bench to put on his skates. She turns to Meghan. "Good to see my brother relaxed."

"He's not always?"

"No," Jane says, trying to spot her son skate. "I wish he'd settle down. He'd be a good dad."

"He loves his nephew."

Jane grins. "He does. That's for sure."

"Is your husband here?"

"Yes, he's here on a business trip. I decided to make it a family event," she says. "It worked out nicely."

"Aren't you coming?" Jared calls from the open boards. "I know you wanna," he teases.

"You go, it's your family skate," Meghan says.

"It's my brother." Jane winces and the two of them laugh.

"You can skate with Beckham," Meghan says.

"I don't think it's a good idea."

"Why?" Meghan asks.

"Jared doesn't know," Jane whispers. "But I'm eight weeks pregnant. I don't want to risk it."

"Congratulations!" Meghan shrieks, with a clap of her hands. "That's exciting news!"

"It's a secret." She lowers her head.

Meghan brings her finger to her lips. "I won't say anything, promise."

"Thanks."

"Aren't you coming?" Jared asks.

"All this pressure," Meghan teases.

"No pressure," he says.

Jane hands her the skates.

"I don't know," Meghan says. "I'm working. I shouldn't."

"I need to skate with someone," Jared says.

"You have Beckham," Meghan says.

"He's already gone," Jared says. "You don't like skating?"

"I do!"

"Haven't you ever been on skates?"

"Last time was at a high school field trip."

"Come on," he says, waving his hand. "You'll be fine."

Meghan looks at Jane. "Thanks. See what you've gotten me into?" The women laugh.

"Go!" Jane tells her.

"I could get into trouble," Meghan says.

"Jared wants you to skate with him," Jane pushes. "You should go."

"But—"

"Put the skates on!" Jane urges.

Meghan takes the skates and sits on the bench to put them on. She looks up to see Dana's worried face.

"What are you doing?" Dana asks.

"Going for a skate." She ties up the boot, her fingers are so jittery that she has to retie it.

"You brought your skates?" Dana asks.

"They're Jared's sister's. She wants me to take her place."

"You're brave. I wouldn't be caught skating with these guys. I'd be laughed at for holding on to the boards."

"That'll be me in a few minutes." Meghan tightens the skate and stands up, her legs finding balance. She's trying her best to hold still with each step. "Wish me luck."

Meghan takes a small step on the ice, unable to hold herself up. She grabs the boards firmly with both hands, trying to get her balance. Her knees are bending as she can feel her legs wobble like those of a fawn standing up for the first time.

"Bend your knees a little more. Find your balance," Jared insists.

"I'm trying."

"Let go of one hand," he says.

"No. I don't want to fall," she calls out. Fear is setting in.

"I thought you said you've done this before." She can tell by his voice he is amused.

"I have." She can't look at him, afraid she'll slip. Nice and steady, she tells herself, moving one foot in front of the other. It's more of a forward and backward glide, hardly moving.

"Did you use the buddy bar?" he asks.

Meghan's face is feeling warm.

"Okay, okay. No biggie. You just have to get your balance and let the blade glide you until you can lift a foot."

"I'm not lifting anything! I'm going to fall!"

Her heart is thumping so hard in her chest she's afraid she's going to bail. What a scene that would be in front of her peers and Jared, who seems to be paying attention to her every move.

"You're not going to fall," he reassures.

"You have more faith in me than I do myself." Meghan's knees are buckling and her legs are feeling wiggly. "I think I better save this for another day."

"You're doing the moonwalk." He is laughing.

Meghan starts to laugh with nervousness. "I can't help it."

"Go forward."

"I'm trying," she says, watching her feet. If she looks into his eyes one more time, she'll lose her concentration. "I'll never make it around the rink."

"Don't worry. I'll help you. Take my hand," he offers, reaching for her.

Meghan looks at his hand; it's strong and could probably pick her up if he tried. She then looks at him and she can't move. "Come on, take it." His smile is wide and his eyes are a gentle stare.

Slowly she lets go of the boards, her legs wobbly again. Her arm starts flapping as she tries to get her balance. Jared grabs her hand before she falls, the other pulling her into his chest. A tingle runs down her spine. She feels safe now, just how she imagined she would, given the chance to be held by him.

"Don't worry, I've got you," he says, giving her hand a squeeze. Suddenly she believes him and a part of her believes that he's enjoying watching her struggle. "Move your left foot."

Meghan tries to push her foot forward.

"Now the next one," he tells her, paying close attention to her.

Meghan does and slowly with the help of Jared for balance, she is moving at a snail's pace, but managing to keep her feet moving, which pleases her. Kids are laughing and skating fast past them reminding her of her twelfth grade skate, when her laces had been done up so tight that her feet had started to fall asleep.

"I think I have this if you want to find Beckham," she says, not wanting him to feel obligated and taking up all of his time. Doesn't he want to socialize with his family or teammates?

"He'll come find me if he wants to. He's playing tag with Buckley's kids."

"Hey, Jare, are you giving private lessons?" a guy shouts out as he skates past them.

Jared chuckles.

"Seriously," Meghan says, trying to look at him, but afraid to lose her concentration watching her feet. "I don't mind if you want to find your nephew, I'll be fine."

"You'll be fine?" He smirks, his lips arched at the side. "We're halfway around the rink and you want me to leave you?"

"You're not here to coach me," she says.

"I sure can't have you stranded at the boards. What kind of guy do you think I am?"

"Uncle Jare!" Beckham yells, skating up to him. "Watch me! I can do a crossover." The boy demonstrates his new move.

"Very good! Don't forget to bend your knees a little more. Yeah, like that. You got it!"

The boy yells and skates as fast as he can.

"Beckham's a sweet boy," she says. "He loves your attention."

"I don't see him much."

"He looks up to you." There's a pause. "Any children of your own?" Meghan asks.

"No." His answer is so soft that she wonders if he wishes he had or it's triggered a memory of someone he used to be with. It wouldn't surprise her if he answered yes. He strikes her as a family man considering the affection he has for Beckham.

"How about you?" he asks.

"Me? A mom? No. I'm an aunt. My brother has two kids."

"How old?"

"Six and eight."

"You didn't bring them today."

"It's for the players," she says.

"Thanks for doing this."

"It's my job," she answers. She's never had a player thank her before, although by the looks of it, she's the only staff member on the ice. Meghan glances at her watch. "Oh, it's time to do the announcement. I gotta get back."

"What's the announcement?"

"Ted Walker wants to thank everyone for coming." She wobbles back and forth trying to get her balance. A wave of panic flows through her. Meghan's back arches and her head flings back, knowing she's going to fall, but just then, Jared's hand grabs her waist and he pulls her in close.

"I gotcha."

"Thanks," she says, drinking up his blue-eyed stare. Her stomach rises and falls. "That would have been embarrassing."

"For you or me? I'm the skater. I couldn't let you fall. The guys wouldn't let me live that one down."

"There's Ted. I have to move faster. I don't know how he feels about his employees taking part in team functions."

"He won't see you," Jared says. "And what's he going to say?"

"That's what I'm afraid of." Meghan looks ahead to how far she has to go. "He's going to see me. What am I going to say?" She grits her teeth. *Don't panic.* Jared can't see her stress. She's got this. "A hundred more steps and I should be there."

"Not even," he says.

Meghan tries skating faster, but the blades are like dull knives, hardly making a dent in the ice. She is skimming the surface barely moving.

"He's coming over! I think he sees me."

"No way," Jared says easily. "He's watching the kids skate."

"I think he's wondering why I'm on the ice . . . with you."

"Relax. Don't sweat. He's just taking it in. It's not often there's an event just for the players, right? So he's just checking it out, seeing who's here."

"Yeah, he sees me." Meghan bites her bottom lip. "I'm in trouble."

"No, you're not." Jared pulls her from the boards.

"What are you doing?"

Jared secures his hand around her waist and takes her left hand in his. "Glide," he says.

"I don't want to fall."

"You won't fall. I've got you." His voice is firmer. She believes him.

Meghan squeezes her eyes shut for a second feeling the cold air tingle her nostrils, her legs getting the hang of it, even though her legs are shaky.

They reach the opening.

"Mr. Walker," Jared says. Meghan is trying to gain her balance; she prays Jared won't let go of her. She can barely stand on one leg as she eases her foot off the ice.

"Jared," Ted says, and turns to Meghan, lowering his full face to meet her eyes. "I see this turned out to be a good event. Everyone showed up, I see. Are you enjoying yourself?" He shoves his hands into his pant pockets. "Is Keri around?"

Meghan gives a quick glance to where she expects Keri to be. "Yes, she's by the refreshment table."

"Is she cutting the cake?" he asks. "Or are you?"

"Um . . . that would be me," Meghan says.

"You're busy," Ted says. "I'm sure Keri can."

"No, no, I'm doing it," Meghan says, taking a step forward.

"I asked her to skate with me," Jared interrupts.

"Well then, let's get the cake cut," Ted tells them.

Meghan hurries to the bench to take off the skates. As she unties them, she notices a pair of Bauer skates loosely laced. She looks up to see Jared standing in front of her. "You didn't have to cover for me."

"He looked upset. I didn't want you to get into trouble. It's supposed to be a fun time, right? I don't think it's a big deal."

Neither did Meghan, but hosting events is part of her responsibilities, she has to show the owner and Keri that she is more than capable of being part of the festivities.

Meghan slips on her flat shoe. "You didn't tie your skates."

"I don't need to. Not for something like this."

His legs must be stronger than she thought and his ankles must be like rocks.

Meghan stands up. "Thanks for the skate."

"Anytime. When are we doing this again?"

"There will be another family skate before play-offs, at least that's when I'm trying to schedule it."

"No, I mean us. We should go skating."

"Us?"

Jared laughs. "Yeah."

"Here? At the Dome?" she asks. "I don't think that will happen. These functions aren't easy to book. I gotta look at the Dome's schedule. Maybe at a local arena."

"I didn't mean—"

"Do you know how many kids would go nuts if you showed up for a public skate?"

"No, I—"

"It would be insane! You wouldn't be able to skate."

"I . . . I didn't think about that."

"I have to get this cake cut."

"Right. Well, we could—"

"I'll see you around," she says with a quick wave. "Thanks for the skate!" Meghan hurries over to the dessert table where Keri is standing.

"Where have you been?" Keri asks.

"Skating."

"Skating?"

"With Jared Landry. He asked me to join him," she says, trying to hide her grin.

"I didn't know you had an interest."

"I don't know how to skate," Meghan admits.

"No, I mean with him."

"Oh." Meghan looks away. "Jared was helping me. He skated with me."

"Like held your hand?"

"A little, yes. He mostly kept me at the boards and made sure I didn't fall."

"Oh."

"I almost fell a few times." Meghan laughs. "I didn't know I'd be so wobbly. Jeez, it's not easy getting your balance. He makes it look so easy. Well, they all do. It's been a long time since I've been on the ice . . ."

"Do you want to start handing out cake?" Keri hands her a plate. "Don't forget napkins."

"Right." Meghan grabs forks and places them neatly on each plate. As she turns around, people are holding their hands out for a slice. The cake is half done when Jared approaches her. Automatically, she hands him a piece.

"No thanks."

"You don't want double chocolate with custard filling?"

"I'll give one to Jane and Becks." He takes two plates.

Meghan watches Jared disappear into the crowd.

"He's something else, isn't he?" Keri asks as she organizes the table with more napkins.

Meghan grins. "He's all right."

"My friend used to date him."

"Is that right?"

"Yup. He broke her heart. He's not one for commitment, apparently."

"Did he cheat on her?" Meghan asks, intrigued.

"No. He told her he was done. Wanted to date other people."

"He's not with anyone now?"

"I don't think so. I don't know."

Meghan sighs.

"Are you interested?" Keri asks.

"Me? No. Not me."

"That's good. I'm pretty sure they'll get back together. He said they were on a break."

"Did he say why?"

Keri shakes her head.

"I'm going to collect empty plates," Meghan says, wandering into the crowd, keeping her eyes peeled for Jared. Did he ask her out? Maybe he wants company since his family isn't living here. It doesn't take long before her hands are full and she unloads at a nearby garbage can.

"Thanks, Meghan, for putting this on," Jane says. "We're leaving now. It was nice meeting you."

"You as well. Thanks for coming. Where's Beckham?"

"With Jared. We're off to grab an early dinner."

"Good luck with everything," Meghan says, giving her a reassuring smile.

"I have a good feeling about this one," Jane says, referring to the pregnancy. "I'm going to tell Jared later. Are you free tomorrow? If you're not busy, would you be around? I'm free . . . and, well, I don't have anything going on."

"That would be great," Meghan says.

"Jared has practice tomorrow and Beckham and I don't have any plans in the afternoon, just wondering if you want to grab tea or something? I'm not comfortable venturing out by myself."

"That would be great. Here's my business card," Meghan says, pulling one out from her pocket. "It has my cell number on it. I always keep a few on me when we have these functions. Never know who needs to contact you."

"For sure!"

"Talk to you tomorrow."

Chapter 7

Meghan and Jane carry their hot beverages in paper cups as they stroll Lonsdale Quay. They pass the water fountain where a busker is strumming a guitar and a photographer is selling scenic photos on a display table. It's a late afternoon, but the tourist attraction is very much alive.

"Mom? Can I have money?" Beckham asks.

"Money for what?" Jane asks.

Beckham points to the fountain.

"Maybe when we come back you can make a wish," Jane says, watching her son run ahead. Beckham tries to catch his rubber ball.

"Watch out for people, Becks!" Jane yells.

"He keeps you busy," Meghan says.

"Yeah. He reminds me of Jared when he was Becks' age. Full of energy."

"Jared is full of energy?" Meghan asks. "He seems mellow, but maybe he gets it out playing hockey."

"He was more talkative at the family skate than usual."

"It was the event. He had family there."

"No, I think he's finally coming around," Jane says, keeping an eye on Beckham a few steps ahead. "He came out to see us two months ago and he wasn't very talkative. I thought something had happened, like a breakup or something job-related. But being here, Jared seems like a different person." Jane sips her tea. "I don't know why I'm telling you this. I guess 'cause his friends are distant and family is far away. We don't see him as much, so it's hard to figure out what's happening in his life."

"I don't really know your brother," Meghan says. "I've met him a couple of times."

"Oh," Jane says with an arched eyebrow. "I thought . . . um, you and Jared were kinda seeing each other."

Meghan laughs. "No." Only in her dreams. "What made you think that?"

"I got a sense that the two of you . . . never mind, sorry," Jane says, playing coy, stopping in her tracks and reaching out a hand to touch Meghan's arm. "I hope I didn't offend you. It's just that the two of you were friendly at the event. Jared held you on the ice. He was smiling and the only things that make him smile like that are Becks, sushi, and a girl he likes."

Meghan's stomach flits thinking about Jared holding her body up and making sure she didn't fall. She had liked the way his arms had been around her, concerned that she was going to fall. His hand had been strong and made her body weak.

"He's happy because his family is here," Meghan says.

"No, no, I don't think that's it. Something's changed in him and I thought that the two of you—" She pauses. "Sorry. It's probably hor-mones," she says giddily. "I'm feeling a lot more emotional this time than I did when I was pregnant with Beckham."

"Don't worry about it."

"I shouldn't be talking about my brother with you. I figured since you worked with him you might see things that he doesn't tell me."

"Like what?" Meghan is interested. She can finally learn a little more about the left-winger. The lives of hockey pros are always a secret to the public.

"Anything. A woman hounding him at events."

Meghan laughs. "No, I haven't seen anything like that. Of course there are fans. All the guys get swarmed if there's not enough security."

"How about friends? Have you noticed who he's hanging around with?"

"Jane, I don't know Jared," Meghan says softly. "I don't have any-thing to tell you."

Jane blinks. "I'm sorry. You're right. I'm just concerned. I don't know anyone on the team. His friends play with different teams and they wouldn't know if something was wrong."

"Why do you think something is wrong?" Meghan's eyebrows furrow.

"He has a past."

"Everyone does."

She throws her head back. "No, he's had some crazy ex-girlfriends."

"I'm sure. A guy like him, professional athlete."

"I'm worried that his ex-girlfriend will try to contact him again. She was obsessive and I don't know if she's psycho enough to try stalking him."

"Would Jared take her back?"

"He says no, but the girl had some power over him. He couldn't say no, except when she told him to marry her."

Meghan gasps.

"Oh, yeah," Jane says, and laughs. "I shouldn't be saying. Sometimes Jared, he gets distant with people, but I didn't see that with you."

Meghan grins. "He probably flirts with all the girls."

"Jared is sometimes hard to please. He doesn't open up too often."

"He seems friendly with everyone," Meghan says.

"Becks! That's too far!" Jane yells after her son.

"My ball!" he yells at his mom, pointing to the twenty-five-cent ball rolling under a bench.

Jane walks faster to get to her son and when she does, she squats and reaches under the bench to retrieve the toy. Beckham takes it out of her hands and bounces it again.

"Did you tell Jared the good news?" Meghan asks as they proceed to walk again.

"I did."

"Have you two always been close?"

"I think so. He left home at fifteen though to play junior, so we lost that family bond because he was only home occasionally and I had my life. I'm two years older."

"Must have been hard for him to be gone." Meghan looks at Jane, recognizing the same rounded chin as Jared's, the fair skin and height.

"It was harder when we lost our cousin. He was like a brother to Jared." Jane takes a sip of her tea and looks out onto the ocean.

"I'm sorry to hear that," Meghan says. "Devastating."

"It was. I think it's still hard for Jared at times. They were the same age and working toward the same career."

"What happened?"

"He died when he was eighteen. It was an accident." Jane stops, strains her eyes, looking for her son. She sucks in a breath. "Becks! Becks!" she yells, straightening her neck to see past the people in front of them. "Where is he? Do you see him?" Jane runs ahead surveying the site for Beckham. Meghan looks around and doesn't see him either.

"Beckham! Beckham!" Jane yells. She stops running and looks around her. "He was just right here!" she cries. "Where did he go?"

Meghan is looking furiously around them, focusing on any small area where the boy might be. There are a dozen small takeout restaurants and gift stores. Did he wander off with someone? Did he find another kid to play with? The thoughts race through Meghan's brain and she fears the worst. She should have been watching Beckham too. How could she not see him disappear? He was walking in front of them, a few feet away.

Jane runs to the pavilion, racing through the building, checking every corner, behind every counter. Meghan meets Jane outside. "He doesn't take off," she yells to Meghan. Her face is dewy and her eyeliner is smudged. "Beckham! Beckham!" she shouts. Strangers are looking and following her gaze to see who she is yelling for.

"Did you lose your child?" a man asks. "What does he look like?"

Jane breathes out before speaking and talking with her hands. "He has short, blond hair." She stops to take a breath. "A little long at his neck." Jane uses her hand to comb down her hair as she explains. "He's four years old, wearing a blue hoodie, jeans . . ." Jane brings her hand to her forehead. "I feel sick. Where is he?" She turns, looking all around her.

Meghan starts asking people if they've seen Beckham. She sees Jane dash past a building yelling her son's name. Meghan stops to ask the hot dog vendor and the lady at the ice-cream stand. No sight of Beckham. As the minutes pass, Meghan becomes more concerned. She doesn't see Jane. Meghan decides to walk to the green space past the pavilion. She has her head down and watching for small bodies. How many minutes have passed? Should they call the police? How long should they wait to notify help?

The water fountain! Meghan thinks, and beelines it to where they started. How does a child, no more than five feet away, get lost? Would someone take him? Did he follow someone? Another child and then forgot where he was? He wouldn't know to trace his steps, would he?

Meghan looks impatiently around the area, scoping it out, hoping she'll see a glimpse of the little boy with messy long hair. The guilt of Beckham's disappearance gnaws at the pit of her stomach. She feels sick. Pressure to her head and a tightness in her throat. It's been fifteen minutes and it feels like an hour she's been searching. She doesn't even know where Jane is. She may never see the two of them again after they find Beckham. Will she get blamed for not seeing him disappear? Maybe she's to blame for the distraction of talking about Jared. Meghan is looking every which way as she walks through the crowd and back around toward the water fountain. There are a lot of people and it wouldn't take much for him to walk behind adults and then get confused and not know where he is. He must be scared, not knowing the area and losing his mom. He's probably crying. She doesn't hear an emotional child, which makes her think that he's not there.

Meghan decides to go back to where they first noticed Beckham was gone and hopefully he'll be there waiting. It only takes a few minutes to get back to where they were, but no Jane in sight. She stands in the middle of the waterfront path with her hands on her hips, pivoting around. Nobody is watching her though. People pass by as she calls out as loud as she can, "Beckham!"

Meghan and Jane make eye contact. Jane shouts as she runs in boots toward her. Tears are in her eyes, mascara imprinted on her eyelids and dark circles have appeared around the tops of her cheekbones.

"I'm sorry," Meghan says. "We should call the police."

Jane nods, her eyes glossy and full of worry. Meghan can't imagine how sick she must feel.

"We'll find him," Meghan says, grabbing for her hand. "He's here. He's probably in one of the stores."

"I checked! I didn't see him."

"Or at one of the vendors?"

"I checked that, too." Jane takes a step to leave, rubbing her eyes. She no longer has the tea she was drinking. Her hands are waving around.

"Mom! No, Mom!"

The women turn their heads in the direction of the child's voice.

Jane's mouth opens to respond, but it's another boy calling for his mom to tell her he doesn't want his coat on. Jane cries. "Maybe he ran ahead, I'm going to look some more."

"I'll go this way!" Meghan shouts. Jane keeps running and Meghan's not sure if she heard her but continues to look in a new direction. Meghan walks to the water fountain. Where else is there to look? It's not a very big place unless he's wandered into the market, but Jane's been there. She wanders around until she spots the little boy trying to bounce his ball as high as he can. Beckham. He's oblivious that he's lost. Meghan sucks in a breath, she can't believe she found him, yet he's totally fine playing with his ball. "Beckham!" she shouts in a not so alarming voice. She doesn't want to scare him, but shouldn't he be scared that he's all by himself?

"Beckham!" she yells, and scurries over to him, reaching out her hand. He doesn't flinch. He stands there with a bright smile, staring at her like he's looking up and admiring the autumn sun.

"My ball can bounce really high," he tells her. "Wanna see?" And he throws the ball down so hard, but stops on the grass.

"The ground is too soft," Meghan says. "You have to do it on pavement for it to bounce."

"I've done this before." He's looking at his ball with a hard stare.

"Let's go get your mom," Meghan says, and leaves her hand out for him to take.

He doesn't take her hand, so she keeps hers at her side, available and ready for when or if he wants to take it. She doesn't let him out of her sight and slows down her pace to be walking with him as she scours the area for Jane. Meghan lets out a breath, stumped at where Jane has run off to. "Let's stay here until we find your mom," Meghan tells Beckham, stopping by a bench.

"You can sit down if you want."

Beckham continues to bounce his ball and catch it with two hands.

Meghan sees Jane running toward them screaming, "You found him! You found him!" She gets closer and yells for her son. "Beckham!" When she reaches them, Jane bends down to grab her son and cradles him in her arms and cries. "I thought I lost you. You made Mommy very scared. You can't run ahead of me. Never! Ever! You understand?" She pulls him away to look at him in the eyes. "I was really scared, Beckham. Don't ever scare me like that again." She hugs him. "I love you! I thought someone had taken you." She cries on her son's shoulder. She then lets go of him and stands up to face Meghan. "Thank you." Her face is textured with running makeup. "Where did you find him?"

"Just over there," she says, pointing. "I saw him with his ball."

Jane exhales again and holds on tight to Beckham's shoulder. "Thank you," Jane says, and without warning, wraps an arm around Meghan's shoulders and squeezes. "I really thought he was gone. I don't know what I would have done. I don't know," she says in a daze. "Thank you."

Chapter 8

Jared wanders up to Meghan's office and stands at the doorway, watching her shuffle papers from one side of her desk to the other, clicking her keyboard and mumbling something to herself. Her hair is parted to the side and left down in its wavy state. He enjoys watching her busily working on something that appears to be important. She glances at the doorway, back at her computer, and then makes eye contact with Jared. She raises her eyes, stunned to see him standing there.

"Hi!"

"Sorry, didn't mean to startle you," he says, taking a step inside. "Your door was open."

"It's always open," she says, her hands resting on a stack of files. She smiles pleasantly. "What can I do for you?"

A lot of things. I could stand here and watch you for a while.

He notices her green eyes have flecks of gold in them, her glossy lips are tasteful, and he inhales, stepping inside the small room. He can smell her floral perfume. He takes another step closer, inhaling her scent that is driving his mind wild. He wants her in his bed. Tonight. What would she say to that?

"What?" she asks.

"Nothing," he says, unable to tell her what is playing on his mind. She would probably throw something at him or worse, tell him he's a dog and send him walking, never wanting to speak to him again. He wouldn't want to blow his chance. What will it take for her to spend the night? Could they even go out for an evening? Could she put her work to rest?

"What brings you by? I've never had a player come to this part of the building before, let alone two times. It's unheard of."

She doesn't have the time to small-talk?

She is wearing that necklace again, the one that hangs low to her chest. He can't tell what it is, a stamped rectangle? A name written in calligraphy? Her short-sleeve blouse shows off her shapely arms. If he stares any longer she's going to catch where his eyes are going. "I can't thank you enough," he says.

"For what?"

"For finding Beckham."

"It's fine. I'm glad he's okay."

"Beckham is Jane's world. He's everything to her. And to me, too."

"She's his mom."

"I know . . ." He nods. "I can't imagine him gone. . . ."

"I'm glad he's safe. I happened to be at the right place at the right time."

"Jane says he got carried away with his bouncy ball, he didn't even notice where he was."

"It happened so fast," Meghan says, recalling the moment.

"You're busy," Jared says. "I just wanted to come by and say thank you."

"No problem. Will I see you tomorrow at the library for the Warriors Reading Campaign?"

"Right. Yes. I will be there. Ten o'clock?"

"That would be awesome." She smiles wide.

Jared takes in her warm appreciation. He could stand here and watch her work. Her smile is infectious. He can't stop smiling back. He leans against the door frame. "Do you have plans tonight?"

She freezes, looks up. "Why?"

"I dunno. Thought you'd want to join me for dinner."

She stares at him for what feels like a long time before she answers.

"Do you have plans?" he asks, giving her reason to decline. He doesn't understand why she would.

"Probably not a good idea," she answers, giving him a lasting stare.

"Why?"

"It wouldn't be a good idea. I mean, you're the hockey player and I'm the . . . the . . . I . . . we work here together and I don't think—" She stops herself.

She is so damn cute when she's blushing.

"It's just a thank-you for finding Beckham," he says. "That's all. I thought I could buy you a drink, take you to dinner."

"You don't owe me anything. Goodness, I would hope if it were me in that situation it would be a good outcome."

"It's just a thank-you, but I understand. You don't want anyone to see me with you."

"No! That's not it at all. I'm flattered. I don't want you to go out of your way to think that you have to thank me. That's all. Really. I don't need anything for it. Jane would have found him, I'm sure. She was close by."

"Jane said she wasn't even close to where Beckham was."

"We weren't too far," Meghan falters.

"Jane said she didn't even know where you went looking for him and you took it on your own to look somewhere else. My family is very grateful. I'm very grateful. I'm taking you out tonight."

"You are?"

She gives him a smile that makes his insides turn upside down. What he would do with her. Damn he wants her bad.

Jared has a feeling Meghan might be harder to convince than other women. Although, no other woman has made him this light on his feet and eager to get to know her. He wants to know who Meghan is, physically and emotionally.

"So do you have a boyfriend? Wouldn't want to get into trouble."

She giggles, finding him funny for asking. "No. I thought you said it was a thank-you dinner," she says.

He can't stop smiling. "It is." He claps his hands together. "Okay then. It's official. I'm taking you out." He holds back from saying the word *date* in case she doesn't feel the same. Why wouldn't she, though? He's a successful hockey player with a name that rolls off the tongues of people in this city. Maybe she's playing shy.

"I'm off at five. I can meet you somewhere."

He can't stand still. If only he had practice now to skate off the adrenaline.

"Where do you want to meet?" he asks.

"I don't know. This was your idea."

I have other ideas.

"How about the Oasis Pub? Six o'clock?" he suggests.

"I'll be there. Six thirty," she says.

"I'll be waiting."

* * *

Jared waits for Megan at a square table at the back of the pub. He is trying to hide himself from the loud, middle-aged men sitting at the bar. They are commenting on the sports highlights and the prediction that the Warriors will have a good season now that they have players like Mason Ward and Eli Cooper. Strong players who can score goals and be tough. It's a hope that they can play for the cup this season, backed by their fans. The nerves are always hard to control at home games. When Jared plays, he tries to keep his focus on the game and ignore the crowds and the chants that fill the Dome. It's tough some nights especially when they are losing. Warrior fans get louder just when he thinks the building can't handle any more yelling and chanting. That's what he gets for playing hockey in this city. It's the way things are for Vancouver. Every night he plays, he thinks of his cousin and puts out his hardest effort for Luke. If Luke is looking down at him, Jared hopes his cousin is proud.

Jared takes a gulp of his frothy beer, sits back, and watches toward the entrance for Meghan. He's anticipating her beauty that leaves him breathless. Her legs are long with calves like apples, small and round. She definitely works out. Her body lean, her lips taut and glossy. Just the thought of kissing her makes his body rise with desire. If he whispered her name and kissed her neck, would it make her body fall into his? Would she be easy enough to take home? How much convincing does she need? He's not asking for a relationship with her, just one night, or multiple nights, depending on how well it goes. There is something different about Meghan though. A woman eager to do business and who flirts with the idea of having fun. He's sure that Meghan knows how to unwind, she just needs the opportunity. Maybe tonight will be the night.

"Jared Landry?" a twentysomething guy asks, walking closer with a curious stare.

Jared sits up straighter and moves his glass away from him, ready to extend his hand. "How are you?"

"It is you!" the young guy shrieks. "I don't believe it." He smacks his forehead and runs his hand through his hair quickly before offering a handshake. "It's great to meet you. Wow. I was just having some drinks with some buddies when I saw you. I didn't think it was you, but then I looked up your picture just to make sure and . . ." He talks with his hands. "Here you are! I wish I had something for you to sign."

He looks around him. "How 'bout a picture instead?" He takes out his cell phone and turns to the waitress walking by. "Excuse me? Can you take our picture?"

The waitress isn't bothered by Jared's status. She takes the phone, taps a few times, and hands over his phone. The guy thanks Jared and leaves.

"You don't look so alone," Meghan says as she steps up to the table and takes a seat across from him.

"I am."

"Drink?" the waitress asks Meghan.

"Vodka and cranberry," she answers.

Jared observes her loose-fitted black shirt and round studs in her ears. Her hair is pulled back into a low ponytail with a couple of long, wavy strands shaping her face. Her skin looks fresh like she just had a shower.

"You changed your clothes," Jared begins with a sideways grin, liking what he sees.

She stares into his eyes for a moment making his heart beat a little faster. Her lengthy, black lashes bat in dismay.

Damn she looks good. I thought by starting off with a little flirting I'd have the upper hand, but she's got me pegged. I can see it in her eyes. She can take it. I like this about her. She doesn't back down.

"I'm not working," she says, leaning back in her chair so that the waitress can set down her drink in front of her. "Thanks," she says, and lifts the glass to her mouth.

"It's working for me," Jared says with a smirk he can't quite erase. He licks his lips and takes a drink, trying not to be too proud of his flirting abilities. What does she expect from him tonight? He only hopes she wants something from him. Is she looking for a one-night stand or something more? "So, is your boyfriend okay with you being here tonight, with me?" he teases.

She laughs, putting down her drink. "I told you I don't have a boyfriend."

Now she won't feel guilty and we can both breathe easily tomorrow.

"I remember," he says. "I find it hard to believe you're not with someone."

"Is that what women tell you until you find out they're taken?"

"I thought for sure you were with someone."

The waitress comes over asking for their dinner order.

"Do you know what you want?" Jared asks Meghan.

She flips open the menu. "I can't make a decision." Her finger scrolls down the page. "Do you know what you want?" she asks, looking up over the menu. He answers yes and places his order. Meghan orders a wrap and hands the waitress the menu.

"What were we talking about?" she asks. Her stare is airy and light, but with an intensity that has him eager for more, and he gazes straight back into her bright eyes.

"That you're not with anyone," he says.

"Right. And you?"

He presses his hand on the table. "Not anymore, but I want to hear about you."

She looks up thinking, batting her coated eyelashes. "I was with some-one for five months. We broke up. It was after the cookbook signing."

"Are you hurt about it?"

"No. Turns out he was a lying bastard who cheated on me. Jerk." She winks.

"Jerk."

"Who does that to someone?" she asks.

"Not a guy you want to be with."

"Cheating. You know what happens when the lies start? They never stop." She takes a long sip of her drink. "It didn't start off that way."

"No?"

"It was nothing too spectacular. He was someone I met at work. We did the same thing. He fell for the intern."

"Why did you go out with him?"

"He took me for a ride on his motorbike and he bought me my own helmet. Well, I found out it was his ex's." Meghan plays with her glass. "He knew how to make me swoon. How about you? Are you seeing someone?"

"No." Jared shakes his head. A little stunned by the question. "I wouldn't have asked you out tonight if I were."

"So you're not a cheating bastard?" she asks with a laugh.

"Nope. Never." It was true. Jared was fair. If a girl wasn't working out, he ended it. Ever since his last girlfriend, he's hesitant about re-lationships. She did it to him. Wanted him every second of the day. He couldn't breathe without telling her where he was and checking in when he arrived at a hotel. She bragged about being together and told people they were engaged. He wasn't planning on it, she wasn't someone he pictured as the mother of his children. Not that he's even considering finding someone who fits the bill, but when dating becomes serious it seems like that's all women think about.

"Did you love the jerk?" Jared asks. He needs to know how hurt she really is about the breakup. That will make all the difference as to how far they go tonight. If he plays the "poor you" card, she'll go for him. What he could do with her legs wrapped around him . . .

"No. Not a bit," she says. "Glad it's over." She drains her glass and sets it down. "Sorry, I shouldn't talk about it."

"Doesn't bother me." He shrugs it off, gripping his glass.

"My friend Brie would give me the third degree if she heard me talk about Stu. She doesn't think he deserves a mention."

Jared is speechless; watching her smile makes him happy. He's forgotten about his life and is interested in hers.

"I'm sorry, sorry." She waves her hands. "I gotta stop. I want to hear about you."

He leans back in his chair. "You know about me. You met my sister, my nephew—"

"Will Jane be coming out again?"

"I doubt it. Although she didn't say." Knowing his sister, she'd want to stay home and get some rest. "She said you two had a good time, despite Beckham's disappearance."

"We found him safe and sound," she says. "That was a relief."

"Thanks to you."

Meghan shrugs. "I'm sure she would have found him. I was in the right place."

"Jane is very thankful, as is the rest of my family."

The waitress puts down their dinner plates. "Another drink?" she asks, reaching for the empty.

"No, I'll take a club soda and lime?" Meghan says, then turns her head to Jared. "You can tell Beckham is close to you."

"I try to stay connected while I'm away from home."

"Home being Brampton?" She attempts to take a bite of her wrap.

"Yeah." He lifts his chin. "Jane told you a lot about me."

"Actually, you told me where you're from. At the public signing when we met at the dressing room."

He makes a face. "I did?"

"Yup."

"I don't remember. What else did I tell you?"

There's a mischievous look in her eyes. "We don't have all night."

"I do," he says. "And you don't have anyone to go home to. Tell me more."

"You don't want to hear about me."

"Yes, I do. Are you fighting off guys to leave you alone?"

I sure the hell don't want to leave you alone.

She laughs.

"I take that as a yes."

"No!" She giggles some more, sucks in her bottom lip.

Jared straightens his back to readjust himself, anything to take away from staring at Meghan. She blows his mind. He can only imagine what she's like in bed. He wants to show her what she's missing out on.

The waitress drops off their drinks.

Meghan purses her lips and stares into his eyes. For a moment, Jared's heart is beating faster. It's like she is feeding his soul with liquid pleasure and he doesn't know what to do except seduce her and take her home. What else can he do with an attractive woman who makes him all forgetful and childlike? He hasn't experienced a woman like Meghan before. It scares him. Scares him so much he wants to burn more adrenaline. With her. In his bed.

"If you want to know," she says, squeezing lime into the soda and plunking the fruit into the glass. She stabs it with her straw. "My last relationship lasted five months too long."

"What made you stay?"

"I'm not sure exactly. Convenience maybe?"

He hums. "Convenience is when you go to the store to buy milk and you pick up a bunch of flowers, too, because they're there." He shrugs. "Five months is long enough if you're not with someone you care about."

"I had no idea you were a relationship expert," she says, leaning into the table. "So tell me, what's the deal with you? Have you ever been married?"

He shakes his head. "Nope," he says, cupping his almost-empty glass. He wants to stick to one or two pints of beer considering he has to drive home. He pushes his plate away.

"How about newly broken up?"

"What do you want to know?"

Meghan shrugs. "Was it serious?"

He laughs nervously. Why is he feeling self-conscious? "I guess so," he says. "She wanted to get married, but . . ." He pauses, choosing his words carefully. The last thing he wants to do is scare Meghan into thinking he's not an easy guy to get along with. "I couldn't see myself with her forever."

Meghan's sympathetic grin eases him. He wants to tell her more, but decides against it. She won't go for him tonight if their conversation is dry and serious.

"Jane bugs me all the time about being single."

"Oh, yeah?"

He smirks as he lifts his glass to his mouth.

"I like Jane. She's fun."

"And bossy," he says. "She's two years older."

"She's allowed to be bossy."

He finishes his beer. "You have one of those too?"

"Nope. Two brothers. I'm in the middle."

The waitress comes by. "Another beer?"

"No, thanks." He points his finger to Meghan. "Do you want one more?"

"No, this is it for me," she says.

"We'll take the check," Jared says. The waitress turns on her toes. "Do you want to get out of here?"

"Where would you take me?"

To my house.

Meghan sucks in her bottom lip.

Damn! She's doing that again with her mouth. I want those lips on me. . . .

"It depends." What now? How does he tell her he wants to take her home? Will she agree? Is she easily persuaded?

"Depends on what?"

She's not making this easy for me.

"Late night, early morning?" he hints.

"Early morning for sure," she says. "I have that event at the library and have to be there at eight to set up."

"Right. The event." He rolls his eyes.

She lowers her head to meet him eye for eye. "You'll be there?"

Jared swallows. How can he lie to her? Those eyes are trusting and innocent. Even more appealing to want to take her home.

"I'll try."

The waitress places the billfold down between them.

Meghan lies back in her chair and crosses her arms, staring at him skeptically. "I'll take that as a no."

"No, I'll try. Promise."

"What's going on tomorrow that's more important?"

"I . . . uh—"

She tilts her head. "Do you not like crowds? Is that it? It's not a big deal if that's the reason, but I should know. . . ."

If only he could lie to her and tell her yes, the crowds kept him away.

"It's just not my thing."

"You're a celebrity in this city, you should make it your thing." Meghan sucks on her straw.

Nobody has ever spoken to him like this before. "If you come home with me tonight, I'll show up tomorrow."

"No, you need to show up because it's part of your job. You're part of the Warriors' image. Besides, I'm not going to make a poor decision."

He leans into the table. "You're saying I'm a bad decision?"

"Yes."

"Is that the kind of guy you take me as?" he asks, taking in her relaxed style.

"I don't know," she says, getting out her wallet and slapping down a twenty.

"I got this," Jared says, getting out his wallet and putting cash inside the billfold. "It's on me, remember?"

"Don't want you to think I owe you anything."

"I wouldn't think that," he says, standing up.

She swings her purse over her shoulder. "Is that right?"

"I'm a nice guy."

"Uh-huh."

He wants to touch her and kiss her neck and hear her say his name.

She turns on her toes and he follows her out, watching her legs part like scissors to the door.

"Where are you parked?" he asks, stopping on the sidewalk.

She points. "Right there. The red Fiat."

"I was going to guess you drove one."

"Why is that?"

"Compact car for city driving."

"And what do you drive, a Porsche?"

"Did I tell you that?"

"No." She laughs. "Am I right?"

"You're playing me," he says.

"I didn't know, I swear," she giggles. "You just strike me as a guy with a Porsche. But let me guess." She holds up her hand. "It's not even a 911 or a Boxster, is it?"

"It's a 918 Spyder."

"Never heard of one. Must be expensive."

"Do you want me to take you for a ride?" he asks.

There, I've got her now. She's tempted to feel the need for speed.

She sucks on her bottom lip. "Probably not," she wavers.

Jared steps closer and whispers, "We can take it on the highway."

She blows out a breath, making her bottom lip puff out. Jared's heart is pounding. He wants to kiss her so bad, but doesn't want to spoil their new connection. The one he feels is growing every time they meet. She's not only sexy, but she is smart enough to know what she wants and probably knows what he wants. He's never met a woman who is not only attractive, but polite and interesting to talk to. And although Meghan is direct and speaks her mind, she is kind and delicate.

Would she be upset if I kissed her?

Jared has never put so much thought into kissing a woman before. Why is she getting to him? Why does she make him think of consequences?

"So?" he asks. What does she need to think about?

"So, what?"

"Don't you want to go for a drive?"

"Not tonight."

It is like a flash of light hits Jared's face, widening his eyes and opening his mouth.

"You don't?" he asks, not believing her.

"What is it with guys and their cars?" she asks. Her lips are pulled at one side as though she's trying hard not to grin.

And women.

"I don't know." *Okay that was a lie*, he thinks. An expensive ride and a hot woman is a combination of sexual fantasies. "What guy can resist? Cars are fun." That might have been a lame thing to say, but how can he tell her he wants her so bad. They can go for a drive, find a hideout, and have fun. That's the fun he's talking about.

She nods and smiles, letting out a chuckle.

Her relaxed disposition makes Jared at ease and he chuckles with her.

"How 'bout another night?" he asks. How can she say no to that?

"Maybe."

"Oh, here we go," he teases. "I'm going to hear, 'That depends.'"

"I'm not the only woman you've asked to go for a ride. You've heard this before, have you?"

"Well, I—"

"I'm teasing. I don't expect you to answer that. I don't care," she says.

"I will answer," he says, standing straighter. "I haven't had anyone in the passenger seat. I just bought it."

"Is that right?" she asks, looking at him mysteriously.

"Yeah. Wanna check it out?" He gives her a half smile. If he can take her hand in his, pull her close, and whisper her name, he could kiss her. . . .

"How about another time? I really should get going. I have an early morning. Lots to do. I've got a meeting to set up with the media and phone calls to make. I need to get a good sleep."

Jared takes a step closer. Raises her chin with a sweep of his fingers. She freezes. "I've wanted to kiss you," he whispers, but his mouth is already on hers. She doesn't tell him to stop, so he closes his eyes, enjoying the moment. Surprisingly, she kisses him back. Her lips are as soft as he imagined. Her bottom lip hugs his, making his body on fire. He slowly puts his hand behind her head, not wanting her to let go and he rubs his hand on her hair, bringing his fingers to her ponytail.

Meghan closes her mouth and pulls away. "I'm still not taking a ride with you."

"I was hoping you'd change your mind."

She holds a grin. "I get the feeling you're after something more."

"Only if you're willing."

Meghan opens her car door. "You'll be disappointed."

"I find that hard to believe."

She smiles as she sits in her car and turns the ignition. "Good night, Jared. See you tomorrow." She shuts her door and drives away.

Jared runs his hand through his hair. Meghan's going to be a tough sell. How is he going to make her want him?

Chapter 9

Meghan gathers strings of balloons, tying a bunch together. She gets a tingle up her spine just thinking about last night as she holds her phone between her ear and shoulder.

"Is he a good kisser?" Brie asks on the other end.

"Yes! Really good! I couldn't stand still," Meghan tells her friend.

"And he asked you to go for a drive?"

"He did!"

"But you didn't?"

"No. I had to keep a clear mind. That's what happened with Stu. He took me for a ride on his motorbike on our first date and then that's all he wanted to do."

"You didn't go home with him?" Brie asks. "Are you crazy?"

"I can't. I have this job."

"Who cares! It's Jared Landry! He wants you!"

"No, he doesn't," Meghan says. "He was just looking for a one-nighter. You know how guys are."

"But it's Jared Landry! He should be the exception."

Meghan won't admit that she was a little disappointed for not taking Jared's offer, but she wants more from a guy than his car and a one-night stand. "You know that's not me."

"It would be good for you."

"I want something more and I'm not sure he can give me what I want."

"Listen to you! He's a hot guy who wants you!"

"No, he doesn't."

"Yes, he does! Go for him! This is good practice for you."

"I'm not changing my ways."

"You're crazy not to," Brie says.

Meghan switches ears as she tries to tie a bunch of weighted balloons together. "It won't last."

"How do you know?"

"I just do."

"And you're looking for a guy to marry you?"

"It would be nice," she says, dropping the balloons in place behind the table and chairs. "Although, not from a guy who has women all over him. That's what he wants, someone to be hanging off him and be his girlfriend on a string. That's not me."

"It beats going out with Stu, doesn't it?"

"I don't think he's for me." Meghan holds back saying Jared's name in case anyone is listening.

"He's hot, isn't he?"

"Uh-ya."

"And he drives a fancy car, probably lives in West Van. What's not to like?"

"Oh, I like him. I just don't think we want the same things."

"You don't even know him! What's going on with you?" she shouts.

"Nothing." Meghan looks around her to see if anyone is nearby and is listening to her conversation.

"You like him, don't you?"

"No . . . well, maybe a little."

"You should take him up on going out one night and then you can say if you like him or not, but I think it's clear, you like him a lot."

Meghan drops the weighted balloons beside the autograph table. "I don't think he wants me like a girlfriend. . . ." Her voice trails as she drags the banner in position. "I think he was testing me to see how I would respond to him. Guys get their kicks from that like they give themselves a reward for who they sleep with," she says softly.

"If he asks you again, you better take him up on his offer or you'll miss your chance."

"I'm okay with it."

"Are you?"

There's a pause.

"Sure. He's not after someone like me."

"Get out! Of course he is! You're attractive and smart. He would be stupid not to ask you out."

"That's nice. Thanks, Brie."

"You are! Is he there at your event?"

"Not yet. He probably won't show."

"Is it not his thing?"

"He hasn't been showing up to every event. Frustrating. He said he would be here."

Meghan cups her phone and swings her head around to see who's beside her. Keri. Her face warms.

"He will if he knows you're going to be there," Brie says.

"I better go."

"Jared's there, isn't he?" Brie asks with excitement.

"Nope, but I better run."

"Mike's having a Halloween party. You should see if Jared wants to go."

Meghan laughs.

"Ask him!" Brie tells her. "It'll be fun. This year, Mike hired a DJ and even has a floating floor for dancing he's going to set up in the living room."

"I hate dressing up."

"Go as a nurse. Guys like that. You'll for sure have Jared all over you."

"That's not what I'm after." Meghan can't stop giggling.

"Right. Well, you have a couple of weeks to think about your costume."

"What are you going as?" Meghan watches Keri talking to someone.

"Mike is going as a caveman and he wants me as his cavewoman."

"I'll let you know if I'm coming," Meghan says.

"You have to! I might have a mermaid costume from a few years ago you can borrow."

Keri makes eye contact.

"Brie, I gotta go!"

"Call me later!"

Meghan hangs up and tucks her phone at her side.

"How's it going so far?" Keri asks.

"Great! Everything is going well. The players are here." Meghan pauses. "Except Jared. He's a no-show, again. But everyone else who's on my list is here."

"It looks good. We have a great response," Keri says. "Before I forget, I wanted to remind you that a bunch of my girlfriends are meeting for drinks tonight if you want to join us. I thought that maybe if you weren't too busy, you'd want to come out."

"Thank you. I just might," Meghan says, hoping it will ease the concern of personal calls at work. She wouldn't want Keri to think she's not working hard enough.

"We'll be at Buckley's. My friend Lauren works there. Make it easy for her."

Lauren? She hadn't heard that name in a long time.

Meghan recalls her old childhood friend. She had the life every girl dreamed about. Clothes that sparkled, a playhouse that had real furniture—wood, not plastic—and dress-up clothes that were really fancy costumes.

A man approaches and Keri turns around with a smile.

"Keri? I'm Bill Braxton, reporter for the *Vancouver Daily* newspaper. I want to ask you a few questions."

"What do you want me to do?" a male voice whispers in her ear.

The hairs behind her neck are all prickly. She looks up to see Jared standing there. "Hi. I wasn't sure if you were coming."

"I told you I'd be here," Jared says, casually dressed in jeans and an unzipped jacket.

She watches his lips move, bringing her back to last night. Those lips . . . on hers . . . They were warm lips, smooth and eager, which made her want to kiss him longer, except she couldn't. It would be too easy to fall for him when he doesn't want her permanently. Flashbacks of Stu are a reminder of what she doesn't want.

"I wasn't sure," she says, gazing at him.

"So, what do you want me to do?" he asks again.

Kiss me again.

She's caught in his admiring eyes. They are so blue and deep-set that she can't take herself away. She blinks and takes a step backward. "We can go downstairs and see if there are more books to hand out."

"That's not what I was thinking," he says as they walk together down the corridor toward the stairs.

"What do you mean?" Her stomach feels all fluttery.

"I came by to see you."

"Me?"

"I thought we could grab a bite after this, seeing as last night didn't work out."

"I thought it worked out just fine."

He saunters with his head hanging. His hair curls below his ears where she notices a small scar on his jawline. "Okay, look, I won't—"

"Where do you want to meet?" she interrupts, remembering what Brie said. He wants her, that's why he showed up. She has a hard time believing it though. He wants something from her, but what? She wishes she knew. Meghan reaches for the railing as they make their way down the stairs.

"Why don't I pick you up?" he asks.

"Okay."

"Are you all right with that?"

"For sure." She'll have to cancel with Keri.

She smiles at him, taking in his charm. It's good practice for her. Flirting worked, now a practice date. She has a date with Jared! How did that happen? What is she going to wear? "What time will you come by?"

"Is six okay? I have a game tomorrow and I have a schedule . . ."

"Sure. Yes. Six it is."

"I need your address," he says, taking out his cell phone from his back pocket. "What is it?"

They exchange addresses and phone numbers. "Are you going to stick around for a bit?" she asks.

He nods. "What do I do?"

Meghan reaches her hand into an open box of children's books. "Hand out one per person and it doesn't have to be a kid," she tells him. "We're promoting literacy and reading to children. Take two, one for Becks and one for ah, for Jane, in case she has another."

She looks up at him watching her and freezes.

"She told you, didn't she?"

"Told me what?" Meghan plays coy.

"That's she's pregnant."

"She might have mentioned it." She passes him a book. "You may be asked to autograph something, that's why there are tables set up."

"Jane doesn't normally tell people . . . stuff. We're a little alike."

"That's why she didn't want to skate."

Jared nods. "I stand here and hand out books? Is that all I do?"

"There are newspapers, too," she says, turning around and pointing to the stack beside them.

They hang out at the table with other players, talking to the public.

An hour has passed and from a distance she sees Keri talking to a blond woman, and players chatting with their fans.

Meghan leaves to see if she can find any more boxes of books, and when she returns, she tries to catch a glimpse of Jared, but she doesn't see him. Could he be gone already? What is it with him and public appearances? She needs to know. What's the big deal? People come to see the team—they're fans—and they don't even get to meet him. That's disappointing for some.

Meghan walks over to Keri. "Sorry, Keri, I'm busy tonight, but maybe another time?"

"Are you going out with Jared?"

Meghan's face feels warm. "Uh, well."

"I saw you talking to him. I guessed by the way he was looking at you."

Meghan can't help the smile planted on her face. "I don't think it's anything to talk about." She tries to push the idea aside, afraid that people will start talking about something that doesn't exist.

"I've never seen a player talk to one of us so extensively. He hasn't left you alone. Are you sure there isn't something between the two of you?"

Meghan shakes her head.

"Are you sure?"

"Absolutely!" Meghan replies.

"Be careful. He breaks hearts."

"You told me. Thanks. It's just one . . . date."

"That's all it takes."

"I'm just about done here. I'll see you tomorrow."

She picks up the leftover newspapers and leaves them on the table while she takes down the banners and signs. She tells two employees to inform the players they are free to go and to fold up the tables and stack the chairs to be returned to the office.

Lauren's face pops into her mind. Is it possible that the woman she saw earlier was her childhood friend? The only way to find out is to talk to her. If only she had time to stop at Buckley's before meeting Jared, it would give her the answer she's dying to know. If it is Lauren, could they be friends again?

Meghan decides to drive home to shower and change for her date. She laughs at the thought, not quite believing it, although her body has been filled with jitters since she spoke to him. Where is he planning to take her? What should she wear? Meghan decides on a pair of jeans and long-sleeve sweater. As she opens her closet, she sees her wedding dress. She touches it. The white satin with a sequined bodice was what caught her eye in the store window. It was sleeveless, a mermaid style with shimmer along the skirt. She fell in love with it. The saleslady had commented on the dress, saying the style was perfect for her small frame.

Meghan takes the dress down from the rod and holds it up to her body, staring at herself in the mirror. She imagines herself wearing it again one day. Without a wedding of her own—it's too fancy to wear out—the dress had to stay at the back of her closet. She sways in the mirror, remembering how excited she was to buy this dress. She loved it so much. It was too hard to sell it and now she realizes she could never wear it again. The dress reminds her too much of Colton, her ex-fiancé, unless she alters it in some way, she thinks, hanging up the dress. Thankfully, she didn't marry him and Meghan came to her senses in time. The dress and all the planning were pricey, but not as expensive as marrying someone who wasn't a good fit for her.

She met Colton at a casino. It was Brie's birthday dinner and, afterward, the women decided to try their luck with slot machines. Although, after losing twenty bucks in five minutes, Meghan wandered over to the roulette table, nudging herself beside Colton where he had the best luck of all. She was drawn into his fast predictions and landing on the winning calls. She remembers smiling and laughing along with him, feeling his excitement and energy that seemed to last for hours. She stood beside him watching the game and found herself cheering him on. When it was time to place his bet, Colton handed her a stack of chips and asked her to pick some numbers. She didn't know how to play, but she placed her chips down as quickly as she could, gritted her teeth, and waited for the outcome. The next thing she remembers is Colton shouting, throwing his hands up and giving her a kiss on her lips. Three years into their relationship, Colton started to hang out with new people and Meghan found herself seeing little of him and paying for everything, even their wedding. Colton said he wanted to contribute, so Meghan thought it was best for them to have a joint bank account. Once she saw the statements of his personal finances, she wondered how she could marry someone who was so careless with money and didn't care about saving for their future. She wanted a house and a family one day. If Colton didn't take their earnings seriously, then he didn't care enough about her. She found out he was spending more time at the casino and a lack of funds was what drove them apart.

Meghan applies makeup to her eyes and adds a touch of gloss to her lips. Her phone buzzes. She looks down at the text.

I'm here. Waiting outside.

Meghan's heart beats faster. She pushes everything into the bathroom drawer and slams it shut.

I'll be right down, she types. She throws her phone into her purse, slips on her black boots, and grabs her jacket and keys as she runs out the door, locking the dead bolt behind her.

She takes a couple of deep breaths to calm herself before opening the apartment front door. She can't miss his car—it's parked right out front. She's never seen a car like his before, but that's what happens when you make eight million a year. She only remembers his salary because she heard people at work talking about contracts and how much certain players make.

He gets out of the driver's side and walks around the car to greet her. Does he do this for all of his dates? He must be trying real hard to score.

"Hi," he says with lit-up eyes, leaning against his car.

Her stomach feels like it's rising and falling the closer she gets. He opens her side door and she gets in as slowly as she can, making sure she doesn't hit his door with her boot. A scratch on a car like this can make a grown man cry.

"Are we taking a drive on the highway?" she asks, smiling.

Jared pulls out of the entrance and onto the street. "Maybe next time. Have you eaten? I know a great sushi place."

"Sounds good. I'm hungry," she says, remembering when Stu would take her out to dinner, he would ask her why couldn't she finish her meal if she said she was so hungry. Then he would tell her she could use the extra pounds, which always got to her. She was happy with how her body looked; she worked hard at her toned legs and arms thanks to running. Why hadn't she seen the way Stu was before? On the other hand, it's just a dinner date and maybe a kiss if she's lucky. There will never be anything more; he wouldn't want more from her.

She's excited sitting next to a hot guy, in an expensive sports car. This is what she needs, to be out with someone she least expected, a time to clear her mind of any past relationship woes. This is her time and she's going to make the most of it and practice dating. That's what it is, she tells herself, and she grows calmer.

"Great! I guess I should have asked if you like sushi."

"Love it!"

"I found a place not far from here that I've been going to."

Meghan takes in the interior, rubbing her hand along the piping of the leather seat.

"What made you buy this?"

With one hand on the steering wheel, he looks over. "I've always wanted one."

"I've never heard of a Porsche Spyder before." But then she doesn't know a lot about luxury cars.

"My cousin . . ." He clears his throat. "We said when we got our jobs we'd buy Porsches because that's what we both liked."

"So your cousin has a matching one?"

"No," he says, staring straight ahead, his face changing. "How's your Fiat? Like it?"

"Good." She laughs at his seriousness. "It gets me to where I need to go."

Jared parallel parks in front of the restaurant. Thank goodness it's dark, Meghan thinks, or people would all be staring at them and wondering who was driving this car. Even though she doesn't know much about cars, this one is hard to miss.

"Hello," the hostess greets them. She leads them to a booth by the window, setting down menus in front of them.

"What do you like?" Jared asks, leaning over the table. "Do you eat the raw stuff?"

She feels all tingly at the back of her head. He is so good to look at, with his broad shoulders and oceanlike eyes.

"No, I stick to the vegetable rolls and miso soup."

"So do I."

The waitress comes by asking if she can take their order.

"Miso soup?" Jared asks Meghan.

She nods.

"Okay, we'll have two miso soups," he tells the waitress and then looks at Meghan. "Do you like chicken teriyaki?"

"Yes." She smiles at him.

"We'll have two chicken teriyaki dinners, please, and an order of kappa and avocado rolls." Jared turns his attention to Meghan. "Anything else?"

"No, that's good."

"That's it," Jared says, handing the waitress their menus.

"So tell me," Jared says, "Are you from Vancouver?"

"I grew up in White Rock. I moved into the city when I was working for a public relations firm. It was too long of a commute to live outside of Vancouver."

The waitress places their bowls of miso soup in front of them.

"How do you like living here?" she asks, stirring her soup with the spoon and watching the broth turn cloudy before taking a sip.

"I like it." Jared brings the bowl to his mouth.

"You must miss your family?"

"I'm used to it." He shrugs. "I haven't lived in Brampton since I was fifteen. It's home because my family is there. I miss seeing my nephew. He's the kid I don't have."

Meghan decides to pick up her bowl and drink from it.

"He's a good kid." Jared pushes his empty bowl to the edge of the table.

A plate of rolls is placed between them along with side plates. Neither makes a move to take one.

"I wonder how Beckham will be with having a sibling."

"I'm sure he'll be a good big brother. Are you close to your brothers?"

"For the most part. My younger brother enjoyed tormenting me." She takes a sip of her soup. "Most brothers do, I think."

"I couldn't with Jane." Jared breaks apart his chopsticks and rubs them together. He mixes soy sauce, ginger, and wasabi together in a bowl before dipping a roll in it. "She was tough. I remember cutting her dolls' hair off. She freaked out and pulled apart my Transformers." He smirks. "I grew up not messing with Jane."

"She got you to fear her, didn't she?" Meghan says.

"It worked." He laughs, using his chopsticks to pick up a roll. "Jane kept her eye out for me though. She was like another mom."

"I think she misses you."

He swallows. "She's big on get-togethers. Loves entertaining."

The waitress places a dish of teriyaki in front of them.

"I always wanted a sister," Meghan says, pushing her empty bowl to the side and taking a roll from the middle plate. "We want what we can't have."

Like you.

Jared nods and eats another roll.

"That's true," he says after he swallows his food. "Or sometimes we have what we want and don't realize it until it's gone."

She watches Jared take a bite. "You must be grateful for what you have."

"Always."

Meghan scoops the chicken teriyaki onto her side plate, taking small bites and eating as carefully as she can with her chopsticks, afraid of making a mess. Why does she care what he thinks of her? They are just having dinner. Jared is probably lonely and needs someone to eat with. After this, she won't see him again. There will be another woman flagging him for attention, then she'll be forgotten.

"Did you have big dreams?" he asks.

She smiles. "I don't know . . . I guess I'm living my dream, doing what I want to do. I didn't realize that until I broke off my engagement."

"You were engaged?"

"I know, it's sounds pathetic, but I learned more about myself after the fact." She shakes her head, looking down at her saucy meal and wondering why she is telling him all of this. He doesn't want to hear her sob story.

"Are you talking about the same guy you just broke up with?"

"No. My ex-fiancé, Colton. Thankfully I didn't marry him. Gosh, I don't know why I thought that was going to work out."

"Why didn't it?"

She puts down her chopsticks and glances at him hesitantly, not knowing what he thinks about her. He's definitely not going to want to see her again. Who wants to hear about someone's past?

"He spent more money than he made . . . drinking with his buddies became more important and I couldn't get him to see what he was doing to . . . us."

"Then why did you accept his proposal?"

"You're really interested, aren't you?" she teases, smiling because he's smiling. For a second she imagines that they are a couple and how much she can't wait to go home with him.

"Sorry, I shouldn't ask. It's none of my business."

"No, it's okay. I haven't spoken about it for some time." Meghan folds her arms together, leaning on the table. "I thought I loved him because it seemed like he wanted the same things as me, but before our wedding, he was acting like he was still single, going out with his friends until early morning, arriving late for work. He wasn't taking us seriously. He took advantage of me because I was always there, taking care of him, cooking dinner and doing what I needed to do. He changed. . . ." She looks out the window at the sprinkle of rain and people are stopping to ogle at Jared's car. "Do you ever get used to all the attention?"

"Nah." He takes a bite of a roll, reaches for his cup of green tea, and sips to wash it down. "That I can do without."

His eyes are soft and she imagines what he is thinking about. He rubs his thumb along the grooves of the pottery cup. "It's not easy."

"People wanting a piece of you?" she asks, meeting his eye.

"I get that people like what I do and I'm flattered." His voice is low, seductive.

Meghan holds on to every word, trying to understand him, but she still doesn't get why Jared can't suck it up and make appearances. It's not like he gets all the attention and is required to make a speech.

"It gets a little much sometimes, but that's the job. I can't complain."

"There's sacrifices with every successful career," she says, pushing her plate away.

"I guess there is," he says, and asks for the check when the waitress arrives to clear dishes.

"Game tomorrow," she says as they walk out of the restaurant.

"Against Montreal," he says, pulling out his keys, unlocking his doors. Jared ignores the people gawking at his car and he slides into the seat with ease. As he pulls out onto the road, he punches the gas. Meghan's back presses against the seat. The humming of the car vibrates her insides, or is it Jared that's causing the excitement?

"Do you have any pregame rituals?" she asks.

"Huh." Jared stares out the window. "I don't know."

"I heard about this one guy never washing his shirt before a game or another guy who ate almond butter with breadsticks before a game. Stuff like that."

"No, not me." He watches the road and then snickers.

"What's yours?"

It takes him a few seconds to respond. "I have a key chain that I have to touch before leaving the dressing room." He slows down to turn the corner, checking in his side mirror and watching the road in front of him. He pulls to the side of the road. "I have a few superstitions."

Meghan raises an eyebrow. "You pulled over to tell me that?" She then laughs.

"I have to kiss a girl the night before the game."

She lowers her chin, staring at him. "You're kidding."

"Nope." He's leaning in closer.

Meghan glances out her side window and when she brings her head back to meet Jared's, he has brought himself closer. She swallows hard, staring into his eyes. She can feel his breath on her face.

"I don't want to be just a girl to kiss. That means you've had plenty and that's not for me," she whispers, looking at his clean-shaven face and cheekbones. His eyes are what's drawing her in. She bites her bottom lip. Jared leans into her and grazes his mouth on hers. What she thought would be a quick peck turns out to be an enjoyable reaction. She kisses him back, feeling her body sink into the seat a little more. She will not touch him, she tells herself. As much as she wants to curl his hair around her fingers and run her hand down his neck and feel his muscular back, it's taking every effort to keep her hands to herself. Is she done with the flirting? It feels over faster than it started. She's mastered it now. Practice makes perfect and if she can call herself a master at getting a guy this far, she's done it.

The kiss intensifies, making them each hungrier for the other.

He lets go and sits back in his seat and drives away.

It takes a moment to cool off. "Don't blame me if you have a crappy game," she teases.

"I should be good to score one goal at least."

"You have more rituals? And don't tell me you sleep with a woman either," she teases.

"How did you guess?" He smirks.

"Your sister was right, she said you knew how to relax."

"What else did Jane say? You've got me now. I'm curious."

"She did tell me you are a private person."

"There's reasons for that."

"Tell me."

"Maybe another time." Jared drives another block.

"What's your other ritual? Or is that a secret?"

He gives her a half smile. "I can't tell."

"Tell me! I want to know."

"I don't have anything crazy to tell you."

"How long have you been hanging on to that key chain for?"

"Ten years." He turns down her street.

"I guess it's working for you."

Jared parks out front of her building, turns off the ignition. "It keeps me focused."

There's a moment when they are looking at each other.

"Thanks for dinner," she says.

"Am I going to see you again?" he asks as she clicks open her door.

"I don't know." His question surprises her.

"You don't want to see me again?" he asks, turning sideways and throwing an arm around the steering wheel.

"It's not that."

"What is it?"

"I . . ." She stops herself, finding the words to tell him that he doesn't want her, he wants someone who isn't looking for serious. How does she tell a guy that she doesn't want him because she knows what he's after? She grins and changes her tune. "Sure. You're going on the road this week, right?"

"I'll call you when I get back."

"The day before Halloween you're only doing the West Coast," she says.

"That's right. We're playing in California and then we're home."

"Don't forget, there's an event happening at Children's Hospital."

"When's that?"

"The day before you go."

"You know my schedule better than I do."

"My job depends on the Warriors' schedule."

"Thanks, Meghan. I had a good time."

She smiles and gives a little wave. "Good luck tomorrow," she says, and shuts the door, making her way to the front entrance. As she opens the door and steps inside, Jared watches her and then drives off.

What does Jared want? It's hard to believe he would want the same things as she does.

As Meghan walks to the elevator, she tries to shake Jared out of her mind, but the thought of kissing him again is burned into her mind. She wants more of him like she's never wanted anyone before. If she can practice a little more, see how far she can get with him, then call it quits; it will help her to find out what she really wants from a guy. She won't let herself fall for him, although she knows that she's never felt like this before about someone. It scares her to think she likes a guy she can't have. Imagining having him to herself has her wondering if she has a chance.

Chapter 10

"Hey, man," Mason Ward says, holding a tall-neck bottle of beer in one hand and shaking Jared's hand with the other when he comes through the front door of his penthouse suite in downtown Vancouver. "You made it. No costume?"

"I brought a mask," Jared says, taking it out of the back pocket of his jeans. "Batman."

"Did you steal it from some kid?"

"I picked it up at the drugstore."

"Grab a beer, cooler is open in the kitchen," Mason tells him.

"Thanks."

Another player shoves him on the shoulder. "Good to see you." Jared keeps walking to find the beer. He needs to relax. He should have invited Meghan here. She would have fit in. It looks to be mostly the team, a few unrecognizable faces, probably because it's a Halloween party. He reaches into the ice cooler, pulls out a light beer, and gets stuck talking to a group of girls, one wearing a bikini with a crown on her head and a Miss Universe banner across her body. The other is a cheerleader and her friend is a nurse.

"Where's your costume?" Miss Universe asks, cuddling up to Jared's arm.

"Dressing up isn't my thing." He brings the bottle to his mouth.

"It's not?" she asks, batting her eyes. Cheerleader joins him on his other arm. "We could change that, couldn't we?" She swings her hips, causing her pigtails to sway.

Jared drinks his beer, thinking about Meghan. Why didn't he ask her to come with him tonight? A pang of guilt hits him. He should be with Meghan. If he is serious about getting to know her and wants to be with her, why not call her to see what she's up to? Although he can guess, she's not home.

As he looks up, across the room, there's a woman wearing a bridal gown with long, blond hair. His heart feels like it stopped beating as he studies the woman in white and wearing a veil that is covering her cheeks. She is talking, laughing with another woman.

It's her.

He can't even hang out at a teammate's party without running into his ex. How did she get in here? Doesn't she get that they're over?

Jared knocks back his beer. "Excuse me, ladies. I'll be back in a bit," he tells the girls. He grabs for his cell phone from his back pocket and wanders off to find a place where he can call Meghan.

"I feel like I've been shrink-wrapped," Meghan says, talking to Brie in Mike's open kitchen. Her black cat outfit is snug in all the wrong places.

"I thought you didn't have an outfit."

"I lucked out. Someone didn't pick up her costume for tonight. It was a choice between a fairy and black cat."

"Have a drink," Brie tells her, handing her a vodka and cranberry.

Meghan plays with the straw and aims it in her mouth, sipping it down.

"Why didn't Jared come here tonight?" Brie asks.

"I didn't ask him."

"Why not?"

"I dunno. He just came home from being on the road. I'm sure he's tired. We're not together anyway."

"Yeah, right." Brie drinks her splashy pink drink. "Finally you have a guy who's worthwhile and you don't invite him to hang out with your friends? What woman wouldn't want Jared?"

Meghan makes a face.

"You're not flirting enough with him or he'd be here," Brie says.

"I've been practicing. I'm taking it slow," Meghan admits.

"You like him."

"A little."

"A lot," her friend says. "You only date guys who you don't care too much about, that way you're not hurt when there's a breakup."

Meghan listens carefully, sipping her drink.

"You don't want to waste precious time," Brie says. "Make it happen with him or Jared will be snatched up by someone else. You know he will."

"I have time." She can't be bothered to get all caught up in the hype over Jared. It's not like he's making time to see her. If he showed more interest in her then he would be here. Meghan looks around the room. "I hardly recognize anyone."

"You know almost everyone here."

"You know what I mean. It's a different crowd."

"Mike invited people from his football league. Oh! Sara's here too."

"Good." Meghan places her empty glass on the island.

"Mike? Can you make Megs another?"

"Coming up!" he yells, taking her glass and dumping the ice into the sink.

Meghan watches him pour vodka into a shot glass.

"No Jared tonight?" Mike asks, topping her glass with juice and handing her the drink.

"Not tonight. And we're not together." Why does she feel she has to clarify?

"She didn't ask him to come," Brie says with a twist of her bottom lip.

"Why not?"

"Because he would be hounded," Meghan says. "Impressions count."

"Protecting him already," Mike says behind the counter. "Sounds serious."

Meghan smiles as she puts her straw up to her mouth. "It's not."

"That's what she says," Brie chimes in. "I don't buy it."

"We've been out a few times." Meghan says. It's hard not to smile when thinking of the passive left-winger.

"Are you seeing him again?" Brie asks.

"I don't know. Maybe." She shrugs.

"Maybe?" her friend yells. "What are you hiding?"

"Nothing. I'm telling you the truth. There's nothing between us," Meghan says.

"Why not? He's a Warrior! He has the looks. You're crazy not to go after him."

"I'm seeing how it goes. Didn't we just go over this?"

"Do something about him before he finds someone else!"

"Leave her alone, baby," Mike interrupts.

"Is he with someone else?" her friend presses.

"Not that I know of." Meghan is sure he isn't, she would know.

Jane would have said, unless he has a girlfriend back in Brampton or Carolina. Meghan's stomach knots. She shouldn't care if he does. They're not together. He probably does have a couple of girls at his leisure. The thought makes Meghan's insides hurt. She swallows another sip.

There's a loud commotion in the living room. People chanting and throwing their arms up in the air cheering at a Dracula bobbing for apples.

"You'll have better luck with your real teeth!" someone shouts.

Dracula takes out his fangs and tries again.

"That game is impossible," Meghan says with a huff.

"You don't want to give it a try?" Mike asks.

"No thanks."

Meghan looks down at her phone in her black purse that is camouflaged by her outfit, thinking about Jared.

She looks up and spots Sara dressed in a maid's costume. "You're here!" Meghan gives her friend a hug.

"I didn't want to miss a party."

"Picture time!" Brie yells, handing her camera to Mike. She poses between Meghan and Sara.

"I'll take one more," he tells them, and clicks away.

"Let's do a shot!" Brie says, jumping away from them. She gets out a tray from the fridge and hands out the colorful glasses.

"Jell-O shots?" Meghan asks. "I don't know. . . ."

Brie nods. She has a devilish grin. "Strawberry."

"I'm going to feel this tomorrow," Meghan mutters as she brings the shot to her mouth.

"On the count of three," Brie instructs. "Mike! Can you get a picture of us?"

Mike grabs the camera.

"One, two, three!" Brie yells.

Meghan knocks it back, licking her lips.

"Want another?" Brie asks.

"Later," Meghan says. "I have to let this digest."

"Let's dance!" Brie says, grabbing for Sara's and Meghan's hands. The living room is cleared of any breakables and the coffee table so that there is room for dancing. The girls move to a couple of songs before Meghan needs a bathroom break.

She disappears down the hall and into the powder room where she attempts to unzip her costume. It's snug. With one hand under her arm, she tries unzipping, but it doesn't budge. It's stuck. Her legs wiggle as she doesn't know how much longer she can hold it for. She becomes frustrated that she can't get the zipper to move, so with one grunting pull, as hard as she can, the zipper moves and she hears the fabric come apart at the seam. "Oh, no!" she gasps, looking to see how bad the rip is. She then gently pulls the zipper down a little more. It's challenging but she manages to slide her arms out and push the outfit to the floor.

Just then, her cell phone rings.

It will have to wait.

As Meghan pulls up the vinyl material, she fiddles with her zipper; it's only going up midway. She tries it again, but it doesn't budge. There's a gaping hole under her arm. She gives up and leaves the bathroom with her arm fixed at her side to hide her costume malfunction.

Remembering her cell phone rang while she was preoccupied, she dips her hand into her purse as she walks into the living room and pulls out her phone. Jared. Just reading his name on the screen is enough to give her heart palpitations.

"Do another shot with me!" Brie yells when she spots Meghan looking down at her phone.

"I don't know," Meghan says. "I think I've had enough. I'm feeling it already."

"You haven't if you think you've had enough," her friend says, giggling.

"Okay, one more."

The women lift their glasses to their mouths.

"Wait! Wait!" Brie yells, waving her hands in the air. "Mikey!" She waves to her boyfriend. "Take a picture of us."

They hold up the shot glasses, clink them, and knock it back.

"Wanna another?" her friend asks.

"No, and neither should you. You'll be hungover tomorrow."

Brie throws her arm around her friend. "I love yooouuu. You're my bestest friend." Brie puts her cheek up to Meghan's. "Even when you're too busy to hang out with me."

"I'm never too busy. What are you talking about?"

"Ya, you dooo." Brie lets go of her and stands up with a little hunch. "Like when?"

"You're busy. We don't hang out anymore." Brie pouts. "We used to get our nails done every month and go to the gym. . . ."

"I like running and you always want to do yoga."

"I looove yoga." Brie's eyes are squinting, as though they're too heavy to open.

"I know you do."

"Sara knows how to do the Toe Stand." She leans against Meghan, giggling. "Show her, Sara," Brie says, waving her hands.

"I don't think I can in this outfit," Sara says.

A guy standing behind them holding a beer is staring at them. "Please do," he says as though he's going to witness something X-rated.

"I can't get my balance. My thighs burn when I do it."

"Our instructor is sooo impressed," Brie says. "Megs, you need to come with us. Right, Sara? You'll like it once you try it. I know you will. It helps with stress and flexibility. It's sooo good for you."

"You're not going to change my mind," Meghan says. "It's not my thing."

"Sara, show Megs!"

Sara hands Brie her drink and squats, getting her balance before bending one leg over the other.

"See? See? Amazing, isn't it?" Brie says.

Meghan remembers she was checking her phone. Jared. She wants to hear his message if he left one.

Hi, Meghan. It's Jared. Wondering what you're up to. Call me.

His voice is relaxed. Is he bored? There's music playing in the background. Sounds like he's not doing anything. Maybe she should have invited him to the party. But then she wasn't sure how he'd be with everyone if he hated big crowds. She saved him the agony by not inviting him.

Meghan steps outside on the deck where the cool air seeps through her costume. She keeps her arm down to prevent a draft under it.

"Hi, Jared, it's Megs, Meghan."

"Hi," he says. "At a party?"

"Yeah. At a friend's house."

"How is it?"

"Good."

"What are you dressed up as?"

She laughs.

"What's funny?"

"Oh, nothing. It's just, I'm a cat without whiskers. Most of the black lines have come off my face and I've managed to rip my costume."

"Sounds like a wild party."

"You can stop by if you want. And don't worry if you don't have a costume. You don't need one. You can go as Jared Landry!" She laughs to herself realizing how ridiculous she sounds, but feeling good thanks to the alcohol in her system.

"Are you going to be there all night?" he asks.

"I'm cabbing it home in a bit."

"How far are you from home?"

"I dunno. Not far."

"In the city?"

"Yup."

"I can come and get you."

"You don't have to come pick me up. You might get stuck here and I know how much you like big crowds."

"That doesn't bother me," he says.

"Sure it does."

"No. I'm fine with it."

"I thought it wasn't something you liked."

"I don't hate them."

"Huh. Then why are you always late or don't show up?"

He takes a moment to answer. It's not a difficult question, she thinks. There must be a reason.

"It's my style," he finally says.

"Your style?" She makes a face. "Why do you need a style? You're a hockey player. It's your job to make appearances. People want to meet you, touch you, and whatever else; they get a kick over meeting you. This city is nuts about their hockey team. Why can't you make the effort to show up? Huh? I don't get it."

"We can talk about it another time," he says. "I'm coming to pick you up."

Did he not hear that she was telling him to get over himself? What's with him? He's more stuck up on himself than she first thought.

She blows out a breath and can see it in the air. "Okay! Where are you taking me this time?" she asks, not believing him.

"Where do you want to go?"

"Anywhere you want," she says, feeling the cool air finding its way under her arm into the gaping hole. "I'll text you the address."

She hangs up and walks back into the house.

"Where's your drink?" Brie asks. "Mike! Megs needs a drink."

"No, I'm fine," Meghan says. She doesn't want Jared to see her all tipsy, even though she feels light-headed already.

Brie grabs her arm. "Let's dance."

They join a group on the dance floor. People are bumping into each other and Meghan feels someone behind her. A guy is rubbing his leg against hers and is pressed against her, following her moves. She doesn't know him and isn't impressed by his approach, so she dances away from him and he follows her. Brie is dancing with her drink held in the air, eyes half closed, grooving to the music. The guy is still behind her. Every step she takes he is right beside her.

"Hey, cowboy, I need some space," Meghan tells him, moving away. She doesn't recognize him, must be a friend of Mike's.

"Come on, kitty cat," he says. "I wanna play."

"I'm dancing," she snarls, and moves toward Brie for protection. Surely she would tell this guy to leave her alone.

"Are you here alone?"

"I'm Brie's friend," Meghan says, overstepping his question.

"Is your boyfriend here?"

She wants to be polite and say she doesn't have a boyfriend, but that would only make this guy bug her more. "He's on his way," she lies.

He unclips his lasso and holds it up. "What do you say we get tangled in my rope?"

Meghan makes a face. "I'm not interested. I have a boyfriend!"

He gets closer to her. "But if he's not here . . ." He leans into her and whispers into her ear, giving her chills down her spine. "I want to hear you purr." His breath is in her ear, so she sidesteps to get away, but Cowboy follows her into the kitchen where she hears commotion.

She feels someone behind her. She turns around to meet the cowboy's brown eyes and says, "I told you I'm not interested."

"You don't mean that," he says with a hand on his hip. "This cowboy can take you places you've never been before."

"You'll have to find someone else." Meghan turns away when she feels a pull at her arm and is tugged backward. She jolts as she tries to stand still. "Please, let go of me." She holds his stare. "I told you I'm not interested," she says in her firmest voice. It takes a moment until his hand finally releases and drops to his side.

"Everything all right?" a guy asks from behind her. Meghan is staring Cowboy down, but he is looking past her in a daze.

"Yeah, everything is fine," she says, her eyes still fixed on Cowboy.

"Meghan." She feels a hand gently touch her arm. "Are you okay?" the guy asks, hovering over her. She slowly turns around to see who is talking.

It's Jared.

With his over six foot height, relief washes over her and her body relaxes. She feels protected and overcome with joy to see him.

"Jared Landry," Cowboy says with a shaky voice.

Jared puts an arm around Meghan's waist and leads her out of the room. "Wanna get out of here?"

"Yeah." She's walking in a daze too. Maybe it's the vodka. Maybe it's being hit on by a total loser that has her wanting to leave. "How long have you been here for?"

"I just got here," Jared says, when he gets bombarded by people talking to him and asking for autographs. Lights are flashing off cameras.

"Are you going?" Mike asks. "Let me get you a drink."

"I'm fine, thanks," Jared says.

"You don't want to stay? I've got a full bar," Mike says.

"Sounds like trouble," Jared says, making eyes at Meghan. "We don't have to go."

Meghan nods. "I'm done." She gives Mike a hug. "Thanks. Make sure Brie drinks lots of water."

"I will." Mike holds the front door open. There's a crowd seeing them out. "Maybe the four of us could hang out sometime."

"Sure!" Meghan says as Jared grabs her hand to help her out, leading her to his car.

He opens the passenger door for her. "Were you done because I was there?"

"No, it was time to go. I would have cabbed it home had you not shown up. Cowboy was getting on my nerves and I'm not in the partying mood."

"Did you not think I was coming?" He turns on the ignition. The power of the engine is felt the moment they drive away.

"I knew you would," she says, glancing over at him. He's so hot. His dirty-blond hair touseled and all she is thinking is running her hand through his scalp and underneath those curls of his. He is wearing a jacket and jeans, casual, and so attractive. She knows that underneath those clothes is a machine of muscle. She would love to see him naked. Ripped and toned. Meghan looks out her window. He's probably used to women gazing at him. He's gorgeous. No doubt, he is as hot as any guy she's ever met.

What is she thinking? He will drive her home and tomorrow will be another day, only with a headache and drinking water, passed out on her couch.

"Do you want to come to my house?" he asks, looking over at her with one hand draped over the steering wheel, the other by his side.

"Yeah, okay." She doesn't want to sound excited. A bachelor's house is probably a dedicated man cave equipped with a pool table, big-screen TV, and La-Z-Boy chairs with drink holders.

"Was that guy really bothering you?" Jared asks.

"He wouldn't take no for an answer."

Jared closes his lips tightly as though he wants to say something but holds back.

"I don't know what gave him the idea that I was interested in him. Never met him before. Don't know who he is. He started dancing with me."

"There's always one at a party, isn't there? A loser like that?"

"I don't know. I don't go to a lot of parties. How 'bout you?"

He shakes his head. "I'm not really into it."

They drive a bit farther. "What were you doing tonight?" she asks.

"I dropped by a teammate's house but I wasn't into the party so I left."

Meghan notices that they've entered West Vancouver. Brie was right, he lives in a posh neighborhood. Her stomach knots, as she thinks about how far he had come to get her.

"You found Mike's place okay?"

"It was easy."

"You drove from your house, West Vancouver, to Vancouver, prob-ably a twenty-minute drive, to get me?"

"Should I have let you cab it home?"

His eyes are full of warmth, making Meghan like Jared even more. *Why?* she wants to ask him. Why does he care how she gets home?

"Thank you for picking me up. I don't know how long I could have stayed there for."

"Are they your friends?"

"Some of them."

They pull up to a driveway with a black iron gate that opens with the press of a button. The driveway winds to the house. Meghan's eyes widen at the massive structure. What did she expect? It had to be an extraordinary house. "Beautiful place," Meghan says as they drive into the garage. She looks through her side window. "You have other cars?"

"A couple." He gets out of his car. The garage door is shutting and he leads her into the side door, shutting off his alarm when he enters.

Meghan can't believe her eyes. The mudroom, if it's even called that, is welcoming with a bench, built-in coatrack, and empty shelves. She takes a seat, unzips her boots, and places them to the side, along with her black socks. Her feet are hot and sweaty. It feels good to air them, even if Jared has heated tile floors. She can feel it as she walks through to the grand kitchen. Amazing. She's only been in houses like this at lotto giveaways when they are raffling off dream houses.

The white cabinets and stainless steel appliances make for a clean appearance. It hardly looks lived in. There's even a waterfall running off the island in the middle of the kitchen. She must look like she's seeing fireworks for the first time because her eyes are dancing around the room.

"What can I get you to drink?" he asks, standing by his full-wall wine cooler. "I have beer in here too."

"Wow," is all she can say as her eyes look around the room.

"I also have soda and juice in the fridge."

"What are you having?" she asks.

"A beer. Don't make fun of me, but I drink light. I got a game tomorrow so I watch what I eat and drink."

"Yeah, fair enough." Her head is feeling clearer than it was at the party. "I'll have a beer."

"Okay." He opens the cooler and hands her a can. "Do you want a glass?"

"No. This is fine. Thanks." She cracks it open and watches him sip, taking note of his succulent lips. "Your house is gorgeous. I love the kitchen." She takes in the glass cupboard without any dishes in it and uncluttered countertops. "Where do you hang out when you're home? Do you have a man cave?" she asks, wanting to know more of the real Jared.

"When I'm at home I'm usually in the basement."

"Sounds like a cave."

He smiles. "It's not. It's my favorite place to be."

"Show me."

Jared leads her down the staircase to a wide-open room where he flicks on the lights.

Meghan doesn't know where to look because there's something in every part of the space. A sectional couch, cushiony chairs, pool table, just like she guessed, a full bar, foosball table, pinball machines, and, "An ice rink? You have an ice rink in your house?"

"Yeah, I use it to practice my shots."

Meghan puts her hand on the red plastic railing. It looks just like a real rink except smaller. The ice isn't real, it's plastic. She stares at it and then looks around as though in a museum.

He looks at her and then chuckles.

"Those sticks must be special." She points to the collection of hockey sticks hanging on the wall.

He nods and points. "That one there is from my first NHL game. And that one over there is the one I scored my first NHL goal with. That one there, is the one I used to score my first hat trick. . . ."

They both are looking at the wall.

"Have you ever played?" he asks.

"Hockey?" she asks, tilting her head.

"Sure."

"Do I look like I play hockey?" she laughs.

"I don't know. Jane used to play."

"She did?"

"Oh, yeah. For years."

"I wouldn't have guessed."

"Do you want to take some shots?" he asks, taking a stick down from the wall.

"Oh, no, I couldn't." She waves her hand to stop him. "I don't know how."

"I'm sure you do." He hands her his stick.

"I wouldn't want to break it."

He laughs. "You won't be able to break it."

"I could put a chip in it," she says, faltering.

"It's aluminum."

"Put a dent in it then?"

"Come on," he says, opening the door to the rink and stepping on the artificial surface.

"Look at that!" she says. "It even has a center ice."

"Here," he says, handing it to her.

"I don't know what to do," she says. She can figure it out, but having a pro watching her moves makes her nervous.

"You can hold a hockey stick." He puts it in her hand. "Like this." He moves her body gently and comes behind her, pressed up against her. She can feel the strength of his muscles under his shirt. His biceps are evident through the fabric, giving her a little squeeze. She's trying to focus on what she is doing, but his arms around her body envelop her so she can't move. She doesn't want to move. Her insides are like a loose circuit, all jittery. He takes her hands and wraps them around the stick. "Like this," he says, putting his hands over hers. Jared moves the stick in a slow swinging motion. "Make sure your bottom hand stays a little loose. That's the hand that will give you the direction you need." He lets go and grabs a stick from the corner of the rink and slides her a puck. He takes one and they stand at the red line. "Do you want to shoot first?"

"No, you go," she says, nervous.

Without coaxing, he takes a shot. Right into the hole of the practice board that is attached to the net.

"I won't be able to do that." She laughs, setting herself up on the line and taking a shot. She misses and the puck hits the boards. "Oops."

"That's okay. You did it." He shoots again and gets it in the top hole.

She tries again and slaps the stick, missing the puck and almost falling. Her cheeks warm. She bites her bottom lip.

"Put some power into it."

"I'm trying."

"Here, let me show you again." Jared comes behind her and wraps his arms around hers. His firmness keeps her still. He rests his head on hers so that they are both looking in the same direction. A brush of his lips against her hair makes her head all tingly and the feeling radiates down her arms. He swings the stick as though going to take a slap shot when there is a tearing sound. He stops in midair and looks at her. "What just happened?"

"My costume." She looks under her right arm and there's a big rip. She laughs hysterically. "Looks like I'll have to pay for this one. I've got matching holes." She puts up her other arm and reveals the broken zipper.

"I'm sorry," he says, laughing.

"It's fine. Really." She shrugs it off. "I may be going home in rags when we're through." He smiles at her and she gushes with laughter. "I'll try this again."

Jared hands her the stick and places his hands over hers, just like before. "Ready? Top corner," he calls, and pulls back the hockey stick. He shoots and they get it right where he was aiming for.

"You're pretty good," she says, feeling him loosen his hand, but he hasn't moved. His body is touching hers sending a glittery sensation down to her toes.

"Just pretty good?" His mouth is at her cheek.

It's a thrill to feel his breath on her skin. If she turns around, their lips will touch. If she stands still and waits for him to move, she's lost her opportunity.

"Well, you know," she begins saying, and slowly turns around. The hockey stick falls to the ground, making a clunking sound. Their lips are a breath apart. Her eyes find his and there is a moment of desire that is so strong, she wonders what is happening between them.

He leans in to kiss her. It's not just a kiss, it's passionate and sincere. It makes her body surrender and fall into his waiting arms. He holds her tight, one hand against her back. She is kissing him with such pleasure, she wants more of him. She forgets about everything—what she's wearing, why she's there—and lets herself fall into his arms. It's okay for this to happen. They are attracted to each other. What more do they need?

His lips coast her cheek and down to the nape of her neck. She throws her head back enjoying the unplanned moment. She has one hand on his bicep, the other on his chest.

As their kiss heats up, so do their bodies. She can feel it under her vinyl suit. She wants to see what's underneath that shirt of his. She wants to touch him, feel him, and admire his form.

"Can I take this off?" he asks, running his hand all over her back, finding the zipper under her arm. He tries to unzip her, but it's not coming apart. He can't see what he's doing because his lips are on hers. Finally, he breaks away from her and looks at what he is doing. With one hard pull, the zipper loosens, ripping the material as the outfit comes undone. "Looks like I need to pay for this." He unwraps the costume over her shoulders and pulls off the arms, revealing her pushed up cleavage in a silky bra. He begins kissing her neck, running his fingers behind her ear. She whispers his name and suddenly, with one breezy lift, he scoops her up and carries her to the long sectional.

She is sitting up, her head against the pillow, and Jared falls to his knees and slides off her bottoms like peeling back wallpaper. He begins kissing her legs.

She watches him slowly make his way to her stomach. As he gets closer, her mind is racing that she is in his house, practically naked and wanting him badly. Will she regret this tomorrow? Maybe she's had a bit too much to drink. Although she is feeling fine, a little giddy, but she's sure Jared has something to do with that.

Meghan reaches for his shirt and with two hands she pulls it up. Jared helps her and lifts it over his head. She sucks in a breath, in awe of his body, and she runs her hands along his washboard feeling the ripples of every muscle. He comes up closer so that his lips meet hers. As they kiss, he unbuttons his jeans and kicks them off, revealing a fitted pair of boxers.

"Are you okay with this?" he asks, taking her bare foot in his hand.

She nods and blinks her eyes. More than okay. Her knees are weak, her legs melting. He massages her foot, watching her expression change. The sensation is felt behind her neck and down her arms.

"I can take you to my room," he says. The deep kisses rattle her senses and the next thing she knows Jared's hands are on her waist and he pulls her on top of him. As his lips come together with hers, she fingers his hair, wrapping his strands around them.

"I love your curls," she whispers between breaths. It feels like silk.

Jared places his hand behind her head and massages her, making her eyes close and the sensation grows all over her body.

"You're sure you're okay with this?" he asks.

She looks him in the eye and nods. He slips her bra strap off her shoulder and kisses her skin, trailing his tongue to her nipple. She holds on to his curls, making her fingers tangled, pushing him back and bringing her lips to his. He is a good kisser. Everything about him is good.

It doesn't take long before Jared takes off her panties and his boxers, edging toward her with excitement.

"Do you have protection?" she asks.

"Yeah. Yeah, I do. I got something." He jumps up and fishes for his jean pockets, pulling out a condom wrapper. It takes him seconds to put it on and push himself inside her.

Meghan is on top of him, his hands on her lower back. She lets out a moan as he starts moving. He's kissing her lips, her neck, her ear.

It's all happening so fast, but the timing is just right. She wants him so bad. She's never wanted a guy as much as she wants Jared. The heat between them is like a summer night.

Jared rests his hands on her small waist, moving her with his body. He is looking at her with dreamy eyes while saying her name when the intensity rises. He whispers if she is okay and then kisses her on her wide-open mouth. Their bodies as one, lusting for each other, they move in rhythm until they both have satisfied their need.

As Meghan slides off him, Jared touches her arm and pulls her back into his chest. "Not so fast," he says, wrapping his arm over her.

Meghan curls up at his side, resting her head on his bare shoulder. He traces her arm with his finger. She reflects on what she just did and if she'll have any regrets in the morning. What does Jared think about her? She told herself she wouldn't fall for him, not wanting him to break her heart, but she's fearing she's already liking him more than she imagined she would.

Jared props himself up to the side of her, looking into her eyes, and touches her chin. He gives her a surprise kiss. "What do you say we take a shower?"

She could do with one, but then the only clothes she has is the catsuit that she dreads putting back on.

"Come on," he says, helping her up.

She grabs her bra and puts it on and then grabs her underwear from the floor. As she stands up, Jared extends his hand and wraps hers in his as though leading her to a secret getaway.

"This way." He takes her up two flights of stairs to the bedrooms.

The whole way there, Meghan can't quite believe her eyes. She is in the biggest house she's ever been in and can't remember which way they went to get to the master bedroom.

"I don't have any clothes," she says, stepping into his bedroom. It's nothing she's ever seen before. Naturally, a king-size bed, two dressers, and lots of space. The room could use a chaise and table to fill the open area.

"I've got something you can borrow," he tells her, opening his bathroom door.

White marble floor throughout and the sinks have painted flowers in them. The shower is big enough for five people, not that there would be that many at once, but there are rain showerheads above and sprays everywhere along the tiled wall. Jared steps into the shower and turns on the tap. He touches some button and more water starts to spray out of the wall. He takes off his boxers and holds the door open for her.

She can't stop gawking at his body.

"Aren't you coming in?" he asks.

"Turn around," she tells him.

"What? Why? What for?"

"I don't want you to see me." She unhooks her bra.

"I just saw you naked."

"So."

"I want to see you again. You're beautiful!" He extends his hand for hers. "Come on!"

She throws her bra to the floor and slips off her underwear. She holds her arms across her chest for extra coverage and he closes the glass door behind her.

"Water hot enough?" he asks. "Soap is right there."

She lets the water run off her and feels the weight of the spray on her back. The warm water pulsates the back of her neck.

I can't believe I'm having a shower with Jared.

There is so much space between them it feels almost private.

Meghan rinses her face and then her body.

"I can soap you up," he says, taking the bar from her hands. He runs his hands over her back and down her arms, stopping at her fingers. He then rubs her down in small, circular motion, holding her stare. He closes in on her and begins kissing her mouth. *This is like a dream,* she thinks, never imagining she would be at Jared's house, this intimate with him. He must be used to stripping down in front of his teammates after a game and showering.

She feels his erection nudge at her thigh. She doesn't have to ask him what he's thinking because already the kissing is more intense and she lets herself go, into his arms and inviting him to play out the fantasy, or is it hers?

The warm water falls on her head. Jared lifts her up and she straddles him, wrapping her legs around his thighs.

She squeezes his arms.

"I won't let you fall," he says, kissing her mouth with intensity. The *water is running off their bodies from every direction. What can be more satisfying than this?* Meghan thinks, holding on to Jared's muscular arms.

Jared turns the water off when they are finished and opens the door a crack to grab a towel. He hands it to her and she dries off and then wraps it around her body, tucking it in like a dress. As she steps out onto the mat, she sees her reflection in the mirror. Her hair sopping wet, she pushes it away from her face. The makeup has disappeared. The black eyeliner she used for whiskers is gone completely and a clear complexion with a smudge of liner under her eyes is all that's left.

"You look really good," he tells her as he steps out of the shower wearing the towel around his waist.

Admiringly, she stares at his body. This will be the last time she sees him in the flesh. Jared drops his towel and puts on a pair of boxer shorts.

Damn he is hot and she has to leave him. Brie's not going to believe where she's been and what she did.

"My costume is downstairs," she says, reaching for her undergarments.

"I have something you can wear," he says.

"I'm not wearing a jersey," she teases, and follows him into his bedroom. She takes a seat on his bed and falls back, letting her head hit the pillow. He snickers as he digs in his top drawer. "Ah. This is comfortable."

"This should work," he says, pulling out a T-shirt.

She's judging it. A little big but what are her options?

He tosses it at her. His lips come together tightly. Then he says, "I'll be right back, I think Jane left some clothes here." He walks out of his bedroom while Meghan tries on his shirt, which fits like a nightie. He comes in with a pair of black leggings. "These should fit." He hands them to her.

"Okay, well, I should go, it's after midnight and you probably need sleep seeing as you need to be rested for the game tomorrow," she says, putting on the leggings. "I can return your clothes tomorrow. I'll just go grab my purse."

"Can't you spend the night?" he asks.

"I shouldn't." She's going to fall for him and she's going to get hurt. He'll break her heart like Keri said.

"Stay. I'll drive you home in the morning."

"Isn't it morning?"

He looks at his alarm clock. "I guess it is." Jared walks over to her, kisses her gently on the mouth, and then guides her to his bed. He puffs up the pillow for her and then crawls in. She decides to lie down beside him. Their noses are just about touching. They smile at each other. How many women has this happened to? She closes her eyes. She doesn't want to think about that. Maybe she'll stay only for a few hours and then she will go home to the life she knows and this will all be a dream. That is, one she won't forget.

Chapter 11

Meghan opens her eyes, staring up at the ceiling. Her heart starts to race as she realizes she's not in her own bed. This one is softer, and the pillow is firmer. She rolls over expecting to see Jared sleeping, but the bed is empty. She sits up, wipes the corner of her eyes, and combs her fingers through her messy, kinked hair. She still remembers everything about last night. There was no holding back for both of them. Did Jared get what he wanted? He's probably waiting for her to leave. That's why he's not sleeping in. He wants her out of his house. Her time is up. She's going to call a cab and be gone before he knows it.

As she gets out of bed, the shirt she is wearing hangs on her like a maternity dress with lots of room in the middle. She notices her purse sitting on the night table. Did she put it there? She picks up Jane's leggings from the floor and puts them on, taking her purse with her as she leaves.

Meghan walks quietly out of the bedroom, down the hall and around the banister, making her way downstairs. Should she at least find Jared and tell him she is going? Does he care? Then it occurs to her that if she leaves out the front door, will the alarm go off?

She gets to the bottom of the stairs where she hears some shuffling going on in the kitchen. It sounds like the clanking of dishes and drawers closing. Would he be unloading the dishwasher? She has to get downstairs to get her costume. It has to be returned Sunday, tomorrow . . . maybe she can just tell them she lost it . . . it would be better than returning it with two gaping holes.

As she nears the kitchen, she watches for the perfect moment to dash past to get to the landing that leads downstairs. Tiptoeing as quickly as she can, she hurries past. Hearing someone come closer, she moves faster. As she turns around to smile and to explain to Jared that she'll be out of his house in a few minutes, a lady with graying hair tied up in a bun and wearing a white apron comes into view. The maid shrieks at the sight of Meghan.

Meghan freezes and yelps, covering her mouth.

The lady slaps her chest and gasps. "I didn't know Mr. Landry had company," the lady says.

"Sorry, Loretta," Jared says, walking around the corner. "I should have told you I had a friend over."

Friend? Is that what we are?

"You're lucky I didn't have a pan in my hand. Someone could have gotten hurt," the housekeeper says.

"Of course," Jared says. "Sorry." He runs his hand through his hair. His smile is more like a jaw-clenching gesture as though he thinks the situation is funny. Loretta is giving a displeasing eyebrow. Probably the same one she gave her kids when they were up to no good. Meghan bites her bottom lip.

Loretta walks back into the kitchen muttering something under her breath.

He snickers. "Did you sleep well?"

"I did. Yes. Thank you." She shuffles her feet. "I'm gonna go downstairs and grab my costume." She takes a step forward. "Then I'll leave."

"I put it upstairs, in my room, with your purse. You didn't see it?"

"I'll go back and get it," she says, staring at his fitted shirt and remembering how every indent of rock-hard muscle was pure pleasure. This won't happen again, she reminds herself, disappointed.

"Let me," he says. "Do you want coffee? Loretta made a pot."

"I'm okay."

He eyes her swiftly. "Shirt looks good on you. Leggings fit?"

Meghan looks down at her clothes. "Yeah, they do. I'll wash them and return them to you tomorrow if you're home."

"No rush. Whenever."

"Jane's a lifesaver."

"Best not to tell her you're borrowing them."

"Okay. Right. No problem."

"Something to eat? Loretta's making me a huge breakfast. She makes the best omelet. I have to eat, prepare for the game tonight. Care to join me?"

"I should really go." She pouts. She loves being in his house. It's a comfortable place to be. The high ceilings, tile floors, and new furniture. Her eyes wander taking in the décor. "Okay, I could use a cup of coffee," she says, smelling something that is making her stomach growl. It's going to be the last time, so why not take advantage of it?

Meghan walks into the kitchen. The smell is floating through the air and into her nostrils, making her feel hungrier.

"Have a seat," Jared says, walking to a cupboard and taking out two mugs.

She sits down at his long butcher-block table and watches him pour the coffee.

"What do you take in it?" he asks.

"Milk. Thank you." She buckles her hands underneath her thighs. Does he do this with all the women he brings home? Is Loretta used to seeing a different woman here?

He brings over their cups of coffee. "Do you want eggs and toast? Fruit cup?"

"I don't want to be a bother." She realizes how formal she sounds. "What are you having?"

"It's no problem. Loretta's got a skill for making eggs. Do you feel like some?"

She wrinkles her nose. "Not really."

"Toast?"

"Sure. That would be good. Thank you."

Meghan watches Jared take bread out of a bag while Loretta busily creates an omelet, picking up a large dinner plate and placing a heaping amount of scrambled eggs and arranging grilled veggies on top.

"Are you sure you don't want one?" Loretta calls out. "The pan's hot."

"No, I'm okay, thanks."

Jared joins Meghan. They sip their coffees, making small talk.

"Did you hear me get up? How did you sleep?" he asks.

"No. I slept like a baby." She takes a sip of coffee.

"What am I making you?" Loretta interrupts, placing a plate in front of Jared.

"I put toast on for her," he says.

Loretta spins around and goes over to the toaster.

"Does she live here?" Meghan whispers.

"No," Loretta pipes up. "But someone has to look after him."

Meghan lowers her head and smirks. "Does she look after you?" she chuckles, and then reaches for her coffee cup.

"She likes to think she does," he teases back. "I do fine on my own."

"I find it hard to believe you're a guy who needs help," Meghan says. She looks at Jared's breakfast. It's a towering omelet. "You're seriously going to eat all that?"

"It's my breakfast game starter. I always eat a big breakfast on game day."

"And lunch?"

"That too."

Loretta puts down two pieces of buttered toast and a tray of jam, peanut butter, and honey.

"Oh, my goodness. Thank you," Meghan says to Loretta. "I feel like I'm at a restaurant."

"Don't get too comfortable," Loretta says.

"She might come for breakfast tomorrow," he says.

"That's my day off. What will you make her?"

Jared looks at Meghan's plate. "Toast." He laughs. Loretta makes a grumbling sound.

Jared starts to eat while Meghan spreads strawberry jam on a piece of toast.

"What do you have planned for today?" he asks.

"I should probably return the costume, or at least call them to tell them it's lost."

They hold a gaze and snicker.

"Most expensive costume I've ever bought," she says.

"There's more coffee in the pot," Loretta calls out from across the room.

"And I'll give my friend Brie a call. The party was at her boyfriend's place."

"Mike?"

"Yeah, you met him!"

"He offered me the bar," Jared says.

"Yup, he's very accommodating. I wonder how Brie's doing today. She got into the Jell-O shooters," Meghan says.

"Wicked. They go straight to your head."

"Tell me about it." Meghan notices Loretta leave the room. "I guess it's nice to have someone here. Do you get lonely? Living by yourself in a big house?" She swallows a gulp of coffee.

"Sometimes. How about you?"

"I'm busy enough," she answers. *Although living with someone would be better.* "What are your plans today?"

"I have practice in a bit," he says.

"And a game? Don't you get tired? You know, being on the ice, then getting cleaned up and then a game . . ."

"It's what I do," he says with a shrug. "Are you coming to the game tonight?"

"No. I don't have a ticket."

"You can get one, though?"

"Not last minute."

He hangs his head as he forks his eggs.

She finishes her coffee. "If you don't mind, I'm going to call for a cab."

"I'll drive you."

"You don't have to."

"I want to."

"Why?"

"I can drive. No sense in calling a cab. I'll go get your things." Jared runs up the stairs to get the cat costume and returns without breaking a sweat. He pats his leg to feel his wallet and leads her back into the kitchen and into the mudroom to get to the garage.

"Are you sure you don't mind driving me home?"

"Not at all."

"Thanks."

It's only a twenty-minute drive to her apartment from Jared's house. They make small talk, but as Meghan looks out the window, she thinks about their time together and what if anything will come of them.

"Thanks for breakfast," Meghan says before opening her door.

"Anytime." He turns off the ignition and jumps out of his car and around the passenger side. He stands close to her, his hands at his side, noses almost touching. "I had a good time."

They need to say their good-byes. Does he want one last kiss before she goes? She hasn't brushed her teeth, except for rinsing with mouthwash she found under his bathroom sink. Her hair is a mess, she's wearing his T-shirt and his hoodie and Jane's leggings. Her boots are tall. She's embarrassed by the way she looks, feeling cheap, looking trashy, and falling for a guy she can't have for the long-term.

Jared brings his mouth to hers and gives her a peck on the lips.

"You don't want to get too close to me," she says, smiling. "I need to get cleaned up."

"You look good to me." He puts his arms around her.

"You probably say that to all the girls."

"No. I've never had—" He stops himself. "This, this is new to me."

"What is?"

"I don't invite just anyone over to my house."

Meghan nods. Her toes curl. "You have to get to practice, don't you?"

"That's what's keeping me away from you. I have a schedule to maintain." He wraps his arm around her another time and pulls her close. "We'll have to pick up from where we left off. I'm on the road Monday. East Coast for a week and then back home."

It occurs to Meghan that he could have a girlfriend in Carolina and is going to see her.

His arms are braced on both of her arms. Toe to toe, nose to nose. She stares into his eyes. They are full of possibilities, yet she knows this has to be good-bye. They can't kid themselves. She has to get this over with.

"About last night . . ." she says. "It was a onetime thing, right? And I know this is meaningless."

He steps back and drops his arms to his side. "I'd like to see you again. That's not a onetime thing."

"Yeah, but—" Her head sways. "I don't expect you to call me."

"I will."

"And I don't expect to see you again—"

"I plan to."

"Jared, you're a great guy." She reaches for his arm. "I . . . I'm not expecting much. You have a demanding career."

"That doesn't have anything to do with us."

There's an us?

"Thanks for the clothes," she says, looking down at herself.

"No problem. I'll see you soon. I'll call you when I get back from the road."

He kisses her gently, making her heart beat faster. Meghan's body is tingly all over again. Why does he make her feel this good? It's going to be hard to put Jared out of her mind. She won't forget him, or what they shared. It definitely felt like more than a onetime thing, but that's wishful thinking. She doesn't need to practice anymore, she needs to move on. If only she was capable of tossing out the memories of last night and begin new ones with someone else.

"Don't make promises," she tells him. "I'm not looking for any. Thanks for driving me home."

As she walks to the front entrance, she turns around to see Jared standing at his car and then get into it when she steps inside the building.

He doesn't care, she thinks. He's putting up a front. That's why he's so good at what he does.

Chapter 12

Two days later, Meghan walks into the party store with her Halloween costume.

"Is it a return?" the purple-haired teen asks, taking the plastic bag from Meghan. "Do you have your slip?"

Meghan reaches for her wallet and takes out the return slip, sliding it on the counter.

"Cat costume," the teen says, holding it up to examine the seams. "There's a rip in it."

"It's just a little tear."

"Are there two holes?" The girl brings the fabric to her face and runs her hand along the material.

"What happened?"

"I couldn't get the costume off and the zipper got stuck."

"I see that. I'll have to get my manager."

"I can pay for the damage. No need to get him."

"Her," the girl corrects, eyeballing Meghan. "I have to. You might have to pay for it."

"You don't have to bother, I'll just pay for the costume," Meghan says, opening her wallet.

"We'll see what my manager says," she says, stepping away from the cash register. "Can I get another cashier!" the teen calls over to another employee.

"What seems to be the problem?" a throaty voice asks, waltzing up behind the counter.

"There's no problem," Meghan says, grinning. "I had a little accident with the costume."

The manager holds it up. It looks worse than it is. A piece of fabric is hanging off and the zipper isn't even lined up evenly. "It looks like it's been trashed," the woman says, frowning.

"I'll pay for it," Meghan interjects. "How much?"

"Two hundred."

Meghan blinks. "For a cat costume?"

"We have to order another one and pay for shipping . . ."

"It can't cost that much," Meghan says.

"We charge fifty dollars for late, lost, or damaged items." The lady points to the return slip. "You're late and damaged."

Meghan hands over her credit card. She should have told them she lost it to save her from humiliation. But it was worth it. Jared was worth it.

Jared is still thinking about his night with Meghan. It's been three days and he craves her. He wasn't expecting to fall this hard for a woman so soon, let alone one who works for the same organization.

Jared takes off his practice jersey. He's in Carolina tonight and wonders how the crowd will react when he's on the ice. Last season he was booed when he skated on wearing the Warriors jersey. The fans were upset that he made a trade. He could have stayed, but chose to go where the money and fans were. He was welcomed here. Vancouver made an offer and he and his teammate, Devin Miller, were a package deal. It is always strange when the call is made and a player is told he has a plane ticket and must leave with little notice because the new team is expecting him. The media has it covered before he puts on his new jersey. It always amazes him that a player can get new equipment with his name and number on it so quickly.

Being back in Carolina is a mix of emotions for Jared. A little nervous, but then he's always uneasy when he plays a home game in a city he used to live in. He wonders if the women he left behind will be in the stadium watching or if they have a plan to come to the players' entrance after the game to meet the team.

He left behind his girlfriend Chelsea. A pretty brunette with a constantly bubbly personality. She was more concerned about all the celebrity commitments and him as a hockey player than caring about him as a person. Once the trade came through, it was a good time to end the relationship. She had cried, thrown herself at him, telling him he broke her heart. He didn't buy it. How could she love him in only the eight weeks they were together? When he told her he needed to focus on his career, she begged him to take her. Jared was glad when he arrived in Vancouver that he came alone. Chelsea wasn't wife material, neither was his newly now-ex-girlfriend. If he had brought Chelsea, she would have driven him nuts and sponged off him to make her life as comfortable as possible.

"I saw your foundation mentioned on TV," Jared says to defenseman Devin Miller, who started a nonprofit to help men find the help they need to provide for their families.

"It's going really well," Devin says, nodding his head while taking off his shoulder pads.

"I saw a clip on the news. Your foundation has a new facility in Seattle."

"Oh, yeah," he says with a grin. "My wife is really proud of it. We've already helped so many men get back on their feet."

"It's a good cause," he says.

"What's going on with you? Seeing anybody?" Devin asks.

Jared doesn't look up as he loosens his laces. "Kinda."

"No one special, then?"

"I don't know. Still new."

"Not serious? That's okay. You'll find one. You're young."

"I like her," Jared says, surprising himself. He really does like Meghan. She is refreshing to be with. Not needy or clingy like the others. Maybe she didn't like him as much as he liked her.

"What's the problem?"

"I don't know."

"She's not like that girl you're trying to get away from?"

Jared takes his skate off and puts it to the side. "My ex?" he asks. "Not at all." He ravels clear tape around his socks.

"It's hard to find someone when you have this career. You want someone real. When this career is over, will you still like her?"

Jared chuckles as he wipes down his blades with a rag. "I guess you're right." His heart swells as he thinks of Meghan. What happens if she doesn't want him as a boyfriend? Maybe this fling is all she wants. Jared's stomach tightens. He wants to get to know her more. When he gets back from the road trip, he needs to do something about it. At least talk to her and find out what her intentions are. He knows what he wants. They can only carry on this affair for so long until one of them lets go and finds someone else. He can't let that happen. He likes her, he tells himself. He's just not sure what to do about it.

* * *

Meghan and Brie meet up at a restaurant near the mall.

"Are you up for a little shopping after lunch?" Meghan asks. "I need to look for a cocktail dress for the black-tie event. I still haven't found anything and I don't want to leave it until the last minute."

"You gotta get something Jared will drool over, like a short skirt, none of this long, flowy, waste-of-fabric type dress."

"I'll be wearing it for a work function. It has to be somewhat sophisticated."

"And Jared will be there, right?"

"I told you there's nothing between Jared and me," Meghan says, holding back a giggle. Every time she thinks about him, she gets all giddy inside.

"Come on," Brie says, "I saw the way he took your arm at the party and led you out like a prince capturing his princess. He came for you. Swept you away." Brie waves her arms, her straight, brown hair moving with her actions. "Not many guys go out of their way for a woman. So what's he like?" She blinks. "Is he an animal in bed, or a charmer, making you fall into his spell?"

"He's a romantic." She gives a sideways grin.

"Is that right?"

"Amazing."

"I told you you'd find someone at work."

"I still can't believe it."

"When are you seeing him again?"

"I don't know. He's on the road."

"You haven't spoken to him?"

"Three days ago."

"Why?"

"I don't know. He's on the road."

"You're scared. I can tell. You don't pursue and take action. Do you have competition or somethin'?"

"I think so. Jared's in Carolina as we speak. I'm sure he has a woman there."

"You don't know that."

"It's where he was traded from. A hot guy like him? I can only imagine the women he has."

"But you slept with him?" her friend reminds her.

"Yeah. I'm not expecting anything from him," she stresses, pushing her wavy hair that feels all frizzy from the cooler weather.

"You should if you like him."

"I don't want to get hurt."

"If you found out he was with someone, would it bother you?"

"Of course it would!"

"Then why not do something about it?"

Meghan thinks for a moment. "I don't think he wants anything more from me, that's why."

"You know that for sure?"

"Well, no . . . I'm saying it because look at him! He's a celebrity here," she hushes, getting her face up close. "You don't think he's going to want to be with someone like . . . uh, a model or someone with a name?"

"You do have a name," her friend interjects. "You are Meghan O'Riley, Public Relations Coordinator for the Warriors. That's a name." Brie snaps her finger.

Meghan smiles. "You know what I mean."

"You are that person, Megs. I think he wants you. You need to talk to him."

"And say what? Marry me, please!"

The friends laugh.

"He doesn't take my job seriously. He hardly shows up to events that I ask him to, or he's late." She nibbles on a crumb of her sandwich that she tore apart. "I'm afraid the practice is over."

"That's it? It can't be over!"

"Now what? I haven't heard from him since Saturday, not like I was planning on it this soon, but I was hopeful. You know? I'm glad it's turning out like this. Easier to let him go. I can move on. I'm pretty sure I have succeeded and now I'll be ready for when someone else pops into my life."

"Just like that? The guy is just going to appear?" Brie snickers.

Meghan shrugs and takes a bite of her sandwich.

"I don't have any doubt that Jared is seeing someone right now. He used to live in Carolina, you don't think an ex-girlfriend is calling him up, asking him to come on over for a quickie?"

"I don't know about that. Call him. Find out! Then you'll know where you stand."

"I know where I stand. He likes his freedom of having women at his disposal."

"You don't know that."

"Then why hasn't he settled down? He's twenty-eight. Most of the guys his age who are professional athletes have a wife and kids by now."

"Maybe he's looking for someone like you."

Meghan chuckles. "Not me. I haven't seen him."

"Call him. You should call him right now."

"I can't. He's working."

"You can call him. He's practically your boyfriend."

The thought of Jared as her boyfriend makes Meghan's stomach feel like she's just gotten off a roller coaster. A combination of nerves and excitement floods her body. "I can't," she manages to say, pushing her plate away. "I don't know what to say."

"Ask him when he's coming back and if he wants to hang out when he's home."

She tilts her head. "He's back here in a few days and I'm sure he has an excuse not to see me. He's a professional lady charmer, I swear."

Her friend laughs. "Isn't it worth a try? At least talk to him and find out where you stand. Then you'll know for sure whether to move on." Brie's eyes are filled with concern.

"I'm not sure if I want to. I like him. I need to leave it at that."

"You're going to forget about him? Just like that? Let him meet someone else and pretend this fling you two share never happened?"

"I am."

"I don't believe you," Brie says, leaning forward. "You're going to regret it."

"No, I won't."

"Yes, you will," Brie says, firmly.

Meghan holds her friend's stare. It's as if she can read her mind and she knows what she's going to say next.

"You don't want to let him go. I bet Colton has regrets."

Meghan opens her mouth to speak. She hasn't heard her ex's name in a long time. "I doubt it."

"He does. Sara and I ran into him—"

"You ran into Colton? Where?"

"He was taking a yoga class."

Meghan bursts into laughter. "He would not do yoga."

"He was doing it," she says.

"With whom?"

"I don't know. Sara and I were at the other side of the room, but I saw him. There's only a couple of guys there."

"Was he with someone?"

"Not sure," Brie says, sounding skeptical. "I talked to him after class. He was asking how you were doing and if you settled down. I told him you were with someone." Brie looks down and picks up her napkin, folding it over and over.

"I'm not with anyone."

"I know."

"You told him I was with Stu?" Meghan grumbles.

"I told him you were seeing Jared Landry."

"You didn't!"

"I did."

"Why?"

"You kind of are."

"There's no kind of. I'm not. We're not together." Meghan holds her head. "I can't let that go around. What if it gets back to Jared and he denies it? I'll look like a loser."

"Not at all. Colton was surprised, naturally, but wished you the best."

"He didn't say he regretted us breaking up, then."

"Well, no. But I could tell by his face he did."

"I'm sure he's doing fine."

"Are you going to call Jared?" Brie looks at her watch. "What's the time difference?"

"I don't know, but it's gotta be late afternoon there and I don't want to talk to him while he's on the road."

"Are you afraid that if you find out he has a girlfriend you'll be crushed?"

"Not at all!" Meghan says with a forced smile. Her stomach flutters as she thinks about Jared and the intimacy they shared. It was a dream. She had never given herself so freely to someone before, until now. He was all she could think about. The way he kissed her neck, massaged her foot, caressed her body. "It was—" She sinks into the booth. She remembers the way his lips felt against her skin. The tingling feeling she didn't want to let go of.

"Are you sure?" Brie asks, her eyes a cold stare as if she didn't believe her.

"I think he has a girlfriend anyway. I'll give him space."

"And when he calls you and wants to have sex with you, you're okay with that?"

"It was a onetime thing, okay? It's not going to happen again. I'm sure of it."

Brie makes a face.

"I'm serious!" Meghan says.

"So am I."

"It won't happen again. I promise you. I won't let it happen. I'm not going to be that girl, the one he calls up when he feels like it and I jump for his every move. No way."

"You like him a lot."

"Yeah, I like him."

"Then, call him! At least you'll know where you stand with him."

"I told you, he doesn't like-like me, you know, in a meaningful kind of way?"

"Don't you want to know so you can move on, if you have to?"

"I used him to practice my skills."

"And now you can tell him you like him and want something more."

"I'm not ready for that."

"Call him."

Meghan holds her phone, looking at it as though expecting it to ring. "He's not going to answer."

"At least leave a message."

Meghan thinks about what she's going to say. "Okay. I'll leave a message. He won't answer." She finds his number and presses the screen, confident that Jared is busy working. She holds her phone between her shoulder and ear, reassured that her brief message will satisfy Brie and she can put this to rest. If she can get over Jared and their amazing night they shared, it will be easier to move on.

"Hello?"

She sucks in a breath at the sound of his voice. His voice message sounds like he actually answered the phone.

"Hello?" There's his voice again, but he's not saying anything else. Her eyes widen and she takes a deep breath. "Jared?"

"Hello?"

"It's Meghan O—"

"Hi, Meg! How are you?"

"Good. How are you?" *He called me Meg.*

"Great. On my way to the arena. Game tonight."

"Yes, I know. Sorry, I shouldn't have called." Meghan looks at Brie who is waving her hand for her to carry on.

"We have one more game after tonight and then we're on our way home. Maybe we could hook up," he says in a low voice like he doesn't want anyone around him to hear.

"Right, yes, about that."

"Everything okay?"

Meghan looks at Brie. She bites her bottom lip and closes her eyes to clear her mind. "I don't want you to think we have this thing going on."

"A thing?"

"Well, you know, you, me, getting together." She lets the word linger, trying to think how she should phrase their connection. Her cheeks are burning and stomach is sinking. . . .

"We'll hook up when I'm home," he says.

"Oh, no, that's not what I mean," she says, hearing sudden loud voices on the other end.

"Landry!"

"I have to get going," he tells her. "Coach doesn't like us distracted before a game."

Then why did he answer his phone?

"Okay. Sure. There's an event I need you at when you're home."

"I'll call you!"

"Good luck!" she says into the phone, but he's already gone. She tucks her phone into her purse.

"What did he say? What?" Brie asks, talking with her hands.

"I don't think he heard a word I said."

"Sorry," Brie says, scrunching up her nose and twisting her lips.

"He was distracted. I should have known. It was a bad time. I'm sure he has a girlfriend." She pouts.

"See? You do care about him or you wouldn't be disappointed."

"Maybe I do like him. I like the sound of his voice. I miss him." She sinks low to the table and puts her head down.

"That's good!"

She looks up. "He's going to make some girl very happy one day," Meghan says. "Or he already has."

Chapter 13

"Hi, baby."

Jared's spine lengthens at the breathy voice on the phone.

"Hey," he answers, waiting for the woman to identify herself.

"Are you home yet?"

"Depends," he says, trying to place her.

"I'm coming over," she tells him. "I've missed you."

"That's not a good idea."

"It never stopped you before."

"I have to go," he says.

"I'm on my way over. I'm wearing your favorite outfit. The red one," she says with a seductive laugh.

"Lauren, this isn't the time," he says.

"I know how much you like to unwind after a road trip."

Jared runs his hand through his hair. "I'm tired."

"I'll see you in fifteen."

"You can't come over."

"Why not?"

"Because I'm on my way out."

"Before lunch? Do you have practice?"

"I'm going out."

"I know, you said. Where are you going?"

"It doesn't matter. We're not together anymore. I don't have to explain."

"I gave you a break."

"We're not getting back together. It's over."

"I gave you your space that you asked for."

Jared can hear her voice change. He pictures her pouting, puppy-dog eyes, the way she did to get her way. It wasn't going to work with him anymore. She is trying to get him to cave. He won't do it. He won't let her get to him. He can resist her. Meghan is more important. She means something to him. He chuckles to himself. He hardly knows Meghan, but knows her enough that he wants to date her and be with her whenever he can. If he could call her up right now and hang out with her, he would.

"Jared?"

"Yes?" He shakes the thought of Meghan, but keeps thinking about the cat costume and hopes she didn't have to pay too much to replace it. He should have given her money for it.

"I gave you space." Her voice is getting forceful. "Why did you leave Mason's party?"

"About that. How did you get in?"

"I showed up."

"How did you know about it?"

"I came to one of your events," she says, sweetening her voice like she wants something. "I spoke to Mason. He was talking to someone about his party and I happened to be there."

"You happened to be right there?" He doesn't buy it. "Please don't show up to things. We're not together. You need to realize that." His neck is feeling hot, his face changing color.

"Did you like my costume?"

"It was a wedding dress," he says.

"I bought it for us."

"You didn't."

"I did."

He has chills from her laugh.

"That's not going to happen."

"Come on!" Her voice changes. "You'll change your mind. Jared, I'm the wife you need. You need to be married to me. People are talking."

"They're not talking."

"They're wondering about you."

He doesn't buy it. "I have to go. I have somewhere to be."

"You have an event to attend."

"How did you know?"

"I know what's going on."

Of course you do.

"It doesn't start until noon."

"I have other things to do," he says.

"Like what?"

"What's with the questions?" He's getting impatient. "I don't have to tell you what I'm doing. We're not together."

"We should be."

"I don't love you," he says, feeling the pull in his chest. He didn't want to tell her that, didn't want to sound heartless, but how is he supposed to tell her to leave him alone?

"You don't mean that."

"We can't be together. I don't feel the same about you." He breathes out. It was easier to tell her how much he didn't care. Will she ever stop reaching for him? Why doesn't she get it?

"You could at least try," she says, as though she had a pivotal moment.

"I did try. We were together for nine months." He's just about yelling into the phone. Lauren is too much of a self-centered person to take no for an answer.

"Come on," she pleads. "One last time. I know you want me."

He laughs. "It wouldn't be the last for you."

She lets out an evil gasp followed by a laugh. "See? You want me! You miss our time together."

"I have to go. I'm late."

"You told me to give it two months to see how we feel. It's been that, maybe more," she says.

"It's over." He hangs up with an uneasy feeling. Maybe he should change the locks.

"We need to start a new bin," Meghan tells her staff, walking around the taped-off perimeter of the Coats for Kindness campaign, a traditional event hosted outside the doors of the Dome for people to drop off their donations and meet the players. "That one's full."

"That's two bins full," Dana says. "If we can fill this next bin, we've succeeded at our goal."

"What did we do differently this year?" Meghan asks, pushing her arms into her sides after feeling the cool air find its way around her neck. She should have worn a scarf now that the November temperature is dropping, calling for gloves and a heavier jacket.

"The players have shown up to meet fans, that's huge."

"All but Jared Landry."

"He doesn't like coming out to these things, does he?"

"As far as I know he doesn't," Meghan says. "I don't know what his problem is."

"Some people don't like crowds. My brother's like that. He's shy. Doesn't like the attention. He arrives late, leaves early . . . always looking for an excuse to leave."

"I'm not sure Jared's like that," Meghan says, changing her mind from what she first thought of him.

"You know him or somethin'?"

"Jared? Oh, no, no, I'm just guessing. I think you're right. Must be a shy guy. He should make an effort though to come out and show his face. Fans look forward to meeting the team. He doesn't realize that he's disappointing people. Jeez, some people have escaped during their workday to come here. The least he could do is show up." Meghan shakes her head. A chill goes through her bones, making her shoulders rise, and she inhales a breath.

"The lineup is still long," Dana says. "People are happy taking pictures and getting an autograph, I don't think it matters who's here today."

"It does matter. According to the recent online poll we did, Jared is one of the fan favorites. He should be here. What's with him? Is he that important he can't appreciate these people coming out to meet him?"

"You seem to be the one disappointed."

"His name is on the event list! He was mentioned in the radio ad." Meghan feels her heart race. "He doesn't commit when I need him to. He better show up or else I'm taking him off the banners and every event we have left this season."

"It's only November," Dana says. "We still have events going on until March."

"I know. He can't do this to us."

"Can you call him? Maybe he forgot?"

"He didn't forget." She bites her bottom lip and looks out at the crowd of people. She's pleased with the turnout. "I better go see how it's going at the promo tent." Meghan wanders over. She needs to stop talking about Jared like she knows him well. The last thing she wants is people to catch on that there's something going on between them. As she scans the gathering of people, she spots a woman who reminds her of Lauren, her childhood BFF, walking like she's on a mission through the open space, past the crowd. Her blond hair is straight and she has on a bomber-style jacket. She looks back and then hustles down the street. Meghan stares at her, wondering if it was her. It couldn't be.

"Hey, Meghan," Keri says. "Great job today. I'm grabbing a bite to eat after work. Wanna join me and some girlfriends? We're heading over to Milos."

"Okay, sure. That would be great. I'm starved."

"Me too. I'll meet you there," Keri says, and walks off.

After the event, Meghan drives a few blocks to the restaurant. She'll have a meal, show Keri that she can hang out with her and they can be friends outside of work and she doesn't have anything to hide. It doesn't have to be a strict relationship where she only can hang out with her at events. She can get to know who Keri is and what her friends are like. Maybe she likes to do shots at the bar or has a passion for live music. Meghan looked up the restaurant beforehand and found they have a band that plays there Friday and Saturday nights.

She walks in, scouting out the tables to see if she can spot her boss or a large table of women. As she walks in deeper, she sees a group of women bobbing their heads in conversation and sipping from their wineglasses.

"You made it. Great," Keri says. "I saved you a seat!" She points to the empty chair beside her and Meghan gracefully sits down. "Here's the drink menu if you're interested." She slides the laminated menu over. "Let me introduce you." She lifts her hand to the left of her, starting with the woman sitting beside Meghan. "This is Trina, and Charlotte, Chrissy, Lauren—"

Meghan freezes. She can't hear the other names, instead she sizes Lauren up, grins, waiting for her to say something, anything. Where has she been all these years? It's the best friend she lost when she was eight years old. Meghan opens her mouth to speak. Her eyebrows rise, as she waits patiently for Lauren to ask how she is and to say *It's been a long time. How have you been?* But she says nothing. Maybe this Lauren looks like her old friend Lauren, but it's not her. They say we all have a twin. How exciting, a woman who resembles the same girl she once knew. The long, blond hair, narrow wrists, thin nose. Meghan can't stop staring. It's her, it has to be her.

"Did you decide on a drink?" Keri asks.

Meghan blinks. "Pardon?"

"A drink? Did you decide?"

"I'm going to have a glass of white."

"That's what I'm having," Keri says.

Meghan looks up from her menu to study Lauren. It was her today. She must have come by to talk to Keri.

"I saw you at the Coats for Kindness event today," Meghan says, eyeing Lauren.

Lauren looks over her menu.

"You came by the event and didn't say hi?" Keri asks.

Lauren looks up. "It wasn't me."

"It looked like you," Meghan says.

"Nope, not me."

"Sorry."

"Is Keri really bossy?" the girl sitting across from her wants to know.

"Not at all," Meghan says, looking to her right.

"Good answer!" someone says, laughing.

"Does she help out at events?" the woman sitting beside her asks.

"Always!" Meghan says, reassuring her with a pleasing smile.

"You two get along then?" the woman across from her asks.

The waitress steps up to the table and takes her drink order.

Meghan narrows her eyebrows and asks Keri, "Are they putting me to the test?"

"Ignore them. I had an assistant once who drove me crazy, I had to be bossy. She complained all the time and said I ordered her around and she couldn't do her job because I was constantly watching her." Keri takes a sip. "Not true. The problem was she couldn't do her job. Thankfully she quit."

"I hope you don't feel like that about me," Meghan says.

"No, you're doing a great job. You're not planning on quitting on me, are you?"

"No."

"Keri says there's a lot of opportunity to chat with players. Must be fun, putting on these events?" the woman to her far right asks.

"I like it," Meghan says.

"She's always working," a woman with dark hair says.

Meghan just smiles.

"Keri won't tell us, but what's it like working with the players?"

Chrissy asks. "Do you get to hang out with them? Keri has, but she doesn't give us details. We keep asking but she keeps saying—"

"It's unprofessional," Keri says, cutting her off, finishing her sentence.

The woman raises her hand as if to say, that's what she was going to say.

"We talk with players. That's part of the job," Meghan says, reaching for her glass the moment the waitress puts it down in front of her.

"Do you get really close to them?"

Meghan swallows a sip, seeing the waitress standing at the table with a notepad in hand.

"We have to order," Keri says, scrolling her finger down the menu to find what she wants.

They all place their orders and as soon as the waitress steps away, the question lingers.

"So? How close do you get to the players?" the woman persists.

"Not that close," Meghan says, getting flashbacks of their night together, him kissing her neck making her have no control, lost in the sizzling moment.

"We get close," Keri says. "Some of us get closer than others, but it's part of the job. Players need to know they can trust us."

Does she know about Jared?

Meghan clears her throat and holds on to the stem of her glass.

"Would you agree?" Keri turns to Meghan.

She nods.

"You're close to certain players."

"Not really," Meghan says quietly.

Keri looks at her friends. "She says that but I see the guys talking to her all the time, especially one player but I won't mention his name."

"Tell us!" a woman says.

"I can't." Keri lifts an eyebrow at Meghan.

She knows about Jared.

"There is nothing between us, I mean a player," Meghan says.

Keri drops her head as though she doesn't believe her.

"I don't know what you're talking about," Meghan says, feeling breathless. "I wish there was something between—" She stops herself. Jared's name is on the tip of her tongue and then she thinks about Keri mentioning a friend of hers whom Jared used to date.

"Whatever," Keri says, waving her hand. "It happens. People who work together have a better opportunity to know each other, right?"

"That's how Travis and I started dating," the woman sitting across from her says. "We kept bumping into each other in the elevator. Finally, he asked me to have dinner with him."

Meghan's eyes perk up. "Are you still together?"

The woman flashes her hand across the table to show off her ring. "We're getting married next summer," she squeaks.

"Congratulations," Meghan says, glancing at Lauren who has been quiet since she arrived.

Does she recognize me or not? If she has the same laugh, maybe I could tell.

"Where are you getting married?" Meghan asks.

"In Victoria. That's where my family lives and we'll have our pictures taken at Butchart Gardens."

"It's beautiful there."

"Have you been?"

"A few times."

"We just have to send out invites in the spring and I have a dress fitting then—"

"Do you have your dress already?" Meghan asks.

"Yes!" She lowers her shoulders, tilts her head, and bats her eyes. "I fell in love with it in the store window."

That's when I fell in love with mine.

"It's easy to do," Meghan whispers. "So many choices though."

"I knew when I saw it on the mannequin that I had to have it."

"It's the right choice, then."

"Absolutely."

"What does it look like?"

"It's a sweetheart neckline," she says, tracing her fingers along her chest. "Sleeveless. At the waist it flares out like a ball gown."

"Beautiful."

"It even has sparkles in the gown. I can't wait to wear it." She shrieks.

My dress was sleeveless, a mermaid style. I love that dress.

Meghan sighs. "And your shoes?"

"I haven't gotten those yet. On my list of things to do."

"What color are your bridesmaids' dresses?" someone asks.

"Coral. The dresses are above the knee."

"Very summery," someone says.

"I got the idea from Lauren. I never would have picked the color, but when we were shopping, she showed me a similar dress and I thought it would we perfect. It goes with the whole garden feel."

"Where are you going on your honeymoon?" someone asks.

"Costa Rica," she answers. "Lauren's family has been generous, allowing us to stay at their villa for free."

"How nice!"

The woman is glowing with pride and excitement.

"We're so excited. I can hardly wait to lie on the beach and sip a drink from a coconut shell."

Meghan is trying hard not to stare at Lauren. She is certain that her parents had a place in Costa Rica when she was a child. Too many coincidences. Why hasn't she said anything? How could she forget those days of climbing the tree fort in her backyard and buying Popsicles at the corner store after school?

Lauren's parents had money. That was the one thing Meghan remembered about her. She rarely played outside, her mother didn't want to ruin her white wool carpet.

"Meghan?" a voice asks, taking Meghan's attention away from Lauren.

Meghan looks up, stunned to hear her name.

"Are you getting married?" the woman asks.

Meghan shakes her head. "No, I've never been married."

"Sorry, I thought, just assumed you were, you really seemed interested and well . . ."

"I was engaged. It didn't work out."

"That must have been hard," Keri says. "Sorry."

"I'm fine now." Meghan gives her a lasting grin. The waitress puts down their dinner plates. Meghan's cell phone rings. She reaches into her purse and pulls it out, sees the number. Her stomach turns as she sees his name come up. What can she say to Jared? He's blowing her off. Now he's calling because he's home and wants her at his disposal? She can't talk to him now. She tosses her phone back into her purse and begins to eat. She's not that hungry though. Thinking about Jared makes her insides go haywire. If only she could forget about him and the sex they had, then maybe she would be able to move on and pretend that what they shared didn't happen. If only it was that easy.

Her phone rings again. She unzips her purse and again, she sees Jared's name. She clicks off the ringer and puts the phone back into her purse. She needs space from him. It's the only way she's going to be able to forget about him. Unless he hunts her down, but she is doubtful. He's not interested in a real relationship. He wants an affair and she won't have any part of it.

Chapter 14

"How can Lauren not remember me?" Meghan asks Brie from her cell phone. "We were sitting across from each other."

"Maybe she had a brain injury and she doesn't remember her past, like amnesia or something."

"She was looking right at me!"

"Why don't you go see her? Talk to her?"

"I could. What if she doesn't want to talk to me?"

"You were eight years old. Why wouldn't she want to talk to you?"

"I don't know. She was the rich girl. Maybe I don't fit in her circle of friends."

"You're doing pretty good for yourself."

Her desk phone lights up, catching her eye. "There goes my phone again. I better go. I have a meeting at two o'clock."

"It's two now."

"I gotta go!" Meghan disconnects and carries it with her along with a binder and pen, not bothering to answer her desk phone. She runs into the boardroom where everyone is sitting around talking until she is at the door. Keri gives her a stern look.

"Sorry, I had something to finish up." Meghan takes a seat, opens her binder, and picks up her pen.

"We'll get started," Keri says, standing up at the head of the table. "The end of the year is fast approaching and we have some events coming up. One is at Metrotown, where we will be collecting toys for kids."

Meghan's cell phone vibrates on the table and the screen lights up Jared's name.

Keri clears her throat. "We'll have a tent set up and there will be appearances—" Keri looks down at the phone just when Meghan scoops it up to put her phone on silent mode. "Sorry," she whispers. Her cheeks feel a little warm as she sees Jared's name on her phone.

"As I was saying, we have players who will make appearances. . . ."

Meghan sinks in her chair. Did Keri just see Jared's name? Why would he be calling her? What does he want? *I have to tell him we can't see each other.* It won't work. An affair is one thing, but that's not what Meghan wants. She wants more. Where is she going to find someone to date? She looks around the room. Not interested in any of the guys sitting in the meeting. She should ask Brie or Sara if they know any single guys who are looking for a relationship or at least a date.

"Did you send out the invites yet?" Keri asks, snapping Meghan's attention from her daydream.

"Pardon?"

"For the black-tie event. Did you send out the invitations?"

"No. Not yet. It's on my things-to-do," Meghan says, pointing her pen at her notes.

"When do you plan to do that?"

"Today, actually."

"Good. That leaves roughly six weeks before the fund-raiser. Most people who have come to this annual event already have it marked on their calendar. Did you want to talk about the details?" Keri asks.

"Sure." Meghan stands up and flips through her notes to the page with the information. "It's at the end of the year, December thirtieth, but most of you are aware of the date. . . ."

Meghan talks about the details and once the meeting comes to a close, she makes her way to her office.

"Meg!"

She turns around to see Keri walking toward her. "Do you have a minute?"

"Sure. Sorry about my phone buzzing. I thought I turned it off. I know how much you hate interruptions during the meeting."

"It happens," Keri says. "I want to talk to you about Jared Landry."

Meghan walks into her office. Her feet suddenly cold, her heart racing.

"It's not what it looks like," Meghan says, turning on her toes. She crosses her arms at her chest.

"What's going on between the two of you?"

Meghan hesitates.

"I've never seen a player hang out and contact one of us because he's interested in an event. He obviously likes you. I saw how the two of you were together at the skate and at the library. I couldn't help but notice that he called you in the meeting."

"About that—"

"You don't have to explain. I'm just worried that you'll get hurt. Jared is kind of a . . . playboy. I've seen him with other women and I don't want you to get involved without knowing the consequences."

"I'm fine. There's nothing between us," Meghan reassures. "We've hung out, but I haven't spoken to him in a while."

Keri eyes her sternly. "Be careful. I'm sure you're aware that he's had lots of relationships. He doesn't have a problem getting what he wants. It doesn't last long . . . from what I know," Keri quickly adds. "He gets what he wants because of his name. I'm sure. Besides, he's getting back with his ex."

Meghan shuffles her feet and lets out a nervous laugh. "That's fine. We're not together, anyway." Her stomach is flipping around. She feels sick. She knew she wouldn't get him.

"I'm just warning you he's bad news."

"He is? Really?"

"Trust me on this. If you and Jared haven't started anything, you're lucky. You won't have anything to lose then."

Her stomach turns.

"Don't fall for his stories. He may say he's single, but he's a player."

"Then why is your friend seeing him?"

"She loves him."

Meghan takes a step backward. "Before you go," Meghan says, clearing her throat, trying to digest the news. "I have a question about your friend Lauren."

Keri perks up. "What is it?"

"I used to have a childhood best friend named Lauren. Blond hair, blue eyes, similar to your friend. I'm wondering if it's the same person."

"Did you ask her?"

"I didn't want to put her on the spot. Has Lauren always lived here, do you know?"

"She did. Although she moved to Calgary for a few years and then moved back here. Her parents own insurance companies."

"I remember her having wealthy parents," Meghan says, mentally taking note and trying to see any parallels. "They own a place in Costa Rica."

"So do Lauren's, my Lauren. It's probably coincidence."

"She remembered me. That's why she didn't talk. Did she think I'd forget her? We were best friends. We did everything together in second grade. We rode our bikes to the store to buy Popsicles and my brother would let us hang out in the tree fort as long as we wouldn't play house." She laughs at the thought.

"Do you want Lauren's number?" Keri asks.

"She doesn't want to talk to me. I'm not the same status as her. She's the rich girl and I'm the average."

"Lauren doesn't use her parents' money. She works two jobs. During the day she works at a marketing firm for a clothing company and works a couple of nights a week at Buckley's. Lauren wants to work for what she has and not depend on her dad."

"I don't know what it could be then," Meghan says, humming. "It doesn't matter."

Keri walks out of her office. Perhaps Meghan needs to stop by Buckley's one night and talk to her. Find out what Lauren's problem is.

Keri's phone is ringing. "I better get back at it," she says. "Do you want me to talk to Lauren?"

"No, it's okay," Meghan says. "I'll talk to her myself."

Jared walks around with his phone between his shoulder and ear as he pulls out the milk carton from the fridge and pours himself a tall glass.

"Our family is having Christmas dinner at my house this year," Jane says. "You will be here, won't you?"

"That's the plan."

"Okay, great. You can stay with us if you want to."

"Mom and Dad already asked me."

"Okay. The door is always open."

"Thanks. Are you sure you want to have everyone at your house? What about the baby?"

"I'm good. I feel good. If I have the dinner this year, someone else can do next year, when my hands are full. Are you bringing anyone?"

"For Christmas?" Jared asks, and then gulps his milk.

"Hmm."

"I'm not seeing anyone."

"How about Meghan?"

His heart beats faster. He puts his glass in the dishwasher. "I don't think we're together."

"You like her, don't you?" Jane asks.

"I do," Jared admits.

"She's a nice person and when you're with her you seem different."

"How?"

"You smile more, you're relaxed. . . ." Jane says.

Jared knows he's far from relaxed when he's with Meghan. She excites him. He can breathe again after years of trying to be somebody he's not. Is that why he and Lauren didn't make it? He didn't care enough about her to open up and be human. She only cared about the publicity and all the money that went along with it.

How can he get Meghan to listen to him?

"She doesn't take my calls," Jared finally says.

"Did you have a fight?"

"No. We're not together."

"Then why won't she take your calls? That's strange. You must have done something."

"I don't recall."

"A woman wouldn't refuse a call from a guy unless he did something."

"Or isn't interested."

"Does she have a boyfriend and is blowing you off?"

Jared's stomach sinks. He never gave it much thought. What did he do? He thinks about when he was in Carolina before the game and she called. Totally took him off guard. What did he say to her? He shouldn't have answered his phone. He never does, but there was a sliver of hope to hear her voice. He had thought about calling her and left his phone on. He was unfocused that night and it made for a disappointing game.

"I don't remember our last conversation," he admits. "I was on a road trip. You know how I get in my own space. I can't communicate like a normal person. My head's in the game."

"Did you call her back at least?"

"I did. She hasn't taken my call."

"You care about her, don't you?" Jane asks.

"I guess I do, yeah."

"I think you're afraid of getting close to her because you like her and you're scared of losing her."

"Maybe," he agrees. His cousin comes to mind. He was a brother he never had. They were inseparable as kids and when they both played hockey and moved away from Brampton, they were best friends, staying in touch. They understood each other's passion and the expectations that came along with playing professionally.

"You know what I mean. You can pick your girlfriends, but you don't hold on to them."

"I haven't loved any of them," he says, shamefully.

"Not one?"

"Never."

"How about the one after Chelsea? What's her face?"

Jared thinks about his brief relationship with the skinny blond who always made it clear to him that she was rich, too, and that they'd make a good marriage. Jared wasn't into her the way she apparently felt about him. She took their breakup harder than he imagined.

"Lauren. Not her either," he says.

"If you really like Meghan, which I think you do, then you have to do something about it or she'll find someone else and I know how much you hate to lose."

Jared hangs up with his sister and paces his kitchen. His house is empty. He would love to have a family and fill up the rooms. He can picture the kids running around the island and Meghan yelling after them that dinner is almost ready. Why does he keep seeing Meghan in his head? He shouldn't, they hardly know each other, but he loves being with her. Maybe being away from home has finally taken its toll. He wants a future. The urge is so strong, he can feel it in his gut. His heart swells as he thinks about the only woman who makes him desire a family life, someone he is sure to love.

He decides to give Meghan another call.

Chapter 15

Meghan changes out of her work attire, showers, and puts on a pair of jeans. She isn't sure why she wants to spy on Lauren. Her old friend could care less about her, she was sure. But she does want to find out if she remembers her. After all, they were best friends in elementary school. Why had Lauren acted like she didn't know her the other night? It didn't make sense.

Meghan heads out to Buckley's. She's never gone to a pub by herself before, making it for an awkward evening. Does she sit at the bar? Or find a table and pretend she is meeting someone? Meghan thinks of a plan as she drives, trying to figure out how she should be alone in a place where she rarely goes.

Meghan enters the pub. There are people everywhere, sitting or standing around watching the Warriors play a game. The bar is packed, not one seat is available and tables are loaded with people. Meghan coasts, hoping to spot Lauren or a place to sit. Her shoulders get bumped with every turn she makes and she keeps her head held high to spot somewhere to stand without rubbing up against someone. A burst of cheers explode, stopping Meghan to look up at the big screen overhead. The Warriors just scored, making it a three-two game with two minutes left. She thought by coming here late there would be an opportunity to see Lauren and chat. She didn't think about the game tonight.

She looks around to find a place to sit, walking in circles. She gets to the bar, waiting for her turn to squeeze in and order a drink. As the people in front of her move away with their drinks, she steps up and orders a vodka cooler from the bartender.

The patrons all erupt in cheers. Meghan looks up at the screen to see that the Warriors have won the game. She puts down money and turns on her toes to see if she can find a seat. The more she looks around, the more she feels comfortable standing.

Meghan walks through the crowd to see if she can spot Lauren. Whenever she sees a waitress holding a tray in front of her, Meghan sizes her up.

She puts the bottle to her mouth to sip and at the same time she gets bumped on the back, forcing her to lean forward and tip her drink.

"I'm sorry. I'm sorry," a man wearing a Warriors jersey says, putting his arm around hers to gently apologize.

She meets his brown eyes and blinks. "I'm fine. It's okay."

"Did you spill your drink?" he asks.

"A little, but it's fine. I didn't get any on me."

"Let me buy you a drink," he says.

"Don't worry about it," she says, smiling at the clean-shaven face and ruffled dark hair.

"Are you sure?" he asks.

Meghan doesn't move. Not sure if she should accept his kind gesture and get to know who this guy is, or continue to look for Lauren. After all, that is her mission tonight. The more she thinks about her childhood friend, the more determined she is to talk to her.

The man extends his hand. "My name's Rich."

"I'm Meghan," she says, taking his hand.

"Are you here with someone?"

"No."

"Alone?"

She nods and takes a sip.

"Do you want to have a seat?" He shoves his thumb behind him. "That table there. I'm with some friends."

"Is there a seat?" she asks, looking over his shoulder.

"Yeah, yeah. One person just left."

"Okay." She tilts her head. It would give her the opportunity to spy on Lauren. "It's busy." Meghan follows him to the table.

"Game night."

She sits down across from him and he does a quick introduction of his friends. Meghan looks at her bottle and it's almost empty. Her eyes are dancing around the room, searching for Lauren. She has to be here. There are a lot of servers and they blend into the crowd, although the atmosphere has cleared out a bit since the game is over.

"Where are your friends tonight?" Rich asks.

"I don't know. I came here by myself."

He eyes her as though she is mysterious. "Do you do that often?"

"Never."

This spot is prime. She can see the bar and the restaurant behind her. It's a great view. Rich and his friends must have been here early to get a seat. Every television is visible from this spot.

"Let me guess, you were waiting for someone and they didn't show?"

"I came here by myself," she says, noticing he has Jared's number sixteen jersey on. Damn, she misses him. Misses how he smells, the way he kisses and holds his firm hand to her back to keep her close when they embrace. She has to stop thinking about him or at least try to. He's probably on to someone else by now or Lauren? Keri's friend? Her childhood friend? It all sinks in.

"Are you hungry?" Rich is asking.

"No," she says in a daze, piecing the connection together.

He drinks down his bottle of beer. "You really are here alone?"

She nods slightly. "Tell me, Rich. What does a guy like you do with himself when he's not hanging out at a bar?" Meghan asks, trying to strike up a conversation. She stares into his dark eyes. There is kindness to them and a sense of pride. He's happy, although she's not sure why since he's sitting with friends who have girlfriends seated next to them. He's the only one single.

"I'm in construction."

She finishes her bottle and sets it down. With a quick glance at the bar she looks for Lauren. Maybe she's not working this side of the pub.

"How about you? What do you do?" Rich asks.

"I'm in public relations," she answers, holding off from telling him who she works for. If he's interested he'll ask more questions. She remembers when she got the job, Stu was ecstatic and thought she would have game tickets for every home game. She practically had to beg for a pair to give him for his birthday. He didn't even say thank you. That's when she should have dumped him, but she was caught up in the rugged motorcycle-riding boyfriend that he was and didn't see him for who he really was.

"Do you want another one?" the waitress asks, reaching over her to grab the empty bottle.

Meghan looks up to meet Lauren's eyes. "Hi, Lauren." Meghan is staring, waiting for her to answer.

"Oh, hi," she says. "You're Keri's friend."

Used to be your friend . . .

"Actually—"

"Can I get another beer?" Rich interrupts. "How 'bout you guys? Anyone else?" he asks his friends.

Lauren gets distracted and takes their orders. She then looks at Meghan with wide eyes to get her to speak more quickly.

"I'll have a Pellegrino, please," Meghan answers, and she watches Lauren disappear into the crowd. She stares.

She doesn't remember me as her friend?

"So, you're a Jared Landry fan?" Meghan asks Rich, eyeing his jersey, trying to make small talk.

"Yeah, the guy's pretty good. Do you follow hockey?"

"For the most part." She nods her head, trying not to smile too much.

"They're having a good season so far. Do you go to any of the games?"

"Not really," she says. "You?"

"I go to two or three games a year."

Lauren comes by the table and starts handing out drinks. Meghan opens her mouth to say something, but can't seem to get the words out. *Don't you remember me?* she wants to ask, but as soon as she is about to speak, Lauren turns on her toes and she's gone again.

Meghan takes a drink of her bubbly water, watching the game highlights and trying to keep tabs on Lauren.

"Is that Alex Price and Mason Ward?" someone from the table asks.

Meghan looks toward the entrance.

"Yeah, it is!" Rich says, jumping from his seat to get a better look.

Already there are people touching their arms and patting them on their shoulders. The guys are smiling, knowing they are well loved, looking sharp in their pristine suits. It doesn't take long before they each have a bottle of beer in their hands and are mingling with the crowd. A couple more players waltz in and they too have bottles given to them. The volume has risen and people are pulling out their cell phones taking pictures and asking for autographs.

Meghan gulps down her water. "Would you excuse me? I'm going to the bathroom." She walks through the pack of people standing around, trying to make it to the bar to find Lauren. She spots her taking an order. Her hair is tied back into a low ponytail, her cheeks are flushed and her forehead is shiny. It's not a good time to ask the question, but when will she see her again? Maybe Meghan will get the answers she needs. It's too busy to have a conversation. If she can find out why she doesn't remember her, it would put the obsession to rest. The more Meghan thinks about it, the more troubled she is. What did she do to this friend to make her pretend she doesn't know her?

Meghan waits so when she turns around she can spring her question *Don't you remember me?* on Lauren. It's on the tip of her tongue. Any minute now, Lauren is going to turn around and she's going to give her the answer she has been waiting for.

"Meg?"

Meghan swore she heard her name, but is focused on not losing sight of Lauren. She looks to be almost done talking.

"Meg!"

She feels a hand touch her arm. She turns around and it's Jared. All six feet of him, staring at her with luscious lips and prickly facial hair that hides the small scar on his jaw. He is still as sexy as ever. His hair is touseled, with half curls that fall on his neck. He is wearing a gray suit with a paisley purple tie. She inhales, hoping to slow down her thumping heart. He smells like a dryer sheet.

"Hi." She still can't believe he is standing beside her, mesmerized like she's meeting him for the first time. She is gazing at him. People around them are trying to get Jared's attention, asking for autographs and taking pictures. He doesn't seem to care. He is staring at her with those big blue eyes, oblivious to what's happening around them. Her heart is thumping so hard, she swallows, trying to get control of herself.

"I didn't know you were going to be here," he says, dropping his arm.

"You didn't ask."

Meghan bites her bottom lip. She wished she didn't sound so disappointed, but he doesn't want her, she knows that. He wants nothing more from her.

"Look, I'm sorry if I sounded a bit short on the phone . . ." He pauses. "I was on the road . . . I lose my concentration—"

"You don't have to explain."

"But I do."

"No, you don't," she says, taking a peek around her to see if she can spot Lauren.

"You haven't taken my calls. Who are you here with?"

"Nobody."

He cracks a grin. "You're kidding. You're here by yourself?"

She nods. "Are you seeing someone . . . else?"

He looks past her, runs his hand over his forehead, and narrows his eyes. "No."

"Are you sure?" Meghan wants to give him plenty of opportunity to tell the truth. She crosses her arms at her chest.

She sees Lauren walking toward her. "Just one sec," she tells Jared. "Lauren!" Meghan leaves Jared's side and rushes to catch up to Lauren.

"Yeah?" she asks, dropping the tray to the bar.

"I need to ask you something," Meghan says desperately.

"Can I get two whiskey sours and a double rum and Coke?" Lauren asks the bartender. She shoots Meghan a look. "What is it?"

"Do you remember me?"

"You're Keri's friend," she states.

"We used to be friends. Remember? Elementary school?" She watches Lauren fill her tray and then swing it around.

"We used to go to school together?" Lauren asks, scrunching up her nose. "I don't remember. Are you sure it was me?"

"Positive!"

"Sorry, I would have remembered. I have to deliver these drinks. Excuse me."

How can Lauren not remember me?

Meghan can't move, she's dumbfounded and a little hurt that she didn't stand out in Lauren's mind. How can this be? She thought she would be able to put it out of her mind once and for all, but the obsession has worsened. She watches Lauren disappear into the crowd.

Meghan's blood is boiling. Why is Lauren acting this way? Then, as Meghan heads back in Jared's direction she sees Lauren sail through the crowd like she's on a mission. She beelines it right to Jared, touches his arm, and sways her head back and forth, talking to him as though they know each other. Jared is rocking back and forth. There are people trying to get his attention, but he's having a hard time talking to his fans because Lauren is in his face.

Meghan's shoulders sink. They're together. She watches them carefully.

Lauren throws her head back laughing and then kisses him on his cheek. It looks like he is saying something to her, although he is not impressed. She touches his chest and pats it before leaving his side. She puckers a kiss and goes to the bar. Meghan holds a stare with Jared and for a moment she can't breathe. He is such a player.

He can't have me at his disposal.

Meghan turns on her heel and passes through the crowd to get to the front doors.

"Meghan!"

She ignores Jared. He has enough people here to entertain him to not even care that she's leaving, and he has Lauren.

"Meghan! Wait!"

She looks over her shoulder to see the distance between them. *He won't be able to catch me.* There are too many people trying to reach him, grabbing for him. She hears her name again. As she gets close to the door, she feels a hand at her back.

"Where are you going?"

She turns around, taking in his charisma. That charm he gives out when he wants something. "Home. You have lots of people here who want to talk to you."

"Can I come with you?" he asks, his eyes begging.

"I can see where this might go."

"I just want to talk," he pleads.

"About what?"

"You're not making it easy for me."

"Am I supposed to?"

"Jared!" someone yells. "Hey! Meghan!"

Their heads in the direction of the voice. It's Rich, waving his arms, pushing his way through people trying to get to them. "Thanks for stopping him," Rich says to Meghan. "I can't believe it." Rich is shaking his head. "Can I get my jersey signed?"

"I need a pen," Jared grumbles.

Someone behind Rich hands him a Sharpie. Jared signs, and shakes Rich's hand.

"I have to buy you another drink," Rich says to Meghan. "What's it going to be this time?"

"I'm okay," she says. Jared is taking it in and she can tell he is wondering how they know each other.

"Just one?" Rich asks.

"Actually, I'm heading out," she says slowly.

"I should get your number and we should do this again sometime," Rich says.

"Oh," she sighs. "Probably not."

"She's with me," Jared says.

Rich drops his head. His brown eyes are wide with amusement. "Okay, then. I uh, didn't know . . . you didn't say . . . I bumped into her and, and she spilled her drink, so I bought her one and we talked. That's all we did is talk and now this."

"It's all good." Jared gives him a nod and grabs Meghan's hand, pulling her with him toward the door. "You let that guy buy you a drink?"

"He was nice."

Jared swings the door open and the rush of cold air shocks Meghan.

"Nice enough to sit and talk with him?"

"He was wearing your jersey!"

They're walking faster, trying to keep warm.

"Is that why you picked him?"

"I didn't pick anyone," she hisses.

"He wanted to take you home," Jared says, stopping, jolting her toward him.

"Look. I'm not looking to pick someone up, I was here for different reasons—"

"Like what?"

"It doesn't matter."

"Yes, it does. I want you," he says, reaching for her face and kissing her hard on the mouth. His hand stays on her face and she kisses him back, but her emotions are all over the place. Why is she letting him get the best of her? He wants her for different reasons.

"I have to go," she says, rubbing her arms. The cold air is getting into her bones.

"Did you forget your jacket?"

"I'm parked up the street." She walks faster.

Jared unbuttons his suit jacket and throws it over her shoulders as they walk in stride down the sidewalk.

"You don't have to do this," she says, crossing her hands on her chest, her fingers securing the coat so it won't slip off.

"Walk with you? I need to talk to you."

"I don't need you telling me who to talk to. Rich was a nice guy," she defends, even though he wasn't her type.

"I'm sorry, you're right. I won't do that again. Were you going to go home with him?"

"No. I've never slept with anyone I didn't know. You on the other hand are a different story." She can't look at him, watching where she is stepping.

His grin widens. "Tell me about it."

"There's nothing to tell. There's nothing between us. Am I right?" She flashes him a hurtful stare.

"That's what I want to talk to you about."

"I'm not the type to run to you because of who you are."

"I figured that."

"I don't care what you do, honestly." She stops at her car on the street, takes off his jacket, and hands it to him. "Thank you."

Jared takes his jacket and pulls at her arm with his other hand, bringing her to his chest. He wraps his arms around her and lowers his head to hers. Nose to nose, he opens his mouth slightly, but her body is trembling from the cold. "You need to get into your car," he says, losing his grip.

She doesn't hesitate. Making her way to the driver's side, she gets in and turns the ignition, blasting the heat and rubbing her hands together.

Jared hops into the passenger side. "Did you watch the game?" he asks, shutting the door.

"The last few minutes."

"Did you see the hit on Grattan?" He whistles.

"At the end of the game?"

"Yeah."

"I heard people shouting about the bad call."

"I don't know why there wasn't a penalty."

"Do you want me to drop you off at the front door?" she asks.

"You want to get rid of me so quickly?"

"Your friends are waiting for you, aren't they?"

"They're not waiting." He stretches out his legs as far as he can.

"Don't you need to hang out with your friends?" she asks.

"You want to get rid of me, don't you? You were meeting someone here, weren't you?"

"No."

"Why were you at Buckley's? Did you know I would be there?" he asks.

"How would I know?" Her legs are shaking from the cold. It's time for her to rethink her wardrobe and wear heavier clothing since it's almost winter. "Do you always come here after a game?"

"Hardly. I try to stay away from here."

"Why is that?"

He flicks his hand up. "There are people I'd rather not see."

"Like Lauren?"

"How do you know her?" His mouth is ajar.

"We were childhood friends." Meghan stares straight ahead. "She wants you back, doesn't she?" A moment of silence makes Meghan feel uneasy. "You want her back, don't you?"

"No, I don't," he says.

"Please, just tell me the truth," she demands.

He looks at her, holding his gaze. "I wouldn't lie to you."

She's happy hearing those words. "Then why were you there?"

"I hadn't been in a long time." He looks out his window. "It's not a place I come to, but the guys asked me to join them," he says softly, glancing her way. "I'm glad you were here tonight. You've been on my mind."

Meghan can't help the sense of pleasure it gives her to hear that he's thinking of her.

Jared rubs his hand on his thigh. His fingers stop and they tap his leg. "I wanted to tell you that we should see more of each other." He clears his throat.

She lets out a breath.

"You don't want to?" he asks.

"It's not that."

"What is it?"

"I can't be that girl, you know? The one who's at your beck and call whenever you're lonely. The one who jumps every time you call. It's not me. I'm sorry if I gave you that impression."

"What do you want?" he asks.

She swallows.

I want you to be in my life, but I know it's not possible.

"I'll admit, I like being with you . . . there can't be anything more between us. You're different, but you want other things."

"What other things? What are you talking about?"

"Someone I know told me—" Meghan looks away. She promised she wouldn't say anything, but how can she not? Meghan knew it would affect their relationship whatever it may be.

"Who told you what?" he demands.

"I shouldn't say."

"It's a little late for that."

Meghan presses her hand against the steering wheel, looking out into the darkness. She sees only the outline of the car parked in front of her.

"You're not the type to settle down," Meghan says. "Not that it matters. You're serious with Lauren."

"Who said? That's not true."

"I'm not looking to settle down right now," she corrects. "It's just that, if you're not interested in one girlfriend, then—" Meghan pauses. "Then I'm not that girl."

There. She said it. She can move on now and be happy with herself. Why does she feel incomplete?

"I just want us to hang out again. Go out for dinner. See some sights. Watch a movie," he says.

"You do those things?" she asks, and then smiles.

"I do get out from time to time," he says. His lips resume their tightness and he asks, "What did this person tell you?"

"I should be careful. You have expectations."

"No, I don't."

"You can't keep promises."

He throws his head back against the seat. "Promises are potential lies."

"You don't commit to anybody."

"I have my own agenda."

"You like your freedom."

"I've never had reason not to like it," he says.

"You've had your heart broken and you don't want to get too close to someone."

"Not anymore."

"Is that true?" She is skeptical. Guys won't admit when they are broken. Her older brother was dumped by the girlfriend he had planned to marry. She was the one until she told him she was seeing someone else. He was so crushed, he stayed home for weeks because he didn't want to talk to anyone unless he was forced to. The thought of doing anything alone scared him and he lost touch with who he was. He didn't know it at the time, but had he not been dumped he wouldn't have met his wife, and they wouldn't have had their two children.

Jared, on the other hand, is a different breed altogether. Meghan thinks it would take a lot for him to be crushed. Although his voice is mild and stays at a monotone level, he's strong, both physically and mentally. He has to be, playing the sport he does. Getting yelled at during practice and being told to fight when he doesn't want to. She only knows this because these rumors float around the office from time to time about all the players. If they're not performing the best they can, there are trade talks or there's the possibility of being benched in a game.

"What do you say we get outta here?" Jared asks.

"Where to?"

"Your house." His voice is sweet like cotton candy.

"Did you drive here?"

"I can grab my car."

"I'll drop you off where you parked."

She's not sure why she agrees for him to come back to her place. She doesn't want to sleep with him, afraid these feelings she has won't go away.

"I have a better idea," she says. "Let's go for a drive."

"Am I driving or you?"

"Me."

Jared's look is mysterious with a cocky raised chin and glazed-eyed stare as though he can't quite figure out what she's up to.

"You don't want to ride in a Fiat?" she says, and laughs, starting up the ignition.

"I guess I better buckle up." He pulls his seat belt over him as she pulls away from the curb. "Where are you taking me?"

"I don't know. Any ideas?"

"Your place sounds good," he says.

She grins as though responding to his humor. "We should do something else." She wants to get to know him.

"What do you have in mind?"

"It's a clear night. I know somewhere we can go. You probably haven't been out of Vancouver much."

"Not much." He rests his head back, making himself comfortable.

"Where have you been?" she asks, watching the road carefully.

Jared taps his lap. "Probably the usual places, Richmond—"

"Because of the airport." She nods her head as though that's an obvious one. Her fingers lift from the steering wheel.

"Been to Surrey."

"Okay."

Jared's quiet.

"Anywhere else?" She looks over.

"Yeah . . . I've been to Cultus Lake."

"Okay, you have been out of the city. That's a long drive for you. Was that in the summer?"

"No, ten years ago."

"You were visiting?"

"Yup."

"When you lived in Brampton? Why did you choose there?"

"I didn't." His voice becomes harder. "I was eighteen." Jared swallows and looks out his window. He's gazing as though trying to recall where he is. Just when Meghan thinks he's stopped talking, he picks up where he left off. "My cousin was playing his junior year in Vancouver . . . I was playing in Seattle. I stayed here before making my way to Seattle and getting settled with my billet family." Jared rests his elbow on the door and rubs his hand along his chin.

Meghan breathes deeply as though she is about to hear something terrible that he doesn't share with anyone. She wants to tell him he doesn't have to go on. He doesn't have to revisit whatever it is that is weighing on his mind. If there is tragedy or a heroic story he needs to tell her, she is all ears. She's a good friend. Regardless where their relationship is going, she is still loyal. He can count on her.

"Luke was invited to stay at Corey Wells's cabin. They were team-mates." He pauses, collecting his thoughts. "Luke asked me to come along. It was supposed to be the last getaway before we started training camp. We wanted to have a weekend we'd never forget. Corey had a boat. His parents encouraged us guys to go fishing for trout." Jared rubs his chin before speaking. He clears his throat. "I was at the camp-site talking to a group of people when I heard screaming coming from the water. . . ." He pauses. "I ran to the shoreline." He stops, looks out his window and then straight ahead. "I saw Corey jump from the boat into the water. I didn't see Luke. . . ." Jared swallows hard. He takes a moment. "I haven't told this story in a long time," he utters.

Meghan nods, looking over at him. His troubled face is the first she's seen of him. Her heart melts a bit as she grasps the event, feeling for Jared and the drama he endured.

"It's okay," she whispers. Meghan turns onto the road that leads up the mountain.

"Where are you taking us?" he asks, looking out his window in awe.

"Burnaby Mountain. Wait until you see the view," she reassures with a smile.

"I remember Luke like it was yesterday. I ran into the water, dove in, and swam as fast as I could. Corey had Luke with one arm trying to keep his face upright. He was unconscious." Jared scratches his temple. "I got into the boat and pulled Luke in. A man and his son came by on their boat and called nine-one-one. We got to shore and by then there was a crowd forming. I was yelling at Luke to hang in there. I was useless." He shakes his head. "There was nothing I could do. The paramedics came. . . ."

Meghan parks her car on the mountain in line with other cars. She turns off the ignition and they stare straight ahead at the sky. There is a haze, but the stars are visible and bright. The ground is clear and the air is crisp.

Meghan takes off her seat belt and turns her body so that she is facing him. "I'm sorry."

"Luke died." Jared's face tightens. His eyes are glossy and he clutches his jaw.

"I'm sorry for your loss," she says, searching for his eyes, but he doesn't look at her. His focus is out the window. "That's a horrible thing to go through and to lose someone so close . . ."

"He was the brother I never had."

"How did he die?" she asks.

"I was told that Luke stood up to grab a drink from the cooler, he wasn't wearing a life jacket, neither was Corey. I don't know why they thought they didn't need to . . . out on the lake . . . Luke lost his balance and hit his head on the bow. He had concussions playing hockey. The doctor said after having two, the chances are greater of having another."

He takes off his seat belt and stretches his legs.

"Do you want to get out and walk?" she asks.

"No, you don't have a jacket."

"Right. Are you comfortable enough?"

"I'm okay. It's quite a view," he says, admiring the unobstructed scenery. "Do you come here often?"

"I don't, but I figured it would be a good place to talk without getting hounded."

"I think we're safe here," he says. "Thanks for listening. It's hard to forget."

"That's a dramatic time of your life."

"I thought by now, ten years later, that I wouldn't think about it as often as I do."

"I'm sure you won't forget. How could you? It's a dramatic event."

"I think about Luke all the time and feel guilty . . ."

"For what?"

"Living his dream."

"Aren't you living yours?"

"Luke wanted it so bad. He had his eye on being drafted by Pittsburgh. The year he died, he was prepared to play one more season of junior but he was already scouted and teams were talking. I have no doubt he would have been drafted that year. He was good."

"So are you," Meghan says. "You wouldn't be where you are if you weren't."

"I love the game."

"It shows."

"Ah."

"Seriously." She reaches out and puts her hand down. She was going to touch his leg, but the way she is sitting, she can't reach. "Thank you for sharing Luke with me. I'm sure he's proud of you."

"My pregame ritual we talked about . . . I think of him every time. He never got a chance to play in the NHL. It sounds dumb, but if I do things for him, it relieves my conscience of that day at the lake."

"I don't understand. Why would you feel guilty? Is that it?"

"If only I was in the boat . . . I could have gone, but didn't feel like fishing. I could have grabbed him before he fell—"

"You don't know that. There are a million what-ifs you can tell yourself, but accidents are accidents and unfortunately as guilty or heartbroken as we may be, tragedy happens and it sucks because it's out of our control."

"We were so close. We were like brothers, best friends. I knew what he would say before he said it, or what his next move was, you know? And if I was in the boat, I would have passed the soda . . . he would have had a life jacket on."

"You don't have to put this pressure on yourself. You can remember Luke for all the times you shared together. Remembering his death will only put a strain on you and not help you heal. Wouldn't Luke want you to be happy and live your best life? Anyone who cares enough would want to see that person succeed and be happy. It's not fair to live your life with this guilt. I'm sorry you feel this way. It's not your fault for what happened, right?"

She waits for him to acknowledge her with a nod and make eye contact.

"I never thought I would tell you this."

"About Luke?"

"Sorry to put a damper on your night."

"You didn't." She grins at him. Her heart swells for him. She wants to wrap her arms around him and tell him he can tell her anything. She likes him enough to not want to let him go yet a part of her knows this is only the beginning of either a relationship or an end. She still doesn't know where she stands. Earlier that night she would have guessed that he was using her for his convenience; now, she's guessing it might be the start of a friendship.

"Tell me, what was Luke like?"

"He was great. A good guy." A wide grin appears on Jared's face. "He was willing to help just about anyone. He coached summer hockey camps, volunteered his time with various activities, and wasn't afraid to show his affection."

"Did he have a girlfriend?"

"Not at the time."

"What do you think Luke would say about me?" she asks.

"He would have liked you," Jared says, smiling, and moving a little closer.

"So you're saying I would get his approval?"

"Maybe."

"What?" she teases. "Just a maybe?"

Jared brings himself to her. "He would have liked you a lot."

"Hmmm . . . and what do you think of me?" she asks, feeling bolder. She needs to know where she stands with him. It's only fair.

"I like you," he says.

"You're a tough sell."

"Am I? I slept with you, didn't I?"

"Don't you do that to all the girls?" she asks, hating herself for asking, thinking about him and Lauren. She's dying to ask more about them. She really doesn't want to know the answer, especially falling for a guy and knowing about his colorful past. Isn't that what Keri told her? He has a way with women and enjoys the single life?

Jared pulls away. "I don't do that to all the girls."

"Okay." She buttons her lips, thinking she's said enough. It's hard to get past the idea of what those lustful lips of his have tasted like.

He eyes her with skepticism. "I've never had anyone like you." His hand touches her arm, giving her goose bumps. "I like you," he murmurs. "I don't know where this is going, but I like it."

She swallows. Does he compare her with other women? Or does she stand alone?

Jared brings his hand to her face, cupping it and slowly drawing his lips to hers. He is gentle and soothing, yet there is something deeper that's felt. The kiss means something to Meghan. It's a step in a new direction. Perhaps he feels it too because he sweeps her hair away from her face, tugs her mouth with his before letting go. They are a breath away. Meghan's body is vibrating from the emotion that has come over her. This is where she belongs. This is who she wants to be with. How can she make him see that he means more to her than what he probably thinks? She doesn't want to fall into that category of every other woman he's been with. Did any of them feel this strongly about him? Probably so. The only thing that will help him understand is time together.

"I'm going to be away for Christmas," he says, letting his hands fall to his side.

"Oh. Right. I guess so."

"Yeah. Jane's having dinner. I'll be gone for a few days, then I'm on the road."

Meghan's stomach sinks.

"That will be nice for you and your family," she says. Doesn't he want to be close to her? They're together now, aren't they? Shouldn't they be together at Christmastime? Their first holiday together?

"I haven't been home since the start of summer."

"It will be good for you." She tries to sound positive. "Beckham will be happy."

A smile comes across his face. "Jane says Becks is telling her what he has planned for us to do while I'm there. He told her that I was to go to his friend's house to play."

"That's cute. Would you ever move back to Brampton?"

"I've thought about it. I've been away for eighteen years. It would be weird for me to go back and live permanently, but you never know. My family is there, so that's what makes it home. I don't know how long I will be here for. I hope for a long time. I like it here. I like the scenery, the hockey club, the mild weather compared to back east and I like what I have. I don't want to change unless I am forced to."

"I guess you can't really plan a future when you have the life you lead."

"Not really. I can only try. It doesn't always work out. I've seen guys play and settle down. Their wives think they are staying where they met, but forget that being transferred is part of the job. I've seen marriages break up because of it."

"They must have known it's what to expect when they married a hockey player."

Jared gives a half grin, rubbing his chin. "One would think."

"Did that happen to you?" she asks, digging into his past again. Wanting so desperately to know about these women he must have loved.

"Not like that, no."

"How serious were you with Lauren?"

His mouth comes together. He rubs his hand on his thigh. "She thought we were."

"But you weren't?"

He shakes his head and makes eye contact. "We're not."

Meghan's face changes shape. Is she a sucker for wanting this guy who's had too many women to count? "Why did you break up with her?"

He swallows. "I don't love her."

Meghan takes in his honest eyes, but she still wonders about Lauren. She was all over him at the bar.

"Do you still talk to her? Are you friends?" he asks.

Meghan blows out a breath. "No. Actually, Lauren is pretending that she doesn't know me. I didn't do anything to her. It's so strange. I don't get it."

"Be thankful for that." He runs his hand through his hair. "She's obsessive. Have you noticed her showing up to events?"

Meghan recalls the Coats for Kindness campaign. "I'm starting to."

"She's not showing up to donate," he says.

"She comes by to see you?"

Jared shrugs. "Seems that way."

"She's friends with Keri."

"Who's that?"

"My boss," Meghan says. Her head is spinning with questions and piecing the mystery together. "Can you tell me more about Lauren?"

"Why do you want to know?"

"I don't understand—"

"I don't want to talk about her," he says. "I'll be honest with you and tell you what you want to know, but when it comes to her, I have regrets."

"Do you have regrets about me?" she asks.

"I wouldn't be here if I did." He smiles at her. "I think you're an amazing person." He brings his hand to her neck, combing her hair with his fingers. "The way you juggle your job and have to answer to people and manage the guys . . . that's talent. I couldn't do it. Why do you care so much about events and who shows up to them? Do you get perks or bonuses or something?"

"I wish!" she laughs. "I don't get anything. It's my job. I care."

"Well, it shows."

"Thanks."

"I'm glad you brought me here." His blue eyes are a shade darker, but the reflection from the night sky through the front window makes them glint. "The stars are out."

"Pretty, isn't it? More than I can count."

"It's a clear night," he agrees. "I'd like to come here again."

"I'm always up for company." She turns on the ignition. "I think it's going to snow soon. It's cold in here." She turns on the heat and plays with the vents. "I doubt I'll forget my jacket again. I don't know what I was thinking."

"I know what I'm thinking," he says, coming close to her. "I gotta kiss you again." He moves his face even closer and whispers, "Do you know a place where we can be alone?"

"I know what you're thinking." She laughs and he kisses her. Every inch of her body is coming undone. Everywhere his hands touch, a shiver runs down her body. Why does he make her feel so alive? He is a great kisser. Knowing there are other vehicles parked around them, she doesn't care. Their arms are all over each other. It's too much to handle for being in close quarters. He takes her hand in his and runs his fingers down her body.

If only they were close to home, she would be willing to take it further. "I guess we should stop," she says in a mere whisper. He pecks her one more time on the lips.

"Why?"

"This isn't the place."

"Why not?"

"There's people around. You wouldn't want to get caught with your pants down. How would we live that down?"

"I'm kidding," he says. "You're right."

"We can go back to my house, but it's late," she says, contemplating.

He begins kissing her neck. She runs her hands through his hair. Why do they have to be so far from home?

"I want you so bad," he says. "You're all I've been thinking about."

"I think of you, too," she says, enjoying his touch. "We should go. I like this, but we have to stop before someone sees us."

He backs away slowly. "I can't get enough of you."

This makes her smile and a fizzle of hope overcomes her. Maybe there is more to their relationship than she thinks. He wants her. She can give herself so easily. Jared is what she wants.

"We can do it right here," he says, massaging the back of her head. Her eyes close and suddenly his lips are planted on hers, again.

It would be easy, she thinks. "There's no room."

"We can make room." He takes a quick look behind them. "Okay, you're right. No room." He places his hand on her thigh and leaves it there. "I'm so turned on."

"Let's drive," she says.

"If that doesn't kill the craving," he says, making her laugh.

"It will cool us down."

"I should probably get my car before something happens to it," he says.

"There's probably people standing around taking pictures," she says. "Your friends haven't wondered where you took off to without your car?"

"They're probably still there. What are you doing tomorrow?" he asks.

"Working. We have an event."

"Do I need to be there?" he asks.

"Yes, I hope you'll be there."

"So you probably won't spend the night?"

Her shoulders sink. She wants to say yes.

"I think about the cat costume . . ."

"I had to pay for that," she says.

"What did they say when you returned it?"

"It was garbage. They couldn't fix it without it looking repaired."

"You had to pay for it? How much was it?"

"Two hundred bucks."

"Sorry. I can give you some money for it."

"Don't worry about it. That costume was a disaster. I should have known when I put it on it would give me grief. It was too tight."

"You looked hot in it."

She beams. "I still have to return your shirt and Jane's leggings. I'll come by this week."

"Are you sure I can't bring you home?"

She breathes out. "I wish I could, but I have a meeting first thing. You don't know how hard this is for me to say no? We have an event this week, it's the second Coats for Kindness campaign."

"Remind me."

"You're not serious," she says. "I e-mailed you the details last week. Do you ignore them?"

"I don't check my e-mail that often."

"That's because you avoid me."

"I don't."

"You don't like going to these things. Is it Lauren?"

"I just want to play hockey." He shrugs. "I've never been big on hanging out at community things. It's not that I'm not supportive . . . I am."

"Then what is it?" She tries to read him.

"I get annoyed by people I don't know hugging me and touching me."

"It's who you are. People feed off your success."

"I know . . . I should be grateful."

"You are, I know you must be."

He leans in and kisses her. His lips taste hers as though he's begging for more.

His lips part. "Are you sure you can't come back to my house?"

"I'd never leave," she says.

"You can stay at my house," he says with a tone that makes her body ache. He could satisfy her need instantly, all she has to do is go to his house or her place and it would be a done deal. She'd know by the deed that they were together . . . a couple, loving each other like two people do when the attraction is so intense.

"Seriously, don't ask because I will." She smiles and kisses him back.

He hums, holding her with a mighty grip, bringing her lips back to his. "I could use the company." Their voices are whispers.

"We'll pick up where we left off when I see you," she reasons.

"Is that a promise?" he asks. "'Cause I don't like broken promises."

"I promise," she says. "On one condition."

"And what's that?"

She pulls her head back so she can dream into his blue eyes. "I want to be the only one."

"Is that what's holding you back from coming to my house?"

"No. I want to know if I'm the only one you are intimate with." Meghan holds back from using the word *girlfriend*, afraid to frighten him. She wouldn't want to scare him into thinking she was cornering him. He might want to run the other way.

He makes a straight face. "You are."

She swallows. "I don't want us to be seeing each other and then I find out you're seeing someone else."

"I wouldn't do that."

She eyes him thoroughly as though she could see if there was anything he was hiding.

"I want us to be honest and when you're on the road . . ."

He lifts his finger to her chin. "I'll be honest with you."

"That's all I want," she says, satisfied.

"I'll be honest right now. I want you so bad." He kisses her neck, making her head fall back.

"It'll have to wait."

"You're not fair," he teases.

"You don't play fair, do you?"

"Always," he says between kisses.

Their lips part and they are a breath away from each other. "We should go," she whispers.

"Go where?"

"You need to get your car." She adjusts herself in the driver's seat and Jared puts on his seat belt. "Do you feel like coming back to my house?"

"I thought you'd never ask."

Meghan drops Jared off to pick up his car and he follows her home.

"I don't have any beer," she says, looking into her fridge. "I have orange juice, a couple of bottles of wine, and cans of 7UP."

"I'm good." He takes a seat on the couch.

"You don't want anything?" She reaches for a can of soda.

He shakes his head, sits back, and stretches his arm out on the couch.

Meghan turns on the TV. "You probably want to watch sports highlights," she says, turning the channel.

"I want to know more about you."

"About me?" She sits beside him, her finger on the tab ready to open the can, but she's stuck looking at those kind eyes of his. "Okay. I think you know a lot about me."

"I don't know," he says, sinking his eyes into hers.

"I think you should tell me more about you."

"What do you want to know?" he asks.

"Why do you have such a big house for just yourself?"

"You can ask me any question and that's all you got?" Jared puts his arm down. "I liked it. I was moving from Carolina and was given a few houses to choose from. I had to make a quick decision and it had to be ready to move into."

She studies his face, the rounded chin, the scar on his jawline . . .

"How did you get that scar?" she asks.

He touches it, knowing exactly where it is. "A puck."

"Ouch. I bet that hurt."

"I felt it more after the game. Adrenaline is like a drug. I was caught up in the moment . . . A guy took a shot, it was a lucky bounce off the ice and hit me. I happened to be in the wrong spot."

"Have you been hurt a lot?" she asks, feeling his ache and the pain he experienced. She can't picture him bruised and cut; seeing him in distress doesn't sit right with her.

"It's part of the game . . ."

"I guess it is." She folds her hands on her lap.

"When can I meet your parents?" he asks.

"Oh, I don't know. . . ." She opens the can and takes a sip. "When do you want to meet them?"

"Christmas?"

"You're not going to be here," she says, taking another sip.

"Maybe after? In the new year?"

"If you want to."

"Did you tell them about us?" he asks.

She puts down her can on the coffee table. "Honestly, I didn't know there was an us."

"There is, isn't there?"

He takes his hand and threads her waves through, bringing her face close to his. He kisses her full on the mouth. He is gentle and sweet. He's kissing her with a soothing motion as though they know where it will lead. There is no competition, no struggle to see who wants it more. They are both making the moment last as long as they possibly can. Meghan touches his face, runs her fingers along his scar and down his neck, circling around his strands.

Jared abruptly scoops her body up and moves it to the other end of the couch, laying her down as he kisses her mouth. Her hands look so small as they wrap around his powerful shoulders. It's like a surge of energy between them, needing and wanting more as though there are time constraints. Jared's body weight has shifted to the outside, letting Meghan be cornered into the cushion. With one hand, Jared pulls off his shirt and throws it to the floor, revealing his oh-so-fine stacked muscles. She can't help herself, she loves touching him. She runs her hand down his chest as he kisses her neck, finding the hem of her shirt. His warm, thick hand finds her bare skin and slowly he ravels her shirt up and over her head. As he kisses her so freely, he unbuttons her jeans and slides them off without hesitation. Then he does his own.

"Let's go to your bed," he tells her, and helps her up. She leads him to her bedroom where he gently lays her down on her pillow.

Why does this feel so right? Is she afraid to lose him? Giving him what he wants so that he will stay with her?

Meghan feels a lot more between them than she should. They hardly know each other, yet it seems like they share a deeper connection. He is making an effort to know her, so why does she sense this isn't going to last? What is she afraid of?

Meghan tells herself that she does know Jared as he pulls her shirt over her head. She likes him a lot, maybe more than she should at this stage of their . . . relationship. She can't quite call herself his girlfriend, as they haven't had that discussion yet. He hasn't made it clear, but she is feeling a bond between them. Does Jared feel it too? Is she what he needs? He's never said, but maybe this is all she'll be.

He sweeps her hair away from her face, touching her cheek and looking at her with a keen eye, before kissing her hard on her mouth. She puts her arms around his neck and he enters her with a thrust, leaning into her, their bodies as one.

As she loses herself in the moment, she realizes how much she wants Jared in her life. She feels a sense of belonging with him, like he truly wants her. A change from what she is used to, being the giver that she is. Will she be just another one of his girlfriends or does he genuinely care enough about her to be exclusive? The way it's going, her heart could break easily if she's not the only one.

Chapter 16

"What's wrong?" Dana asks. "You look like something's bothering you."

"I'm fine," Meghan says, taking out her cell phone to check messages.

"Personal stuff?"

"No."

"Is it the season? It can bring people down."

"That's not it." Meghan puts her phone away. Jared hasn't even gotten in touch with her after he spent the night. He left early in the morning and she hasn't heard from him. Didn't he say he would be here? At least he could be more considerate and tell her where he is and why he can't make it.

Dana lowers her head. "Are you mad because Jared didn't show up again?" she asks in a whisper.

"Oh, no . . . why would I be . . . mad?"

Dana giggles. "You're always mad at events when he doesn't show up."

"He's the only one who doesn't take these events seriously," Meghan mutters under her breath. Maybe she should have reminded him last night that he's expected to show up. Does he think because she slept with him that he has a free pass?

Regardless of what's happening between them, this is still her job. Doesn't he understand that? She wants to make a difference in people's lives. Having this job gives her the opportunity to reach out to a variety of charities and people in need. Why can't Jared be more understanding and giving of his time?

"Why do you care if he shows? He's not the only one who hasn't shown up for something."

"But he does it most often and doesn't apologize. It's like he doesn't care."

"He probably doesn't."

"That's what bothers me."

"Don't let it. You can't make him come to events. Players do it because they want to and it means something to them. I'm sure Jared has his reasons."

"He does have his reasons," Meghan says. "He told me he doesn't care about the events, he only wants to play hockey, but it would be nice if he would take part, at least show his face for his fans. Meghan sucks in her lips. And show up for me. Does he *even care what I think? This is my job, he should be supporting me if he really wants to be with me. Maybe he doesn't and it's his way of telling me.*

"Are you and Jared together?" Dana asks.

"Ah, no, not exactly," Meghan says. She should have been more prepared for this question. "A little. We've seen each other now and then. . . ." She realizes this is the first time she's admitted to seeing Jared to anyone, besides Brie. Will Jared care if anyone knows?

"You have? Really?"

"Shhh." Meghan looks around. "Please, I don't want anyone to think we're together, you know?"

"Well, are you?"

"Kind of. We've been out a few times. Dinner . . . we're friends." She let the word hang on her tongue. If only she could admit they were more than friends.

"You're so lucky."

"Am I?"

Dana's eyes grow wide. "He's gorgeous."

"He is." Meghan tries playing it cool, but the thought of his washboard abs and cheeky smile make her insides turn upside down. Her whole body feels a buzz as she thinks about being with him . . . naked . . . in the shower . . . waking up in his bed . . . in her bed . . . She's getting dizzy. Does Jared feel the same about her? Surely, he feels something. He keeps coming back for more.

"Meghan, are we taking donations on footwear?"

"Just coats," she answers.

"The bin is almost full," one of her coworkers says.

"That's great. There's a lot of people we can help out," she says.

"How long do you need me for?" Alex Price asks, holding a Sharpie in his hand. There are people crowded around, wanting autographs and pictures.

Meghan takes out her cell phone to check the time. "Is a half hour okay?"

"Fine." He walks away and begins talking with fans.

The grocery store has been sectioned off so that it gives Alex Price and Mason Ward room to move without getting ambushed. Maybe Jared knows how popular he is and doesn't want to be bothered by obsessed fans.

Meghan watches over the production of the event to make sure it runs smoothly and is easy for the players. She has a view of the semi-trailer that is parked outside a short distance from where they are standing.

Someone hands Meghan a plastic bag filled with what looks like coats. "Thanks," she says, and takes it outside. As she throws it into the bin, she spots Lauren walking toward the store. She is tall, wearing a long coat and pumps. She doesn't look like the waitress with a messy ponytail, damp forehead, and flushed cheeks. Lauren looks made up and businesslike.

A sense of relief comes over Meghan. Finally, Lauren wants to talk to her and tell her how sorry she is about that night at Buckley's. She wasn't in the mood to talk then and realizes now that she misses their friendship. Perhaps Lauren was self-conscious, unable to spill her guts about how she moved away and was unable to keep in touch with her. How did Lauren know she was going to be here today?

A smile comes over Meghan as she waits for Lauren to approach her. She's excited to talk to her, find out what she's been up to. Meghan keeps her smile as she steps out of the event circle so she can talk to Lauren and give her a hug if she is willing. Meghan lifts her shoulders and eyebrows at the same time when she makes eye contact with Lauren. Is it a hug or just a friendly nod? To Meghan's surprise, Lauren isn't smiling. In fact, she looks really perplexed, like something is troubling her. Maybe she's thought about their friendship in depth and feels bad about the whole thing. Yes, that's it, Meghan convinces herself. She would feel the same had she been in Lauren's shoes. Meghan closes in and gives Lauren a nod, saying hello when she is in arm's reach of her.

"Good to see you," Meghan says. She can't help but feel the joy that has come over her. Finally, they'll be friends again.

"I thought Keri was working today," Lauren says.

"She's in the office today. I'm on location."

"I see. Okay." Lauren stands on her tippy-toes, trying to see over Meghan's shoulders.

Meghan gazes behind her. What can Lauren be looking for?

"Is Jared here?"

Meghan throws her head back and stares at her wondering why she's asking, but Lauren isn't paying attention. She's more concerned about what's happening with the event than talking about the friendship they used to have. She shakes her head. "Can I help you with something?" She has no idea what Lauren would need help with, but there must be something on her mind. Meghan bites her lower lip subtly waiting for Lauren's response. "You were really busy at Buckley's when I saw you," she says, making small talk. Maybe Lauren doesn't know how to start the conversation. Meghan can help her.

"It always is."

"Run off your feet," she says with a light laugh, desperately trying to ease up the tension. Why is Lauren so tense? She could probably balance a plate on her head, she is standing so straight.

"I'm going," Lauren says. "I'll talk to Keri later."

"You were asking about Jared," Meghan says, her head cocked. She wants to get to the bottom of this.

Lauren makes a straight face. "I wanted to talk to him. I was taking a chance, thought he'd be here."

"You're not together," Meghan tells her. What is wrong with Lauren?

"He's my boyfriend."

Meghan's stomach sinks. Her throat is dry and she licks her lips to moisten her mouth so she can ask, "Your what?"

"Jared's my boyfriend. I told him I would meet him here. I wanted to surprise him." She looks around. "Guess I'll run by his house."

"Lauren, you and he used to date."

"We're still a couple."

Meghan bites her bottom lip. The pressure is enough to put a small puncture in it. She wets it with her tongue.

"I need to talk to him."

"Why didn't you call him?" Meghan regrets asking. She can't

imagine Jared and Lauren together. The thought tears her heart apart. She wants him. Lauren can't have him. She's too late.

"I did. He didn't return my calls. I'll stop by his house."

"He was supposed to be here," Meghan says, not sure why she is telling her this.

"I'll find him. He won't be far." She lets out a laugh like she's got an evil plot.

"Do you want me to give him a message? If he, uh, comes by?"

"You can tell him I was looking for him and that I have to talk to him. It's important."

"Okay."

Lauren turns on her toe to leave.

"I have something to ask you," Meghan says, stopping Lauren in her step. "Why are you ignoring me? We used to be best friends when we were in school, then you moved away and now you pretend you don't know me."

Lauren's face softens. "We were best friends?"

"Don't tell me you've forgotten. We hung out all the time. We rode our bikes to the corner store for Popsicles and you used to play in my tree fort. How could you forget?"

"It's one of those things." Lauren looks smug. "You know, I thought it was you . . ."

"Come on, seriously, Lauren. Why are you pretending to not know me?"

"I'm not pretending."

"Yes, you are." Meghan won't let Lauren go without an explanation. "What did I do to you?"

"Nothing."

"Then why are you pretending you don't know me?"

"Okay, okay." Lauren shoves her hands into her coat pockets. "Yes, I remember you."

"And?"

Lauren rolls her eyes. "We can't be friends. You like my fiancé."

"Who's your fiancé?"

"Jared!"

"What? He's your ex-boyfriend!"

Lauren laughs. "Jared's my boyfriend. I know you like him, I saw how you two were talking at Buckley's, but he's with me."

Meghan is stunned. She can't believe what she's hearing. "I had no idea."

"I'm outta here," Alex tells Meghan. He nods at Lauren as he walks by.

"Thanks for coming out," Meghan calls after him, noticing Eli Cooper is still there and probably will be until the very end. She turns to Lauren. "I still don't understand. Why have you pretended to not know me?" Meghan presses.

"Don't you think it's weird that you like my boyfriend?"

Meghan shakes her head.

"You tracked Jared down at the pub—"

"I was there to see you," Meghan says.

"You always wanted what I had."

"You came from a wealthy family. You had what most girls wished for." Meghan looks away, taking note of the event and how many people are left. It's about time to clean up. It went rather smoothly, she thinks. Perhaps people are busily doing Christmas shopping and this event is a stop-by, so the crowds are minimal. If Jared or Devin Miller were here it would be a much crazier event.

"You had a real dollhouse," Meghan says in wonder. "You had money and could buy more than what I ever had."

"My parents had money."

"When you were a kid, your parents bought you lots of stuff."

Lauren puts her hands into her coat pockets. "I have to go and meet Jared."

Meghan's insides feel like they've turned inside out. Jared still has feelings for Lauren? She feels like her heart has been taken out of her chest and squeezed so tight that she can't breathe.

Why didn't she tell him how she felt? Why didn't she go home with him that night? Is that all he wants in a relationship? Someone to sleep with and go with his career?

"You're not together," Meghan says, not believing her.

"We are together," Lauren corrects.

"Did he buy you a ring?"

"Not yet," she snaps. "It's being made."

"I don't get you," Meghan says. Has Lauren always been shallow? "You want Jared back because he's moved on?"

"No. You're after Jared because I have him, and you know he's mine."

"He's not yours," Meghan banters.

"He is mine," Lauren says with a heightened, long, shaped eyebrow. Her stare is fierce, bringing Meghan to a halt. She sees something in her eyes that makes her hold back the fight. She can't have this conversation at work. People can hear them, especially the players who are saying bye as they leave.

Is Lauren telling the truth? Is there no chance for Meghan? Why should she compete for Jared if she's already lost? Lauren has already told her she's competitive, what will happen when she finds out she and Jared have been seeing each other?

"I have to run," Lauren says. "Jared's waiting for me."

Meghan is speechless as she watches Lauren trot off through the parking lot. Her whole world seems empty now and if she doesn't have Jared, well, she can use her flirting skills to work on finding someone who really wants her. Meghan takes down the banner of Jared and makes a mental note to take him off the ads and replace him with Eli Cooper. The young ones are always eager to please.

Jared takes some shots at his empty net in his basement. Being by himself is wearing thin. When is he going to settle down and have the family life he always wanted? He loved having Meghan cuddled into his arms last night. He didn't want to leave her one-bedroom apartment, it was like a hideout, nobody knew he was there. The best part was, he didn't feel alone, he felt wanted. He checks his watch. He should go make an appearance at the campaign. Meghan is probably wondering where he is.

"Jared?" Loretta calls out, stopping him from taking another shot.

He looks up at his housekeeper who is walking the distance to talk to him.

"Lauren is here," she says.

His stomach tightens. "Lauren? What the hell? What's she doing here?"

"She's sitting in the living room. She says she wants to talk to you."

Annoyed that she's in his house and he has no interest in what she has to tell him, he leans his stick against the boards and makes his way upstairs. He saunters down the hall and into the wide-open space. Lauren is sitting on his burgundy plush couch with her hands folded on her lap, rubbing her toes along the edge of the pattern rug under the glass coffee table.

As Jared comes into view, Lauren stands up and says hello.

"Hi," Jared says. "Were you in the neighborhood and decided to stop by?" It is an honest question, but also a familiar one between them. Anytime she came over unexpectedly, she would tell him she was in the neighborhood. It was a long drive from her house, so for her to drive over, there had to be a reason.

He takes in Lauren's height and skinny limbs. She carries herself well. Her hair is the same blond, hanging past her shoulders, high cheekbones and red lips.

Lauren puts her arms out and wraps them around his broad chest, giving him a little squeeze and releasing herself to him, bodies still touching.

"What's this about?" he asks.

"I've missed you. Can't I give you a hug?" She steps back.

"What do you want, Lauren?" He stands still, not hugging her back.

"I came by to see what you've been up to. I was at an event, thought you'd be there, but the promotions girl said you didn't make it."

"What promotions girl?"

"Meghan."

His chest expands. *She probably was wondering where I was.*

"She said you didn't show up."

He shakes his head. "I didn't make it this time." He held off from telling her that he was on his way.

"Afraid of big crowds?"

"I didn't feel like going," he lies. "Why did you stop by?"

"I've been thinking about you. Wondered how you've been."

"I'm good."

Lauren reaches for his arm and rubs her hand down his bicep. When she gets to his hand, she wraps her fingers around his, pulling herself in close. "What do you say we pick up from where we left off?" Lauren skims his neck with her nose and begins kissing him. Her tongue licks him and he jolts backward, unmoved by her touch.

She laughs at his reaction and does it again.

"Stop, Lauren. We can't do this." He breaks away.

"Why not?"

"We broke up. There was a reason for that."

"You're going to say no because we broke up?" Lauren crosses her arms at her chest. "Who is she?"

"Who?"

"What's her name?" Her look is suddenly innocent.

"None of your business." Jared's mixed emotions about Meghan hit him like a punch to the stomach. Why hasn't he made Meghan his? Why is he waiting for her to make the first move? He's so used to women, like Lauren, who throw themselves at him and he takes action, using them as girlfriend material when all he really wants is someone to come home to and be himself with. There hasn't been anyone he can do that with. Until now.

"Then why won't you kiss me back? It's never stopped you before."

"I . . . don't know."

"Then what's wrong with you? Are you not feeling well?" Her face relaxes.

"I'm fine. I think you should go." He steps into the hall and waits for her. Lauren hasn't moved.

"Can we talk?" she asks.

"You never want to talk," he says.

"I think we could make it work again."

He tries not to laugh.

"Why? We have chemistry. We have goals. We have each other."

I didn't love you then and I couldn't love you now.

"We broke up because you wanted to get married. That wasn't me."

"But it is now?" she asks, batting her eyes.

"I don't know."

"You do know. You don't want to say it."

"Say what? That I don't want to marry you? Come on, Lauren. I don't want to hurt your feelings. I don't know why you don't see what I see, but a marriage wouldn't last between us anyway. Why would you want to?"

He knows the question is going to start her up like a wind-up toy and she'll let loose on him, but isn't a marriage supposed to be about two people who not only love each other but want to be with each other? He didn't mind Lauren for a day or two, but anything more than that and he had to make excuses as to why he needed to go to an extra practice or meet up with a teammate. She was okay for putting out, but horrible if she stuck around. That's not what he wanted in a relationship. He wanted someone he could trust and have fun hanging out with. All Lauren wanted to do was have sex and go shopping.

"We care for each other . . . I'm devoted to you . . . I understand your career."

"Is this what it's about?" he asks, remembering when they were together Lauren wanted to be at every function that required a spouse or girlfriend to help out at fund-raisers. "My career? You love the attention and being associated with me because of what I do."

"Isn't that a good thing? I'm proud of you!"

"That's nice, but really, you told people who you were and that I was your fiancé. It was a little much. Okay, too much."

"Sorry. I didn't know that bothered you."

"We weren't engaged!"

"It was hard to explain who I was."

"*Girlfriend* works just fine."

"I'll remember that for next time."

"There won't be a next time, Lauren. We're not together. We will never be together. We don't fit."

"Don't you want to settle down?"

"If I'm lucky. One day maybe," he says.

Her shoulders drop and she wears a frown. "Do you want to have one last go?"

"You mean sex? You'd want to have sex with me and be gone?" He was not going down that road again. At least not with Lauren.

"Why not?"

"I can't."

"You're saying no?" She bursts out laughing. "I don't believe it."

"That would just complicate things," he says, thinking about Meghan and how he doesn't want to lose her. He has to come up with a plan to convince Meghan that they should be together. She is the one he can't stop thinking about. He has to get rid of Lauren. How would he explain her to Meghan? And would she understand?

He opens the wooden door, letting a rush of cold air fill up the corridor.

"Last chance," she says, slipping on her heels.

"Take care," he says, watching her trot down the driveway and into her car. "Oh, and Lauren?"

She turns around.

"Do you have my garage remote?"

"No, I don't."

Jared shuts the door, wondering where it could be.

"You and her getting back together?" Loretta asks, walking down the stairs behind him.

"Nope. I'm surprised she left that easy."

"She'll be back," Loretta says, laughing as she climbs the stairs, keeping her hand on the railing. "She always does."

"I don't think so. She got the point," Jared says. He looks up at his housekeeper. "I'm going out for a bit. I'll be back later."

After Meghan cleans up the event, she decides to stop by Jared's house. Why didn't he show up to the event and what was Lauren talking about? She has to drop off Jane's leggings and his T-shirt. She forgot to give it to him. She has been using it as a nightshirt, unable to get away from his scent. It smelled like fabric softener, but it was his fresh scent that Meghan couldn't get away from. She missed the time they had together and felt even closer to him when they were sitting on top of the mountain talking about stuff that mattered. Jared had opened up to her and she wondered if he had ever spoken to a girl-friend that way and told her of his past. He had to have, but Meghan wanted to feel special and unique so she thought of Jared as her secret crush and played with the idea of Jared being her boyfriend.

She pulls up to his house. The gate is open, so she drives up his driveway and parks her car as close to the front door as she can. Her legs move with excitement; she carries her purse like a sling and holds the items neatly folded as she reaches the door and rings the doorbell. She looks up at the massive entrance, suddenly intimidated by the grandness of Jared's house. What made him buy a house so big? It's beautiful and Meghan loves the thought of living in such a prestigious home. She waits another minute and rings the doorbell again. Maybe Jared is in his man cave shooting pucks or watching a movie.

She hears the door unlock a couple of times. Her heart races as she looks forward to seeing Jared's face. Even though he didn't show up to the event he was supposed to, she misses him and wants to see him. Excitement fills her, thinking of the possible kiss she could endure when Jared sees her.

The door opens and to Meghan's surprise, Loretta is standing in front of her with a wrinkled up nose and forehead.

"H-hi, Loretta," Meghan says. "Is Jared home?"

"No," she says, looking past her. "I should have locked the gate."

"I should have called first," Meghan says.

"Yes, that would have been a better idea."

"I came by to drop off his things." Meghan holds them out for Loretta to take them and after a conscious delay, Loretta takes the clothing. "Thank you. Do you know when he'll be home?"

"I don't. I'm his housekeeper, not his mother."

"I thought you might know. Okay, well, I'll get going," Meghan says, stepping away from the doorway. "I'll try giving him a call."

"I don't plan on seeing him today," she mutters. "I'm going home." She pauses, folding her apron in her hands. "It's none of my business what's going on between you and Jared, but I don't trust the other woman."

"What other woman?"

"The blond, his ex-girlfriend."

Meghan's face falls, her stomach sinks. Does he want to get back with Lauren?

"Jared and I are . . . friends." Meghan swore she didn't want to be that girl, but here she is not knowing where she stands and waiting to have her heart broken unless she acts fast.

Chapter 17

Jared showers and dresses after the game. He is wearing a dark suit. His hair is still damp and his facial hair has new growth. He's going home. He should have called Meghan again, but she's not answering her phone. She did say on his voice mail that she was disappointed with him and upset that he didn't show up for the event. How many of these things does he have to commit to? Why does the team have so many things going on? Jared just wants to play hockey. He didn't sign up for everything else that involves the sport. He loves the game too much to turn his back on charity and wouldn't have the heart to not support the ones that pull at his heartstrings. He's never played for a hockey club that is as involved with events as the Warriors. What's Meghan thinking? Maybe he should talk to her and tell her to slow down, it's too much. If he went to her house right now, it wouldn't be too late. Maybe she would be in the mood and want him to stay. The thoughts of lying in bed with Meghan again get him all heated and focused on driving to her house. He hopes he'd remember how to get there.

Jared can see down the corridor that the visiting team is leaving the Dome. From a distance, he spots a player, dressed in a black suit, looking back at him. His hand is on his hip as he waits for the bus to load their gear.

"Jared," the voice calls. The guy, dressed in a gray suit, heavy black coat, and black loafers, makes his way toward him. He is shorter than Jared and stockier.

Jared's heart races. His chest hurts, muscles are tight. This is the last guy he wants to see, let alone speak to. If seeing him on the ice wasn't enough.

"Good game," Corey finally says when he gets close.

Jared doesn't move an inch for him and says nothing. He stares at him like he has something horrible tasting in his mouth.

"You still hold a grudge against me," Corey says.

Jared looks past the player's shoulder. If Corey only knew how much Jared hated him he probably wouldn't be standing in front of him making small talk.

"It's been ten years . . ." Corey says.

"It feels like yesterday."

"That hit you gave me . . . it was deliberate."

"I got a penalty for it," Jared says. "You're lucky the ref intervened because I could have done some damage."

Corey puffs out his chest. "You think I killed Luke, don't you?"

Jared grunts. Every time he's brought back to that day, it hits him hard like a punch to his gut. Why did Luke have to die? He was so young. He hadn't even lived his dream. He was a kid . . . they were kids. Jared was here living out the life he wanted and he's gone.

"You could have helped him," Jared says as though he's numb. He can barely speak, trying as best as he can to stay the distance with Corey, afraid he could unleash on him.

"I did everything I could. We were eighteen. What could I have done differently?" Corey's mouth is a sarcastic grin. "Tell me. What could I have done?"

"For starters, you weren't smart enough to wear life jackets."

"Luke didn't want to wear one."

"Stop blaming Luke. He's dead! He can't defend himself."

"I shouldn't have listened to him. We were only going to go on the water for a little while. We were hungry and thought we could catch dinner."

"And fry it up?" He laughs. "Luke wasn't an experienced fisherman. The lake has trout, nothing too exciting." Jared remembers because that day there was talk about fishing and the people who knew the lake spoke about where they could rent boats. Someone there had a small boat and Luke and Corey somehow got permission to use it.

"What happened on the boat?" Jared asks, holding that dislikable stare.

"You know what happened. Luke got up and reached for a drink and he fell in, hitting his head on the bow."

"How does that happen? How did he hit his head? He would have had to go backward."

"He lost his balance, slipped on some ice that spilled out of the cooler. It all happened so fast." Corey runs his hand through his hair, looks to the ground before giving him a sobering stare. "If I could have prevented the accident, I would have. We were good friends. . . .'"

Jared nods, trying to accept his explanation.

"I helped the best way I knew how . . . I'm sorry that you think I could have done more. Believe me, I wish I could have and it would have made a difference."

"You know what struck me as odd?" Jared asks. He's never brought this up, it was a question that has been burning inside him since that day. "Luke didn't drink soda. He was the healthiest guy I knew. Luke was scouted and wanted to be in the best shape of his life. His diet was precise. Even when we were away, he made sure that he had meals planned because he didn't want to be thrown off schedule when he went back to Seattle."

"Come on, Luke wasn't all that strict," Corey mimics.

"Yes, he was," Jared says. "He bought power bars by the boxes and drank milk by the gallon. He was the healthiest guy I knew."

"Not the Luke I knew."

"How so?" Jared stares.

"Before we went out on the boat, we smoked pot."

"Luke wouldn't do that."

"We did. We thought it would be funny to smoke a joint and see what kind of fishing we could do. We weren't thinking straight. We were only out there for a few minutes when Luke said he was really hungry and thirsty. I threw in a cooler before we left because it was really warm that day, remember? All I found was a couple cans of soda so I threw some ice on it and we took off, concerned about the drinks being cold and not a life jacket. Stupid, I know." Corey shakes his head.

"Luke never smoked anything. I don't believe it."

"He did that day."

"Did you offer it to him?"

"Someone offered it to us, I can't remember who. We took it, not thinking it was a big deal. We were having fun . . . We got into the boat . . .'"

Jared exhales. He feels so disturbed. Could Corey be lying? Why didn't he know this fact about the accident? Wouldn't the doctors know and say something to his aunt and uncle?

Jared takes a step backward. He wants to go home. He doesn't want to give this guy any more of his time. He changed his life and wrecked Luke's life. If he had of known this in the game he would have pounded him harder against the boards. Jared makes a fist and cups his other hand around it, holding back from the fury that is vibrating his bones.

"We were kids," Corey reminds him. "I made a mistake . . . Luke made a mistake. We weren't thinking about consequences, we weren't thinking about anything else except having fun. We didn't know if it would be our last year playing junior together. . . ."

"That's not like Luke, the guy rarely had a beer," Jared says. "Was he okay? Was he upset about something?" He knew everything that was going on in Luke's head, or he thought he did. He would never guess that Luke would smoke anything at that time of launching his career.

"He was fine. Luke was his usual self, upbeat . . . he was eager to get out on the water."

"So you guys were fishing and Luke just happened to slip on ice cubes and fall off the boat? Doesn't seem logical, does it?" Jared tests. Did Corey really think he'd buy his story?

"That's what I'm telling you."

"Was Luke already unconscious in the water?"

"Yeah. He hit his head like I told you. I jumped in the water, saw blood and Luke sinking. I pulled him up and tried my best to keep him afloat. I couldn't swim to shore, it was too far and I tried lifting him into the boat but I couldn't. . . ."

"If he didn't hit his head . . ." Jared says.

"That's when you came . . . It was an accident. Look, I didn't catch up to you to relive Luke's death. I've been carrying the guilt and it hasn't helped me cope in my life." Corey brings a hand to his chest. "I want you to know that I'm sorry for what happened to Luke. I wish it were a different outcome, I do," he says. "I wish he were alive. I'd like to watch him play. He'd be a hell of a player and probably would kick both of our asses."

That evening, Jared drives home thinking about Luke. How could Luke have smoked pot, gotten on a boat, and not worn a life jacket?

It all seemed so simple, yet he thought he was invincible. Jared thinks about Meghan. He wants to see her. He likes that she is a good listener, is friendly and encouraging. If only she was easy to reach. Why doesn't she answer her phone? He has to talk to her about that the next time he sees her, which most likely will be after Christmas since he's leaving tomorrow for his hometown. Was she mad that she wasn't coming with him? Was she expecting an invite? She had her own family plans; besides, it wasn't like they were serious or even together. As much as he cares for her, they are still at the beginning. Does she think there was more between them? No doubt he is sexually charged whenever he is close to her. He can't help thinking about getting her into bed. But there is also something very different about Meghan. As much as he wants to sleep with her, he wants to be in her company. He realizes that he enjoys talking to her more than he had with any other woman. Meg is easy to talk to and more importantly, she seems like the one person who understands him and just listens without him feeling like she wants to solve a problem. She heard him out and he told her more than most people. It has to count for something. He needs to talk to her again and tell her how much she means to him. Seeing Lauren in his house reminded him of what he didn't want. Lauren isn't good enough. Meghan is what he desires.

Jared drives over to Meghan's apartment, hoping it could lead to a few hours in her bed before he has to say good-bye. He doesn't bother calling. He hasn't spoken to her in a few days. Loretta had told him she had come by to drop off his sister's leggings and his old T-shirt. He was sorry he missed her, but after seeing Lauren, he wanted to get out and do something, so he chose to go out and do some Christmas shopping. He wants to buy Meghan a gift, but doesn't know what.

He thought about calling her earlier in the day, but at the time he was mentally prepping for his game and with practice, he didn't have time or want to mess up his concentration, so he kept to himself. It didn't help matters since their game was a huge disappointment for the team and the fans. He was now officially on winter holidays for the next six days and would be back soon enough to play a couple of games before the New Year. There was never a waste of time for a hockey player. Most of them flew home for Christmas and then back again, making a week not so long when they hadn't seen family for months.

He rings her apartment number, but there's no answer. Why did he think she would be home? It's three days before Christmas. She probably has things to do. He gets back into his truck, an alternative ride in case he has to plow through snow. A light dusting has started to fall, not like home where plugging in your vehicle isn't an option and digging out your driveway was the way it is for everyone. British Columbia was damp and chilly in the fall. People complained when it snowed and complained when it was hovering around freezing. He liked it here. It did feel like home. The weather was easier to get used to, unless he was playing somewhere down south. This was a hockey city and he was thankful for the fans, even though he wasn't interested in making appearances.

Jared tries calling her on her cell phone. He misses Meghan. Thinking about being away from her over Christmas.

There's no answer. He takes the phone away from his ear ready to hang up and then brings it back. What can he tell her? That he misses her? He wants her so bad that he'll wait in visitor parking until she comes home? He quickly says his name after the beep and tells Meghan to give him a call when she can. After he hangs up, he stares at his phone for a moment as though waiting for Meghan to call him back instantly. She could be shopping and trying to pay for something and not be able to answer her phone. He imagines her riffling through her purse for her phone and seeing that he called. She waits until she has her hands free before calling him back, except there's no call made. Jared waits in the parking stall a little longer. She's too busy to take his call. He throws it down on the passenger seat, starts the ignition, and drives home, determined to see her before going home tomorrow.

Meghan goes home to change after work and to figure out what to do about a cocktail dress for the upcoming black-tie event in just over a week. After all the planning, she didn't even think about what she was going to wear. Keri said it's an excuse for her to go shopping, needing a glamorous dress for the party, but Meghan would rather save her money and wear something she already has. It turns out her wedding dress is the fanciest thing she owns.

She pulls out her wedding dress from her bedroom closet and studies the off-white ensemble, holding it up and wondering what she could do to alter it so that it doesn't look like wedding attire.

Meghan undresses and steps into the gown, just as she had

practiced when trying it on for Sara and Brie after she bought it. A thrill had run through her body, as she enjoyed the moment of feeling like a princess. The dress was one she picked out because of the fit and the way it hugged her waist and hung straight to the floor. She looks down at the mermaid-style dress. She stands in front of the mirror, judging herself and the look she is trying to convey. If she cut off the train and brought the sleeves in so there is less pouf . . . Meghan tries to imagine the change, but she can't get past the color. It would still look like a wedding dress. It doesn't matter how short the length or if it's sleeveless, the look still represents purity, unless she dyes it another color.

Later that day, Meghan finds a sewing and alteration company that will change the look of her dress.

"What exactly do you want to do with this?" the dressmaker asks, wearing a pincushion on her wrist. Her black hair is gathered and clipped at the crown of her head. There are white, sparse hairs poking out every which way.

"I want to change the look of it," Meghan says.

"Are you sure you won't wear it again?" the woman asks.

"I'm sure. Why keep it if I'm not going to wear it again?"

The woman looks at her and then down at the dress that is laid out on a table. She brushes the fabric with her hand. "It's beautiful."

"Thanks."

"It's an expensive dress. You could sell it."

"I know."

"What do you want to do to it?" the woman asks.

"Cut the train."

The woman gasps, holding her mouth. "The train makes the dress!"

"I know, but I don't want it to look like the same dress."

The woman touches her chin, studying the dress as though it's a work of art and she's not sure where to hang the piece on the wall.

"How about if we dye it?"

"Change the color?"

Meghan nods.

"If you dye it, you can't get it back to the original."

"I know," Meghan says. "I will never wear it again."

"But if you get married, you already have a dress!"

"I couldn't wear this one again. It reminds me of my ex, but if I dye it and alter it, I can wear it another time or two."

"Okay." The woman hums and feels the fabric. "If I cut off the train and alter the sleeves to be thinner." The woman gathers the lace on the sleeves to show what she's talking about. "And dye it . . . do you have a color in mind?"

"Black."

"Oh!" she gasps. "You want to dye it black?" The woman holds her hand to her cheek. She hums, staring at the dress. "Okay, okay. It will look like evening wear, still very formal."

"That'll be perfect then!" Meghan clasps her hands together. "When can I pick it up?"

"How's next week?"

"I need it by next Friday," Meghan says, and leaves the store to meet up with Brie and Sara for a little Christmas shopping and a light dinner.

The three of them sit in a booth surrounded by their purchases and order drinks and appetizers.

"What's Jared doing for Christmas?" Brie asks as she pulls apart a piece of bread and dips it.

"Going home to Brampton."

"Guess you're not seeing him before."

"Probably not. I haven't spoken to him in a while."

"Why's that?"

"Busy."

"You're too busy for a guy? Especially Jared?" Sara asks. "Come on!"

"He had games and I was working on finishing some things up," she says as though it's no big deal.

"What's going on with the two of you?"

"Nothing." Meghan sips blueberry tea. The liqueur warms her insides and giving her a little pep that she lost while shopping. Her energy level is renewed now that Jared is on her mind.

"I thought you liked him."

"I do! He's Jared Landry. Every woman likes him," Meghan says.

"So that's it? You two aren't together?" Brie comprehends. "You're done?"

"We were never together," she says, trying to believe it herself.

"You were for a little bit."

"Not really."

"What happened?"

"I don't know. He doesn't seem to be interested in a relationship.

We've had a good time together." *A real good time.* Will she ever get his naked body out of her mind? It could be a curse that stays with her forever. Those ripped abs and solid arms. Meghan straightens her back, thinking of the wondrous affection he's shown her when they are together. She sulks. "I think he's seeing his ex-girlfriend."

"Oh," Sara and Brie say in unison.

"How do you know?" Sara asks. "He told you?"

"Not exactly."

"So it's not for sure," Brie says. "I'm not following you. How do you know?"

"Remember my childhood friend I've talked about? Lauren? Well, turns out she's his ex. She tells me they're together when she came to the event looking for him and she's planning their wedding!"

Brie breaks out laughing. "You don't believe her, do you? Sounds like crazy talk to me."

"You still don't know for sure," Sara says lightly.

"I went over to Jared's house, he wasn't there and I tried calling him, but he doesn't answer. I think they're back together."

"How did that happen?" Sara asks.

Meghan shakes her head. "I can't believe it either. Lauren's beautiful! Why wouldn't he want her back?"

"Megs? You're beautiful." Brie dunks another piece of bread in the spinach dip. "You don't know what she's like in a relationship," Brie soothes. "They broke up because it wasn't working out I'm sure. So, if they're together, what's changed?"

"I don't know. Honestly, I have no idea. They have a history and sometimes it repeats itself. In this case, I can see them patching things up." She remembers the way Lauren approached Jared at the bar.

"Do you know why they broke up?"

"No."

"Then you can't assume. I think you should call up Jared when you get home and tell him you want him and see where you stand. No sense playing around."

"It'll have to wait a week. I don't know when he'll be back."

"Did you buy him anything for Christmas?" Sara asks.

"No, should I?"

"Up to you."

"I wanted to, but we're not together. I don't want to give him something cheesy. The guy is rich. He can buy anything he wants."

"He can't buy you," Brie says.

"No, he can't," Meghan agrees. "But I may be too late. Lauren's beat me to it."

"Don't worry about Lauren, worry about what you need to do to get him back," Brie says. "Whatever it takes. You've perfected the flirting, now you're onto relationship building."

"You sound like that psychologist you read to me." Meghan laughs.

"I see what's going on with you," Brie says. "You need to show him you want him. Give him what he doesn't have. Tell him you want him and then throw yourself at him." Brie smirks.

"What are you suggesting?" Meghan asks, fluttering her thick eyelashes. "Have sex with the guy? Is that his gift or mine?" She laughs.

"Think of it as something for both of you," Brie says.

Meghan's smile fades as she thinks about what it would be like to lose Jared and not see him again. "Only in my dreams."

"It wouldn't hurt if you showed up at his front door wearing a bow tied around you," Brie says. The women all laugh. "Best present he'd ever have, I guarantee it."

"But would that make him stay with me? I don't want a fling," Meghan says pouting, feeling a desperate pull of her heart. She thought they had something. There was definitely something between them. More than Colton, more than Stu, which makes her laugh considering she's not even Jared's girlfriend or hasn't been and she feels a strong connection with him. Could it be the chemistry, or was it that they got along and saw things the same way? Whatever it was, Meghan wanted more of Jared.

"You're not going to do it, are you?" Sara asks.

Meghan lifts her cup to her mouth. "I'd need a lot of these before thinking about doing it." She sips her hot beverage. "I don't think throwing myself at him will help matters, I'm sure he gets that a lot."

"Probably does," Sara chimes in. "Who wouldn't if they have the opportunity?"

"Jared doesn't come to a lot of the events he's expected to go to because he doesn't like the attention."

"Really? A guy like him?" Brie asks. "Never heard of that."

"Not everyone wants to be in the spotlight."

"His job makes him so he is."

"He wants to play hockey," Meghan says. "He doesn't want publicity."

"Something happen to him when he was younger?" Sara asks.

"I don't think so." Meghan holds back from telling them about his cousin's death. Maybe that had something to do with Jared's loneliness. Although when they were together he is far from being introverted. He's more outgoing than Stu and Colton combined.

Meghan sighs. "I'm not chasing him. If he wants me, he knows how to find me."

"You're tough," Sara says.

Brie grins. "She likes him. She's playing hard to get."

"It's the only way to know if he wants me," she says, reaching for her phone after hearing a *ding* that she has voice mail. "Besides, if he really wanted to show me, he would have invited me home for Christmas."

"That's a big step. So you're gonna wait around for him to call?" Brie asks.

"Looks like he just did." She holds up her phone. "Missed it."

"I didn't hear it ring."

"Neither did I."

"Are you going to call him?" Brie asks.

Meghan looks at her phone, wondering. "I will. It's the only way to tell if he's serious." It could set her up for heartbreak or make her hopeful. Either way, she's nervous. It would be devastating to lose him, or it might leave her panic-stricken to keep him.

Chapter 18

Jared settles into the spare room and unpacks his belongings in the empty dresser. He uses the bottom drawer for the gifts he bought and would give Jane gift cards to use for Beckham. It was easier for her to pick out what he needs rather than try to guess what his nephew is into.

Jared didn't sleep very well. He got up at four in the morning with Meghan on his mind. He grabbed his phone and saw that there was a message. He ran his hand through his hair. He must have been in a deep sleep to not hear his phone. He listened to her voice, wishing him Merry Christmas, and asking himself why he wasn't with her over the holidays. Unable to go back to sleep for an hour, he got ready to leave, showering and double-checking his bag loaded mostly with gifts for his family.

At five thirty, it was still too early to call Meghan. He thought about her on his way to the airport, on the four-and-a-half-hour flight, and even when he took a cab to his parents' house. He wondered what she was up to and was disappointed that he didn't see her before he left. Was she thinking of him, too? Was she mad at him for not showing up to the event? What more did he want from her? He thought about Meghan moving in with him one day and even pictured her as his wife. A crazy thought for having not been together quite two months, but he felt something with Meghan he had never experienced with anyone else before. The thought made his heart beat faster as he had never imagined the future with anyone; well, he did with Lauren because that's all she talked about and he realized that he didn't feel the same way. He doubted Lauren loved him the way his felt for Meghan. Lauren was a fake and, given time, her true colors would show.

When he got back home to Vancouver, he would need to tell Meghan how he feels about her, then he could put this vision of the two of them together to rest. It was harder by the day, thinking of the possibilities of being with her and unsure where their relationship was going. Of all the women he'd been with, Meghan was the first one not to throw herself at him, which made it harder to judge what she wanted. She was the first woman that he wanted to be with at all times.

"Dinner will be ready in twenty minutes," his mom says, standing at the doorway.

It's a good thing he's hungry. He isn't used to eating at five o'clock, but his parents eat early and go to bed early.

"Great, I'm starved."

His mom smiles. "It's good to have you home," she says. "I miss you."

"Miss you, too, Mom."

He misses Meghan. He would be happier if she was here with him. Why didn't he invite her?

"Are you happy to be home?" she asks. Her shoulder-length hair is a whiter blond, blended with gray, her eyes the same color as Jared's. She is shorter, though; he gets his height from his dad.

"It's good to see family. What's the weather like today?" Jared asks.

"Wet snow, rain . . ."

She nods. "I invited your aunt and uncle for dinner. They should be here by now."

Jared closes his mouth and tries to grin. He isn't in the mood to speak with them. They remind him of Luke. He knew he would see them while he was here, it was Christmas after all, but he didn't prepare himself for talking about Luke. His aunt Debbie always brought Luke up like he was still alive and that always grabbed hold of his heart and squeezed it tight. He had to stop feeling this way, the pressure was too much. Something had to give. Is Luke holding him back? Does he feel guilty for not saving Luke's life? Does he feel guilty because he was living Luke's dream? If he had a choice between Luke or himself playing in the NHL, he would have given it to his cousin, not because he didn't want to play; he would have given it up to make his cousin happy. He wanted the people he loved to be happy, but where did it leave him? He wasn't as happy as he could be, yet he had everything he wanted, except someone to wake up to and he hoped it would be Meg.

The doorbell rings. "That's them!"

Jared's phone rings and he grabs it from the top of the dresser.

"I'll see you downstairs," his mom says, and leaves.

He picks up his phone to look at the call display. Warriors number. He's not sure exactly who's calling. Perhaps Ted Walker? But he had Ted's number saved on his phone.

"Hello?" he answers.

"H-hi, Jared."

Excitement rings through his body. It's a sense of relief knowing Meghan wants to talk to him. Does she miss him, too? He strengthens his smile and answers with a "Hey, Meg, how are you?" He can't help the energy he feels.

"Good."

"What are you up to?"

"I'm at work."

"Right, three-hour time change," he says.

"Oh, sorry, to bother you," she stammers. "What's it like to be home?"

"It's okay. What's the weather like there?"

"The snow has turned to rain."

He chuckles. "That's what I thought. It's minus eight and snowing here."

Meghan lets out a *brr*, making Jared keep his smile.

"I couldn't get used to that," she says.

"I'm only here for a few days. Isn't the office closed?"

"I work a half-day tomorrow and then I'll be back next week."

"What are you going to do with your time off?"

"I've got dinner plans, visiting family. The usual O'Riley gatherings. I'm calling for a few reasons," she says, changing her tone. "First, I wanted to tell you that I dropped off Jane's leggings and your T-shirt, did you know? I spoke to Loretta."

"Yes, thanks."

"Apparently I just missed you."

Jared rubs the back of his head. "To tell you the truth, I can't remember what I did that day."

"That's okay. The other reason I'm calling is because I wanted to clear something up. . . ."

"Yeah?"

"I know you and Lauren have something going on." She pauses. "I just don't understand . . ." Her voice softens. *Is she crying?*

"Wait a minute, I'm not with Lauren. We're not together."

"Then why did she tell me that she was expecting you home?"

Jared throws his head back. "It's not true."

"Why would she say that?"

"Because she's crazy. You know she is."

"It's just that—" Her voice drops, leaving him hanging in mid-sentence. He can tell she is probably wondering if she should believe him. "She told me you two were getting married, so when's that?"

He breaks into hysterical laughter. "I'm telling you, Meg, there's nothing between Lauren and me. She's obsessive."

"I understand if there is. Honestly, I do."

"But we're not—"

"Tell me, did you bring Lauren with you?"

"No! Lauren and I aren't together. We will never be together."

"I see. . . ."

"What's wrong? You have to believe me."

"I do believe you."

"Then, what is it?"

"I'm at work," she says sadly. "I can't get into it. What I really need to talk to you about is the black-tie event that's happening in just over a week. I don't care what events you don't show up to, but this is the big one. The whole team is expected to be there unless there's a crisis and knowing you, there very well could be."

"What's that supposed to mean?"

"You have every excuse not to show up when I need you."

"Is that what this is all about?"

"I need you there, Jared. Okay? And if you don't want to do it for me, do it for the sick children. That's what the event is for. You probably don't know that, but every event we do, it's for charity. It's helping those in need. And for you to not show up because you're too important, well, I know what kind of guy you are."

Jared paces his room. Her demands were fair, yet he feels she's being unreasonable. He's never heard her speak to him like that. Does she really think he and Lauren are together? He tosses that idea out of his mind.

"I'll think about it," he says, scratching his unshaven chin.

"That's not good enough. I need you there. I'm expecting you there."

"About Lauren—"

"My other line is going. I gotta go. Say hi to Jane! Merry Christmas!"

"Merry Christmas," he says, but she already hung up. *She hung up.* He can't believe it. Jared holds his phone in his hands, staring at it until he hears his mom's voice calling his name.

The tone of her voice is the same as when he was a boy and his mom would call him for dinner, except this isn't the house he grew up in. This one he bought for his parents as a gift. A gift to say thanks for believing in him and letting him do what he was dreaming about. He winces at the thought. So many years ago, yet he still remembers his teenage years, living and breathing hockey. Happy times. There was no sorrow then, no broken hearts, just a lot of love for what he was doing with his life, it gave the people around him hope and security to see a young man succeed in their hometown.

Jared walks down the stairs and into the living room where he is met with his aunt Debbie. She runs to him with open arms and squeezes him tight before he can even say hello. His uncle Lee shakes his hand as Debbie is slowly letting go of their embrace as his uncle throws his arm around Jared's shoulders and pats him three times on the back before letting go.

"Jared, you look great, just great," Uncle Lee says with a mega grin. His leafy-brown hair sits thin on his head and his cheeks are red and round. "It's some season you've had so far."

"It's going well."

"I watched you the other night. Winning the game with a minute left." Lee shakes his head. "That was a good game."

"Because we won?"

"I can't stand Vancouver, you know that, but I cheered for them because of you." Lee slaps Jared on the shoulder.

"Do you wear the jersey I sent you?" Jared asks.

"Only when you're playing. My buddies would kick my butt if I showed up wearing it." He lets out a deep-throated laugh.

"Dinner is ready," Mom calls.

"You guys still eat at five," Lee says, walking into the kitchen.

"That's 'cause Dad gets up at six," Jared says, following behind.

"What do you do, that you have to get up at six?" Lee asks.

"I read the paper, ride my bike."

"That's right, you put a gym downstairs."

"How do you like the treadmill, Dad?" Jared asks, sitting down at the table. His parents had decided to buy cardio equipment for their downstairs and he wonders how often they use it.

"Your mom uses it more than me."

"I walk!" she says, bringing the bowl of mashed potatoes to the table.

"I prefer the bike and rowing machine," Dad says.

"I can see that you've been working out," Debbie says.

"You can?" Dad looks at his arms and then puts them down as if he forgot he is wearing a long-sleeve shirt.

Mom rolls her eyes.

"Can you pass the gravy?" Lee asks Debbie.

"Mom, this looks great."

"I bet you can't wait to come home to your mom's cooking," Debbie says, handing over the gravy boat to her husband.

"It's the only time I allow myself gravy and cheese sauce," Jared says, putting a scoop of mashed potatoes on his plate. "And that's in small doses."

"Would you like me to make macaroni and cheese for you?"

"Your mom makes the best, doesn't she?" Debbie says.

"I have a game in five days, I have to stick to my diet or I'll crave it more."

"They don't let you have a long vacation, do they?" Debbie asks.

"Five days isn't so bad," Lee says. "At least it's time off."

"I can't complain."

"You'll be in play-offs before you know it," Lee says.

After dinner, they gather in the living room, Uncle Lee holding on to his short glass of ice cubes and a shot of whiskey. His aunt dangles a glass of wine in the air as she talks to her sister sitting beside her. The guys make small talk, mostly about hockey and where they both plan to vacation next.

"Jane must be excited," Debbie says. "Expecting again."

"Beckham is very excited," Mom says. "He thinks he's getting a brother. We've warned him that he could be getting a sister, but he doesn't want to hear it." Mom laughs. "He is so sure he's getting a brother that he's named him, Jake, after a cartoon he watches."

Jared smiles. "Will I see Beckham before Christmas dinner?"

"Jane said she'd be over tomorrow with Becks. She has a doctor's appointment. I'm watching him while she's there."

Jared missed Beckham terribly. He loves that kid like his own. The thought of having his own children one day scares him. Could he love another child the way he loves Beckham? For some reason, Meghan flashes in his mind. Why was she so upset with him? He wishes he was closer and he would see her face-to-face and find out what's bothering her. Maybe it's Christmas. It's a stressful time for some people. Maybe she's having a bad day at work. He tells himself she is fine. There's nothing he can do, two thousand miles away and talking on the phone isn't the same as being with her in person.

"Do you remember Corey Wells?" Lee asks Jared, erasing everything from his mind.

He sucks in a breath. "What about him?" Jared asks.

"He called us."

"What did he want?" Jared asks, suddenly annoyed. He knows Corey had contacted them once after Luke died to send his sympathy and the second time was to "check in" to see how they were doing.

"He was asking how we were." Lee stares into space. "Wishing us a Merry Christmas."

"He's a nice guy," Debbie says with a slight pout of her lip. "He says he keeps us in his thoughts all the time. Imagine that, a pro hockey player who we don't know very well, contacts us to see how we're doing. I didn't expect that. He makes the time to call. You know," Debbie says, and then pauses. "When you make time for someone, it really shows you care."

"Isn't that right?" his mom says. "A phone call goes a long way."

"He said if he was closer he'd pay us a visit," Debbie goes on. "I wouldn't put it past him."

"Do you think he had nothing to do with Luke's death?" Jared asks.

Debbie's eyebrows raise, her mouth ajar. "It was an accident. A horrible accident."

"Corey should have done more. He could have done more. Why weren't they wearing life jackets? Why did Luke stand in the boat when Corey could have simply handed over a drink? And Luke didn't even drink soda. He was particular about what he put into his body." Jared holds off telling them that Luke also smoked pot before the accident, but then, maybe it's what Corey wants Jared to believe.

"For years, I asked questions," Debbie says, her eyes beginning to water. "I miss him."

"I'm sorry," Jared says, slouching over in his father's recliner. "I can't stand Corey. I hear his name and I want to punch him."

"Accidents happen," Lee says. "I hate to say that, especially about my son, but if we keep thinking that there was something someone could have done, it would kill us. It would." He looks down at his drink.

"I think, sometimes, it should have been me," Jared says.

"What?" His mom gasps, her face wrinkling.

"Luke was the best hockey player I knew and he deserved to play in the NHL," Jared says.

"So do you, honey," Debbie says calmly. Her eyes haven't left Jared's face.

"Luke had charisma and everywhere he went, he met people and had a ton of friends. He was the life of the party. He should have been the one to live."

"You're a great hockey player," Debbie says. "You wouldn't be where you are if you weren't. You put in a lot of hard work and it shows."

Jared hangs his head. "If I was on the boat instead of Corey, I would have swum to shore with Luke. I would have done whatever it took to save him."

"You don't think Corey did his best?" Lee asks.

"I don't think he did enough," Jared says.

"You swam a long distance to get to Luke. You did all you could do," Lee says. "The doctors told us, given his history of concussion, the hit to his head was enough to knock him out. It took several minutes before Corey could dive into the water and keep Luke afloat."

Jared shakes his head. "It shouldn't have taken him that long to save someone's life."

"You guys were eighteen years old. Still young. Your hormones are still out of sync and there's no telling what you could or should have done. Corey feels bad and he has to live with those memories for the rest of his life, just like the rest of us. If we keep pressuring ourselves about Luke's death, it will kill us all."

Jared takes in his uncle's words. "You forgive Corey?"

"There was nothing to blame him for," Lee says. He takes a swig from his glass. The ice cubes clink around when he lowers the glass from his mouth.

"It's easier to blame someone for a mistake that was made," Debbie says. "I just want Luke's memory to stay alive. He's with me every day and there's not one day that goes by that I don't think of him." She wipes the corner of her eye with her knuckle. "The pain will always be there. I will never forget my son. I have to live my life in honor of him. Luke wouldn't want me to be miserable. He was too thoughtful and caring. He wouldn't want that from you, either. If Luke were alive, I'm sure he would tell you that it's okay to be mad, but don't let it take over your life. He would expect you to be happy. Life is for living."

Jared closes his eyes for a moment, picturing Luke telling him just that. All along he thought he was doing himself a favor and remembering Luke whenever he stepped on the ice. Thinking of him when the pressure was on and how Luke would handle situations. That wasn't living. Jared has his own life to live and Meghan had made him feel like he finally had a new lease on life. She gave him a taste of what he had been missing and now it was what he craved. He wants her, wants a life he could be proud of outside of having the best career he could ask for. This was his time. He doesn't get another chance at life. He needs Meghan and he wants her now. He can't wait for his five-day vacation to be up so that he could see her. She has to know how much he wants her. Perhaps she would know by the gift he sent her that she meant a lot to him. He just hopes she would know how he feels.

Chapter 19

"I'm heading out," Keri says, standing in the doorway of Meghan's office. "Are you leaving soon?"

"Yes, I was just finishing something up."

"Have a good Christmas."

"I will. You too," Meghan says.

A guy wearing a blue uniform and badge around his neck appears in the doorway holding a small box. "I have something for Meghan O'Riley."

"That's me," she says, standing up from her desk.

The man hands it over. "Merry Christmas," he says, and leaves.

Meghan repeats his greeting and stares at the box on her desk.

"Who's it from?" Keri asks, walking into her office.

"I don't know. It doesn't say."

"Are you going to open it or save it for Christmas?"

"I'm not sure," Meghan says. "I kind of like the suspense."

"Any guesses who it could be from?"

"I have no idea," she says, reading the address. "I don't know anyone from Ontario." She pauses, staring at the address. Although it isn't familiar, the word *Brampton* is visible. Could Jared have sent her something? She didn't get him anything. They're not together anyway.

"I think I'm going to save it," Meghan tells her. If it's from Jared, she doesn't want Keri to know. She would tell Lauren and who knows what would happen. "Have you spoken to your friend Lauren?" she asks. Maybe Lauren has said something to Keri about Jared.

"I haven't. She's been working double shifts and I have been busy," Keri says.

"Has she mentioned anything to you about Jared?"

"No. Why?"

"Just wondering. They're back together—"

"They are?" Keri asks. "Are you sure? I don't think they would be. She hasn't said."

"Why is that?"

"Because Jared broke up with her. Why would he get back together?"

"Lauren is beautiful! And she fits the type, you know? A hockey player's girlfriend? She was talking wedding the last time I spoke to her."

Keri shoos her. "No way. Jared didn't want to get married and Lauren did. Lauren is the type who doesn't take no for an answer and she was crushed when Jared broke up with her. If they are back together, it's her doing. Jared is a softie."

Meghan sits back in her swivel chair, sinking into the cushion as though it will comfort the ache she has throughout her body. Thinking of Lauren and Jared together makes her sick. Why didn't she do something sooner to get Jared? Why did she let him go? Instead of practicing her flirting, she should have been perfecting it and keeping what could be lost. If they are back together, they will be together permanently. They've resolved their issues whatever they may be.

"Where do you and Jared stand?" Keri asks. "You two were seeing each other?"

"Sort of," Meghan says with a shrug. She stares at the box. What would he be sending her? She's excited thinking about the possibilities, yet terrified to find something that will make her cry. Maybe he sent this before he and Lauren got back together. How long has he been in Brampton for?

"Don't wait around for Jared. From what I know, he's sometimes too laid back and waits for people to make decisions rather than doing it for himself. Lauren used to complain that he wasn't at all serious with her, going out on dates, spending extensive time together. He had his space and when she wanted to move in after being together for I don't know how long, it was more than six months, he wasn't interested. She told him they should get married and that's when he broke up with her. He doesn't want a wife or a serious girlfriend and would rather be a playboy. I don't know what's changed between them. Maybe Jared has changed."

"Maybe," Meghan murmurs. Her fingers touch the edge of the box.

"You're better off without him. If he can't commit and be with one girl, what's the point of getting involved with him?"

I really like him.

Jared is different and if he doesn't feel the same about her, then it won't work. She doesn't want to put Jared on the spot and make him feel bad for not loving her the way she deserves. He can have Lauren, even though he says he doesn't want her. Her heart breaks at the thought. How will she know where she stands with him?

"You're right," Meghan says, trying to believe it.

"Enjoy your time away. Try not to think about work and have a good Christmas," Keri says.

"You as well," Meghan says. It will be impossible to keep Jared out of her mind. She'll open the gift from him, thank him for his generous thought, and not talk to him on a personal level again. It was a huge mistake contacting him and pressing him to come to events when she should have let it go and not care so much about her job. It's just a job, she thinks. She shouldn't let one player get to her and ruin the relationships she has with the Warriors. All players aren't like this, she decides. Never again will she practice flirting and involving herself with a hockey player. It didn't get her anywhere and now she's heart-broken and disappointed that she's no further ahead in the relationship department.

Meghan makes herself hot cereal and as she waits for the microwave to ding, she stares at the parcel. Curious as to what's inside, she's not sure what Jared thinks she is. He's never called her his girlfriend and doesn't treat her that way, more like a really good friend. If she was his girlfriend and he did think of her as someone who means more to him than *that girl*, shouldn't she be talking to him more? Is he hiding something from her? He already told her that he wasn't seeing Lauren. Then what is it?

Maybe she should have bought Jared something, but then, they aren't together. He obviously sent this out of guilt.

The more she thinks about what's inside the box, the more curious she becomes.

Meghan carefully strips off the masking tape from the box, slowly opens the cardboard flaps, and peeks inside. She pulls back the tissue paper, revealing a white card on top of a royal blue box. Her heart starts to race as she reads the hand-printed note.

Meg,
   I look forward to counting the stars again with you, when I
get home.

                                        Merry Christmas,
                                        Jared

Meghan picks up the little box, eager to know what it is. Why did he send her something? Her arms are a tad shaky as she opens the gift. Jared had thought of her. Does he want her as his girlfriend or is this just a memento for what he expects from her when they see each other again? As much as Meghan wants him, she will not be at his beck and call, even if he tells her how much he wants her. Nope. She won't do it, she tells herself. Being with Jared has rattled her senses. Is there someone like him in her future? All this practicing, trying to learn the technique of flirting with a guy, did get her further in love, yet, getting burned had made her distance herself. Did Jared want someone like Lauren? It didn't surprise Meghan that Jared wanted someone glamorous who looked like she could be a model. Lauren presented herself as though she was a celebrity, someone worth a second look.

Meghan bites her bottom lip and begins to open what appears to be a jewelry box. Maybe Jared meant to send this to Lauren, but then he wouldn't have gotten the Dome's address and Lauren's mixed up. Unless he was thinking about sending it to Buckley's Bar and Grill to surprise Lauren at work. But then, they did count the stars that night on Burnaby Mountain. That's what he's talking about.

She looks inside and pulls out a sterling silver necklace with a star pendant attached. Meghan lifts it up and dangles it in front of her face. It's the fanciest necklace she's ever owned and probably the most expensive. This wasn't bought at a department store and certainly not at any street vendor. It's beautiful. She reads the note again, making sure that Jared had written her name and not Lauren's. Had Jared and Lauren shared an intimate moment under the stars as well? She holds the jewelry for a minute, studying it before deciding to put it on.

Did Jared go out of his way to buy her the gift or did someone go shopping for him? Then she remembers a conversation they had. He told her a gift is when you go out of your way to buy something for someone.

Where does that leave them? She goes into the bathroom to look at herself in the mirror, studying the long chain around her neck. She touches the star, remembering that night. Should she call him and thank him for the gift? It would be the right thing to do, yet he's at home with his family, busy catching up with them. She will pay him a visit and tell him to keep the necklace. She can't accept a gift like this, one that tells her he wants her while he loves someone else. She won't let Jared play her this way and she is not going to wait around for him to change his mind.

Chapter 20

Meghan drives with the little box sitting on the passenger seat. She turns up her radio, getting lost in the song and rehearsing what she will say to Jared. She swallows, gripping her steering wheel, reminding herself that she has every right to feel betrayed. He led her on to believe that she was the only one. Why hasn't she spoken to him? He told her he was only going to be away for a few days.

Meghan pulls up to his house. The gate is shut. Is he home? She'll have to call him and that wasn't part of the plan. She was hoping to knock at his door and hand him the opened cardboard box without saying too much. He will know by her actions where they stand.

Meghan gets out of her car. Her boots crunch the snow as she walks over to the intercom and presses the button. Her heart is in her throat. What if Lauren is here and she interrupts them doing whatever they are doing? She doesn't want to think about Jared doing whatever it is with Lauren. What she wouldn't give right now to see him answer the door shirtless, just one last time so she can remember him as the sexy guy that he is. But it's winter so the chances of that are slim.

"Hello?" the woman says through the intercom.

"Loretta! Hi, Loretta! It's Meghan!" she shouts, jumping up and down. She is rubbing her hands together, trying to stay warm.

"Yes?"

"Is Jared home?" Meghan grits her teeth.

"No, he's not."

"I have something for him. Can I give it to you?"

Loretta huffs. "I guess so."

Meghan runs back into her car and waits for the iron gate to open.

She drives up and runs to the front door with the cardboard box. She presses the doorbell and stands tall.

The heavy door opens slowly and Loretta appears, wearing a white apron and black pants, holding a duster in her hands. Her hair is out of place, as though she had taken it out of a ponytail and left it. Meghan wonders how hard this lady works. Can there really be a lot to do in a house that's barely lived in?

"Hi, Loretta," Meghan says. "Did Jared say what time he would be home?"

"No, he didn't."

"Okay, then. May I leave this package with you?" Meghan hands over the box. "And can you please tell him thank you, but I can't accept this when we're not together."

Loretta stares at the box. "It was a gift?" she asks, her voice airy.

"Jared bought me something. . . ." Meghan says, looking down at the box. "It was nice of him, but we're not together, so I can't have it."

"A gift?"

"Yes," Meghan says.

"He has lots of money. Keep it!" Loretta shoos her hand.

"No, I can't. It wouldn't be right."

"Why wouldn't it be? It was a gift."

"I know. But it reminds me of him. Have you seen much of him?" Meghan wants to know, although the answer might frighten her, knowing very well that Jared has probably come around with Lauren.

"No, I haven't," Loretta says. "I'm usually gone before he gets home. With the weather and steep hills, I don't like being out too late. I'll tell him you stopped by. Meghan, is it?"

"Yes. Thanks."

"Did you stop by yesterday? Someone rang the doorbell, but by the time I got to the door they were gone."

"No, it wasn't me."

"Couldn't have been anyone important. Maybe they had the wrong house. Who knows."

"Thanks for telling Jared that I stopped by." Meghan turns on her toe to leave when she sees a white car pull up. Her heart picks up pace as though she's expecting to see Jared in the driver's seat. That adorable smile he flaunts and his wholesome build make her body electrified, yearning for his touch. Kissing him. She stares hard at the vehicle. The white Mercedes stops in front of the pathway that leads to the front doors. It's driven by a blond woman. She puts the car in park.

Lauren.

What's she doing here? She watches her get out of her car. She is wearing black knee-length boots and a long black coat with a tie around her waist.

"Hi," Meghan says, as Lauren walks up the driveway.

"Hi," Lauren says. "What are you doing here?"

"I was thinking the same thing," Meghan admits. "I came by to see Jared."

"I guessed that," Lauren smiles. "Something came up at work? You need him for a promo? He didn't show up and you're tracking him down?" She throws back her head. "He's getting a reputation now, isn't he? I'll have to talk to him about that."

"Loretta says Jared's not home."

"Who's Loretta? Her?" Lauren asks, pointing a thumb toward the door.

Meghan swings her head to look behind her. "Yes."

"There used to be a younger lady. She had to go. I think she was snooping through Jared's stuff. I caught her going through drawers."

Meghan listens carefully, nodding her head slowly, taking in Lauren's story. "So, you told Jared to get rid of her?"

"Yeah." Lauren raises her eyebrows.

"I was just leaving," Meghan says. "You're expecting Jared home?"

"He should be. We're heading out to dinner."

"I see." Meghan takes a couple of steps toward Lauren in the direction of her car.

"He's always late." She blows out some air. "I think I'll get him a watch for his next birthday." She giggles to herself.

She hadn't hit upon that dilemma with Jared yet. "I heard Porsche makes watches." Meghan bites her lower lip. Maybe she should keep some comments to herself.

"How do you know Jared likes Porsches?"

"I heard him talk about it once."

"He has a nice car." Her body lengthens as she stands on her tiptoes and raises her chin to the sky. "I love riding in it. Makes my stomach feel like it's floating on air. Cruising around the city . . . it's a powerful ride."

He told me no one's ridden in the passenger seat.

Meghan nods with anticipation. How much more is Lauren going to brag? It's obvious she and Jared are an item and when it comes down to looks, they suit each other perfectly. Does Lauren fit in his arm like a piece to a puzzle? Does he wrap his fingers in her hair before he kisses her deeply on the mouth? Does Lauren feel the solidarity of his body with hers? Or, every word they speak? Does she dream in his eyes without saying a word? Does he hug her back and ask for another?

A twitch pulls at the side of her mouth. She blinks her eyes afraid they'll water any moment and she can't tell Lauren how much she is in love with her boyfriend. Lauren had him first. They have a relationship and if Jared wanted something from Meghan he would have let it be known. The hard and fast rule of falling for a guy who doesn't fall first, is he won't fall at all. A guy knows what he wants just as a woman does, except a guy draws a line between girlfriend and friend. He knows what woman he wants to be with and clearly, Lauren has it all: the bombshell look and the attitude to go with it. Meghan is just a woman who loves a good hockey game, is comfortable in a pair of sweats, and works out to combat stress. A real woman is what she is and if Jared prefers a little fake n' bake complexion and salon-done hair every day, then Meghan is definitely not for him; no matter how hard she practices, she'll never be the one he desires.

"Are you still working at Buckley's?" Meghan asks, as she takes another step in the direction of her car. She is at a short distance now, wondering where the high-fashion blond will be strutting herself if she's dating a wealthy jock.

"I don't work there anymore."

"You don't?"

"I don't need to. I was saving to pay off my car loan," Lauren says with a wave of her hand at her new Mercedes.

"Fancy," Meghan says.

"I might as well park it and wait for him," Lauren says, throwing her head back laughing as she walks back to her car. "Jared will be home any minute." Her burgundy lips spread like she's forcing her mouth to move as though it's never stretched before.

"Right. I better get going." Meghan's chest feels like it's sinking to her stomach. She wishes she never stopped by. She's not playing this game, waiting for Jared to come home to see both of them as though begging for his attention.

If only she could walk away and leave him as a memory. The idea of Lauren at his house for different reasons of her own makes her angry. She swore she wouldn't be that girl and he'll have to prove to her that she's not.

Meghan gets into her car and drives away, only to pull over on the road where she's not being watched by Lauren. She dials his number and when she gets his voice mail she leaves a message. "Jared, it's Meg. I haven't spoken to you since you got home. I guess . . . I guess I know why. Good luck at tonight's game." She feels a wave of emotions as she drives home. Even if he did return her call, she doubts she'll hear from him tonight. Meghan's sure that his head is in the game and she'll be in bed by the time he gets home. Why did she let herself get involved with him? She knew he was too good to be true.

Chapter 21

Meghan's cell phone rings on her desk, while she's finishing typing on her computer. A quick glance at the display and her heart feels like it's in her throat. Jared. She wants to talk to him, wants him to tell her she's his. She's tired of this battle that she's trying to win against Lauren. Is he worth it?

"Hello?" Meghan holds the phone between her ear and shoulder, leaning her arms on her desk as she concentrates on Jared's voice. That sweet, sexy tone that makes her body rise with anticipation knowing she'll be kissing those full lips of his.

"Meghan!" His voice is direct, sending a chill up her spine.
He's mad.

"What the hell is going on?" he asks.

"You should tell me," she says, playing him a little. "You didn't show up at the event, so I took down your poster and took your name off the ads."

"You did that?" He changes his tone. "Why did you do that?"

"Isn't that why you're calling?" she asks, stringing him along. Why can't he tell her that he missed her and wants to see her?

"No."

"Oh." She bites her bottom lip.

"Why did you take down my name? I'm part of the team! I work hard for the Warriors."

"Yes, you do, that's the point. You need to be there, embracing your fans."

"I do!"

"When you're approached. You're not there all the time. I thought this job meant something to you."

"It does!"

"Then why aren't you showing your team that you belong with them? You don't even show me that I belong to you. If this is your dream job, shouldn't you be respecting the opportunities that come your way?"

"I'm grateful."

"I know you are, but nobody else does. You're playing here because you've proved yourself worthy of it, but when you don't show up for events when I ask you, what can I do? I can't count on you. I thought I couldn't, so I made room on the ads for people like Mason Ward and Eli Cooper."

"You placed Coop in front of me?"

"Jared, you've been ignoring me. I've sent you e-mails to remind you about the events and you don't reply."

"You can call me. You have my number."

"Right. Along with all the others who are supposed to attend. I was scheduling you for campaigns because well, I wanted you there . . . working with me . . . being with me," she says, her voice cracking. She swallows. "I thought . . . I thought we could hang out together."

"I didn't realize . . ."

"You're a popular guy on the team. A lot of people want to meet you. I didn't know it would be a big deal for you."

"I—I didn't know . . ."

"You're much harder to please than I first thought." She stops herself, listening to him breathe. Has she hit a nerve with him? Why isn't he responding to her?

"Jared?" she says his name with gentleness. "Are you still there?"

"Yeah," he says.

"I'm telling you the truth and if you don't like it, that's okay. I'm not trying to hurt you. I wish you could see that you deserve to be a part of these events like everyone else on your team."

He breathes hard, inhaling, exhaling, holding back to tell her something that is bothering him. She can tell, she's had deep conversations with him before. "I don't show up to events because of Lauren."

"Because she's always there?" she asks.

Jared nods.

"She waited for you to come home," Meghan says.

"I have nothing to do with her."

"She seems to be around a lot. I can't be with you if she's thinking there's a chance." Tears are forming. She doesn't want him to think she's weak and easy to persuade. She's holding her ground.

"Why did you give me back the necklace?"

"Because . . . I'm not sure where I stand with you. I can't take something like that and wear it without reason."

"But I bought it for you. Do you like it?"

"Yes, I like it, but I can't have it."

"Why?"

A tear falls and silently she wipes it away without leading him on that she is crying. "I haven't seen you since before the holidays."

"I was on a three-day road trip and then I flew to Brampton."

She shakes her head, phone pressed to her ear hard so she doesn't miss a word. "I know."

If she means this much to him, why didn't she go with him?

"Jared. I was that girl." She pulls herself together. "I don't want to be."

"When can I see you?"

"Saturday."

"Tomorrow? Why not now?"

"Because I'm working."

"I'll come by and take you to lunch."

"That's nice, but I have a lot to do today. Saturday is a big deal."

"So when can I see you?"

"I'll see you at the black-tie event," she says. "I have to go." She hangs up. Her hands are shaking, her body feels exhausted. This job was a lot to handle and adding Jared to her to-do list made it more stressful. She doubts he will be at the black-tie event. He won't be because he's a selfish, cocky hockey player who is only thinking about what pleases him. Meghan packs up her things. If only she could be the one to make him see what he's missing.

As she grabs her purse from under her desk, Meghan's cell phone rings. She wipes her eyes, takes a breath, and says hello.

"Your dress is ready, Ms. O'Riley."

"Great! I'll be down this afternoon."

"Well, um, there's one thing."

"Yes?"

"It didn't turn out very black."

"But it's black?"

"It's black. A lighter shade of black."

"What? A lighter shade? Isn't that gray?"

"Maybe you can come and see it and decide for yourself. I've tried dying it twice and the silk, well, the silk didn't seem to take the dye and I'm not sure why."

"Black's the strongest color. The most potent, isn't it? My dress was off-white, why wouldn't it be black?"

"It is," the saleswoman says, stretching out her words. "It's just a lighter shade. Are you able to come here and look at it?"

"I'll be right there."

Meghan gets to the alteration store and is met by the same woman she's been talking to.

"Ms. O'Riley! Hello! I have your dress. You know, it looks good. I think you'll be happy with it."

"I can't wait to see it," Meghan says.

"Let me get it."

A few minutes later the saleswoman scurries over with the dress wrapped in plastic. Meghan barely recognizes her dress. It's black, or kind of black. Maybe it's the plastic that's causing a shadow and making it appear musty.

The saleswoman unwraps the dress and lays it down flat on the counter.

Meghan can't breathe. The dress is ruined. "It's not black," Meghan manages to say. "This is not black." She stares hopelessly at what was once a treasured piece of her life and now is something ugly.

"I can tell you we used the finest dye. Black is a funny color to use."

"But it's splotchy," Meghan points out. "It's not an even coat of color."

"Some silk will do that."

"How was I supposed to know?" Meghan stares at her dress in tears. "It's not black. It's gray. It looks like it was tossed in a washing machine. How did this happen?"

"I will try dyeing it again—"

"Will it stop the splotching?" Meghan touches the bodice.

"I can't guarantee that, but I can try to dye it again."

"What are my options?" Meghan looks at the saleswoman who shakes her head slowly and then returns her stare at the gown.

Meghan holds her head with her hand and rubs her left eye.

"Do you need this dress soon?" the saleswoman asks, blinking. Even through her glasses, Meghan notices her concern.

"Tomorrow."

"Leave it with me and I'll see what I can do."

Chapter 22

"What are you doing here?" Jared asks into the intercom. "I'm not letting you in."

"I have something you want," his ex says.

He runs his hand through his hair and turns on the TV to watch Lauren. "I don't think you do."

She holds up his garage remote and waves it in the air. "I think I do."

"I'll come out and meet you."

"Let me in and it's yours."

"Don't play these games. I don't want to see you." Jared didn't think he had to be direct with her, but she's pushing him and making him angrier. How does he get rid of her? Why is she not leaving him alone?

"Fine," he says. He opens his wrought-iron gate and heads out to meet her in his driveway. It's cool with just a sweeping of snow, not like at home where he would have to have his driveway shoveled.

He watches her park and get out of her car. Standing, he waits for her wearing his heavy coat. Lauren is dressed in tall boots and a long jacket.

"Hi, handsome," she says, puckering her red lips at him.

He turns away when she kisses his cheek. He holds out his hand for the remote. "I'll take that."

She pulls her hand away. "Don't you want to talk?"

He laughs nervously, wondering what her intentions are. "I have nothing to say."

She stands before him. "You don't want to let me in?"

He looks past her, gathering his thoughts. His jaw is clenched. "No."

"This is your last chance," she says. "Take me back and I'll make you the happiest guy."

He looks at her sternly. "We're over. I want my remote."

She puts it in her bra. "Come and get it."

"I'm not playing games. I'll call the cops and they can give it to me. Your choice."

She pouts. "You wouldn't."

"Try me."

Lauren's eyes start to water. "We had something special. I love you and you turn your back on me like I am nobody. . . ." She sniffles.

Jared's not buying her tears, but he doesn't trust her. Those tears are fake. He would call her on it, but he wants her to leave. The longer she's here, the longer she'll think he'll take her back.

"You weren't a nobody," he says. "We had some good times."

"What is it? Why don't you want me?"

"We don't belong together."

"How can you say that?"

"You deserve someone better. You have a lot to give. You're going to make some guy really happy."

She sniffles again. "But not you?"

"I'm a difficult guy. You don't want me."

"I do."

"No, you don't. I'm not looking for a wife. You're looking for a husband and that's not me."

He's hoping she's buying it. What he would give to settle down with the right person, someone like Meghan. He can be himself with her . . . she would love him for who he is . . .

"Lauren, please give me my remote." He holds out his hand, staring her down.

It takes her a moment before she reaches into her bra and pulls it out. "I bought a dress for the black-tie event."

"Why would you do that?"

"I'm going with you."

"No, I'm going by myself."

"You invited me."

"I don't recall."

"Jared," she whines. "You promised me that I would go with you."

"I don't make promises and if I did—" He stops himself. If he did, it was a lie.

She pouts. "But I want to go."

"We're not together. I don't want it to end this way," he says, fearing the unknown.

Lauren's eyes are perplexed. "You don't?"

"I hope you find someone who deserves you," he says, trying to find the words to please her. He wants her to leave. What's it going to take for her to drive away?

"You don't want to settle down—"

"No, but you do."

"I can be that girl. I don't need to get married."

"Yes, you do."

"I want to be with you," she cries.

"Lauren, listen to what you are saying." He takes a second to find her eyes. "You need to be somebody's wife, somebody who loves you."

She nods, looking down at the white, covered driveway. "Yeah," she says.

"I have to go in," he tells her, shoving his hands into the front of his hoodie.

"If you change your mind, call me," she says. "You know how to reach me."

He watches her get into her car and drive around the cement fountain.

She's gone. Finally. He can get on with his life and be with the one who he wants desperately.

Meghan walks into the alteration shop and the saleswoman scoots over to her, holding her hands up to her face. "It's fixed!"

"My dress?"

"Yes, yes."

"That's great news. So, it's black?"

The saleswoman shifts her eyes. "Not very black, but black. I'll show you."

Meghan stands at the counter where the saleswoman grabs the dress wrapped in clear plastic from a nearby rack. "Here it is!" She takes the plastic off and lays the dress on the counter.

Meghan stares at her dress. It definitely doesn't look like the dress she fell in love with.

"Do you like it?"

Meghan is in disbelief. "It's not black. It's gray."

"It's black. It will look darker with different lights. These lights"—the saleswoman looks up at the fluorescent bulbs—"make it look less dark."

Meghan raises an eyebrow. She doesn't have time to find a new dress, she needs it for tonight. This is all she has, looking down at the once elegant mermaid-style wedding dress. A part of her is sad to let go of the memory because it signals a change in her life to move forward. Now she has. She can forget about Colton and be glad that the past is not her future.

Chapter 23

Keri joins Meghan at the back of the ballroom, which has been converted into a Vegas-like theme with showgirls offering drinks on mini trays and a stage for the band that will play when the speeches are over. There are roulette tables, craps and poker tables; all money-makers for Children's Hospital.

"Everyone's here." Megan looks around. "Except I haven't seen Jared. Big surprise."

"He'll show," Keri says.

"I don't think so," Meghan says, moving her foot around in her heel. Her foot feels achy, so she stretches her toes inside her shoe. "We had an argument. If he's not here by the time the guests have finished their dinner, then I doubt he will be showing."

"Don't worry about him. We have to find Ted. He needs to make a presentation when the dessert comes out. Where is he?" Keri scouts out the room.

"I just saw him," Meghan says, looking at the table the general manager was sitting at. Meghan lets her hand grace her hip, feeling the texture of the fabric that once was a graceful, elegant dress with all its off-white color and what it stood for. Now, wearing it as a shorter, gray dress has her feeling less luxurious than if it had been black; but nevertheless, she is relieved she is wearing it one last time.

"When the presentation is over, people can mingle and gamble. It looks like people are just about done. Can you go find Ted? Also, what players are presenting the donation check?" Keri asks.

"Alex, Mason, and Jared."

"Jared's not going to make or break the event. Sure, he's a big part of it, but if he doesn't show, oh well." She shrugs. "We can pick another player, no big deal. Mark Buckley would be a good one. He's a father and is very outspoken. Why didn't we pick him to do the presentation?" Keri asks.

"Because Jared is popular. He's a fan favorite and his stats are excellent and well—"

"Don't worry about it. We have enough on our hands to worry about one player. We have things to do," Keri says. "We have to find Ted. He's supposed to be making the first speech."

"Right!" Meghan says, looking around.

"Go find him!" Keri demands.

Meghan shuffles around the tables trying to spot Ted Walker. He could be talking to someone at another table, she thinks, browsing around the perimeter, trying to make herself less noticeable by walking sideways along the back wall.

Dana hustles over to Meghan as she is looking around the room for Ted. "We have a problem."

"I'm trying to solve one right now," Meghan says, unable to look at her coworker, afraid she'll miss Ted.

"The lead singer for the band is stuck in traffic. Apparently he went to the wrong hotel."

"How is that possible?"

"What should we do?"

Meghan thinks, backing up so that she's against the wall. "They can play without him."

"They can't. He's also their guitarist."

"I don't know. I guess tell them to play something without the guitar," Meghan says, her eyes straining. "Have you seen Ted? I can't find him."

"Last time I saw him he was heading downstairs."

"Downstairs? He's supposed to be giving a presentation in a few minutes."

"He's probably having a smoke break."

"He doesn't smoke. At least I don't think so. There's a deck on this floor to smoke on." Meghan leaves the ballroom, her head bouncing from side to side as she looks for Ted. There are a bunch of people gathered by the washrooms, all in suits. With one sweeping glance, Meghan doesn't recognize anyone so she moves faster down the hall to the stairs, turning the corner and racing down the stairs on her tiptoes so that her heels won't slow her down. As she gets to the bottom, racing as fast as she can and holding on to the railing for support, she flies around the corner and lets go prematurely, her fingers slipping from the lacquered wood, causing her to spin around and lose her grip. She reaches out to grab the banister, but it's too late, she is falling, her heel catches the edge of the worn carpet of the last stair. She falls forward, there's a snapping sound as she lands on the marble floor.

Gasps come from all over.

She can barely look up.

Someone reaches over for her hand. "Let me help you."

Meghan is slow to get up and shakes herself off. Her face red with embarrassment, she exhales, getting back her composure. There's no time to waste. She has a mission to accomplish. She needs to find Ted before people start to get out of their seats. As Meghan takes a step, her foot bends, and she realizes that the heel of her shoe is broken. She closes her eyes again, takes another deep breath, and walks with a limp to the main entrance. Perhaps Ted went outside for some fresh air.

"Are you okay, miss?" a hotel employee asks.

She nods, looking straight ahead, focused on the main doors. As she gets to the entrance, she only sees taxicabs and a limo parked out front. There is a doorman and a valet attendant. No sign of Ted. No sign of Jared.

Meghan decides to take the elevator back upstairs. She waits, taps her foot, turning for distraction. She sees a bunch of people walking through the hall where she is standing. A blond woman catches her eye. It's Lauren, wearing a royal blue cocktail dress, strutting through the groups of people, on a mission to be somewhere. Is she going to the black-tie event? There's a *ding* of the elevator, and Meghan steps in. Lauren has no reason to be there. Is Jared waiting for her? Her stomach falls as the elevator goes up. She glances at her full reflection in the mirrored wall. Her low bun has come out of the elastic and is dangling like a tail on her neck. She lowers her head, anxiously waiting for the elevator doors to open. She tries not to put pressure on her foot, as the heel is barely hanging on. How is she going to make it through the rest of the night wearing only one shoe?

Meghan takes small steps out onto the floor. Ted must be around here somewhere.

She hears her phone in her purse. She stops to answer it. People are walking around her.

It better be Jared. He better be coming.

She is disappointed when she looks at the call display. "Hello?"

"Meghan. Did you find Ted?" Keri asks, her tone demanding.

"Not yet."

"Maybe he went out for a smoke break."

"I looked. I thought he didn't smoke."

"Check the men's washroom," she demands. "I'm looking in the banquet room. Everyone seems to be done with their dessert. They're getting restless."

Meghan spots a man from afar who resembles Ted. "I think I see him. I gotta go!" She hangs up and walks as fast as she can without a definite limp of her foot and without losing her balance as she tries to hold her heel together. If she can just keep it on for a little longer until the gambling gets under way and she's stuck in the dimly lit room, she may be able to go barefoot.

Meghan races toward the man she thinks is Ted. As she gets closer, she notices his beard, but Ted is clean-cut. Meghan stops and decides to head for the washroom. A busy entrance.

"Hi," Meghan says to the first guy she sees leaving. "Did you notice an older man, white hair . . ."

The man shakes his head and continues to walk away.

Another guy comes out and she asks the same question. The answer is no. As a man is walking in she stops him and asks to look for Ted. She waits outside the washroom for the report and continues to scan the venue. No sign of him. Then she hears commotion coming from the elevators. She looks over to see a group of men walking with Ted. They are having a loud conversation about what teams are expected to make trades in the new year.

Meghan sprints for the group. "Ted!" she says, rushing toward him. "Mr. Walker," she says, changing her tone from friendly to businesslike when she is close enough for him to hear her. "I need you to do the presentation right now."

"I thought I had time," he says coolly. "I'll be right there." He is so relaxed and not bothered by her panic. Meghan walks with him and the group he's with so that he stays on track and gets where he needs to be. People are trying to capture Ted's attention, but thankfully, he keeps walking, heading toward the ballroom.

Meghan leads him to the stage and then hobbles to the side to find Jared. There is still no sign of him. She grits her teeth. It doesn't matter. He doesn't want to be there because of her.

She walks Ted to the stage and gives Keri a thumbs-up as she passes. She still needs to find another player to present the check after Ted's speech.

Meghan makes her way around the back wall to reach Alex Price and Mason Ward, who are standing at the entrance. They are both dressed in suits. She takes note of the men; all of them are here except Jared. She sighs, hobbling toward them to let them know where they need to be.

"Alex," she greets. The bald-headed twentysomething smiles and asks how she is. "Are you and Mason able to present this after Ted is done speaking?"

His eyes widen and he grins, bringing his hand to his face. "Who's missing?"

"Jared. He's not here."

"He's here. I saw him."

Meghan puts her hand on her hip. "Are you sure?"

"I spoke to him."

"Where is he?"

"I'm not sure."

"I can't run all over looking for him," she whispers.

Ted Walker walks on stage and asks to have everyone's attention.

With one quick turn on her broken heel to look at Ted, she feels a snap underneath her, causing her to lose her balance. Thankfully, she puts pressure on her other foot and manages to slip her foot from the shoe. There's no use in trying to wear it, walking with a limp, so she takes off both shoes and kicks them under the tablecloth. She flexes her toes and wiggles them. Her taupe nylons are holding in the heat and are making her feet uncomfortable. Will anyone notice if she took them off?

"What do I have to do?" Alex asks.

"Just read this." She hands him a piece of paper from her clipboard. "We're presenting a check to the board members of Children's Hospital."

"I'm saying one line?" he asks, reading the paper.

"With the generous donations, the sale from tonight's tickets and the Warriors' Heroes Campaigns . . ." Ted says.

Meghan listens for Ted's key words to indicate he's done. "Come with me," she says, picking up her pace heading to the stage.

". . . We have raised enough money to provide this state-of-the-art machine for a much-needed facility." Ted looks to his side at the projection on the wall that has an enlarged photo of the purchase.

As she enters the ballroom, at first the room is quiet. Her stomach sinks and her heart thumps so wildly. The crowd is fixated on the stage, where Mason is approaching the podium. She exhales with relief. This event is almost over. She can breathe again. Meghan has been so involved with pulling off this event, it almost seems surreal that she's in the middle of it. She steps aside, so that her angle is away from the audience. Meghan takes a breath and tells herself everything is fine.

"To present our donation," Ted says, his hands resting on the podium, "let me introduce the Warriors' forwards, Jared Landry, Mason Ward, and Alex Price."

Meghan's stomach sinks. She forgot to tell him Jared wasn't here. Then, strutting onstage are Alex, Mason, and Jared, all smiles, dressed in suits and patterned ties. Her mouth drops. Why didn't he tell her he was here?

Meghan turns on her foot and escapes to the back wall, where she blends into the dark room.

She checks to make sure each gambling table has a worker at it and every player who is there has a job to do. She will pretend that Jared is not there. He probably wouldn't do a job for her anyway.

Meghan escapes to the hallway to redo her hair in a low bun, smoothing the strands against her scalp. She glosses her lips and wipes away the smudged eyeliner that is on the crease of her lid.

As she wipes a finger away from her eye, she is caught off guard by Lauren standing in view. Meghan's mouth opens. She turns around. "What are you doing here?"

"I came with Jared," she says.

Meghan inhales, feeling her insides crumble. She tries to zip up her purse as she walks past Lauren.

Meghan feels a hand on her arm, springing her back, causing her to drop her purse.

"He's mine," Lauren tells her. "Don't think you have a chance."

"Lauren," Keri calls out from the ballroom doors. Her authoritative voice causes Lauren to drop her hand.

Meghan picks up her purse and rubs her arm where she was pinched.

"Jared doesn't belong to you," Keri says, walking toward them. "He's not yours. You two aren't together anymore."

"I thought you were my friend," Lauren says, her eyes piercing with anger. "Whose side are you on?"

"It's not about sides, it's about reality and you can't make someone like you. You can't treat people this way," Keri says.

"Meghan always wants what I have," she says through gritted teeth. "Jared is mine."

"No, I'm not," Jared says, coming into view. "You're not supposed to be here."

"You told me I was your date," Lauren says.

"I didn't say that." He looks at Meghan. Her insides are mush.

"She said you two are—"

Jared shakes his head. "We're not."

"Lauren," Keri says. "I think you should leave. This isn't the place. It's a private function."

Lauren walks up to Keri. "Am I ruining your event?"

"Not yet," Keri says. "Don't make your problem mine."

Lauren's face changes. "Tell her, Jared, tell her I'm with you tonight."

Jared tilts his head slightly. His grin is mischievous. "We talked downstairs. I told you I was coming up here without you. You made me late, you're ruining my life and I don't want to ever see you again."

Lauren throws herself at him, wrapping her arms around his neck, crying. "You don't mean that! I love you! You can't get rid of me that easy." Jared tries to pull her off him, but she is stuck like glue.

Meghan watches Keri signal security.

"Get off me," Jared tells her. Lauren is crying so hard, people are looking now, wondering what is going on. Meghan steps in and tries to pull Lauren's hand away.

"Don't you touch me!" Lauren spits, waving her hand at Meghan.

A security guard grabs both of Lauren's hands and pulls her off Jared. As she's kicking, another guard steps in to help.

Jared runs his hand through his hair. He takes one look at Meghan and smiles. Her heart is in her throat. She hears the band play.

"Are you okay?" he asks.

"I didn't know Lauren was like that."

"I warned you."

"And we used to be friends."

"You would never be friends with her. She's hard to understand," Jared says.

"Did you just get here?"

"No, I arrived as dinner was being served, but then Lauren wouldn't leave me alone . . . I decided to get some air."

"I thought you weren't going to be here."

"I wouldn't miss this." He puts his hand on her arms. "I'm sorry if you think I haven't been there for you. I wanted to . . . I've missed you."

She swallows.

"I planned on showing up."

"You needed to wait to make a grand entrance?"

"That was an entrance?" he asks, still holding on to her arm. His fingers tickle her forearm, the feeling racing all over her body. She wants him so bad. It's not fair that this attraction is so fierce that it rips her insides apart. She will only be that girl to Jared and not the one who stole his heart. They should just say their good-byes and she can recover from the heartache.

"Do you need an entrance from me? Show people what you mean to me?"

She searches his eyes for an explanation.

"I love you, Meg. I've missed you like crazy. The past week has been impossible for me to live. I need you. You are so important to me. I don't want to mess this up. What we have. I know you were waiting for me and I'm sorry for not telling you sooner." He reaches into his suit pocket and pulls out the necklace. "You left something at my house. I want you to have it. It belongs to you. You belong to me."

He unclasps it and puts it around her neck. "It's yours. I wish I spent Christmas with you." He lets go of the necklace, sliding his hands down her arms. "I'm sorry you received this in the mail . . . I'm sorry that I didn't tell you sooner how much you mean to me," he whispers. "When I'm on the road, I want you to think about us and the stars we can count together. That night, looking at the sky made me think of all the things we share."

Meghan's throat is dry. She swallows, staring at his seriousness and how much she cares for this man. It doesn't matter that there are people all around them, listening. She won't hide the fact that the two of them are closer than acquaintances and more than friends. She can see the look in Jared's eyes telling her that he wants her, needs her, and that they do belong together. It's everything she wants from a man.

"There's nobody else," he tells her. "There hasn't been since we've met. I will always be there for you. Whenever, wherever you need me, I will be there. I have never felt so close to anyone in my life as much as I am with you."

Meghan hears someone call Jared's name, but he doesn't look up. His eyes are on hers and he pulls her in closer. Their foreheads come together. All she can think about are his lips on hers.

He glances down at her feet and whispers, "Guess I owe you a foot massage."

A half smile comes to her lips.

"You really need to invest in good shoes," he says.

"They weren't cheap. I thought I learned my lesson last time."

He wraps his arm around her waist. "Meg. I love you." Her heart picks up. His mouth is finding hers and she closes her eyes to feel his touch.

"I love you, too," she murmurs.

This is the man she wants. This is who she craves. There is no amount of practice flirting that can lead to the attraction and chemistry she feels with Jared.

This is real. This is perfect.